THE
DISCARDED

PRAISE FOR THE JONATHAN QUINN SERIES

"Brilliant and heart pounding"—**Jeffery Deaver**, *New York Times* bestselling author

"Addictive."—**James Rollins**, *New York Times* bestselling author

"Unputdownable."—**Tess Gerritsen**, *New York Times* bestselling author

"The best elements of Lee Child, John le Carré, and Robert Ludlum."—**Sheldon Siegel**, *New York Times* bestselling author

"Quinn is one part James Bond, one part Jason Bourne."—**Nashville Book Worm**

"Welcome addition to the political thriller game."—***Publishers Weekly***

ALSO BY BRETT BATTLES

THE JONATHAN QUINN THRILLERS
THE CLEANER
THE DECEIVED
SHADOW OF BETRAYAL (U.S.)/THE UNWANTED (U.K.)
THE SILENCED
BECOMING QUINN
THE DESTROYED
THE COLLECTED
THE ENRAGED

THE LOGAN HARPER THRILLERS
LITTLE GIRL GONE
EVERY PRECIOUS THING

THE PROJECT EDEN THRILLERS
SICK
EXIT NINE
PALE HORSE
ASHES
EDEN RISING
DREAM SKY

THE ALEXANDRA POE THRILLERS
(with Robert Gregory Browne)
POE
TAKEDOWN

STANDALONES
THE PULL OF GRAVITY
NO RETURN

For Younger Readers

THE TROUBLE FAMILY CHRONICLES
HERE COMES MR. TROUBLE

THE
DISCARDED

Brett Battles

A Jonathan Quinn Novel

This is for my wonderful editor Elyse
For making me sound better than I could ever hope

CHAPTER
ONE

ABRAHAM DELGER WONDERED once more if it might be time to get out of the game.

His latest assignment, like most of those he'd been forced to take in the last year or so, had nothing to do with his communications and tech expertise. He could see the reason every time he looked in a mirror. His sixtieth birthday was five weeks behind him. In a world that favored the young, he was an anomaly. When it came to tech work, most clients refused to believe someone his age would even be aware of the latest breakthroughs, let alone understand how to utilize them.

So, in the past twenty-six months, he'd served as a decoy driver, a lookout, a contact point, and a consultant who ended up sitting in a back room throughout a whole operation, the only questions thrown his way having to do with directions to the bathroom and did he know where the op lead was.

And now this.

"I need someone I can trust implicitly," Gavin Carter had told him. The man had flown out to San Diego to meet with Abraham in person. Nobody did that anymore. "I need someone to do the task and not ask any questions. Now or later. Someone I can keep off the books. A link breaker.

You're the only person I trust to do this for me."

It was unfair, really. Abraham had no doubt there were others who could've handled the job. The reality was, Carter was leaning heavily on a debt owed by Abraham that could never be fully repaid, so the older man had had no choice but to say yes.

And that yes had brought him to an abandoned doorway, not far from Osaka Bay, that only partially sheltered him from the rain while he waited to take possession of the package he was to transport—no questions asked.

A damn courier.

About as far down the food chain as an op could get.

The roar of the downpour made it nearly impossible for him to hear anything else. The rain had been falling like this since well before the sun went down, the kind of rain Abraham only expected to see in the tropics, when the remnants of a typhoon temporarily laid claim to the air and the land. The difference was, a tropical storm was warm. This one, not so much. Another few degrees colder and he was sure it'd turn to sleet.

He scanned the road but there were still no signs of vehicles in either direction, only the halos of light from the scattered streetlamps. This was not a neighborhood someone would just drive into, especially during a storm.

He checked his watch. Only a few minutes before eleven now, smack dab in the middle of the twenty-minute window when the drop was supposed to occur. He knew the weather wasn't helping, but it didn't matter. If the deadline passed without the package arriving, he would be gone. That was the way it was in the espionage business. Sticking around could mean capture or death, and Abraham had already put in too many years to risk either option.

The minutes continued to tick by, inching ever closer to time to go.

He adjusted his coat, his mind already preparing for his exit. A dash around to the back of the building, jump in his appropriated car, and good-bye, Osaka.

The rumble almost sounded like distant thunder, but this

wasn't that kind of storm. He looked down the road. The darkness held for another few minutes before twin headlight beams lit up one of the buildings several blocks down. A moment later, a delivery truck turned onto the road.

As the vehicle neared, he could make out writing on the side below a cartoon image of a smiling woman with stars streaming out of her mouth. While Abraham could speak Japanese enough to get by in a pinch, his ability to read the language was limited to the words for *toilet* and *exit* and *tickets*, so he had no idea what the truck was advertising.

Right on cue, the vehicle slowed and blinked its headlights once. Abraham made no immediate move to approach it, content to stay in the semi-protection of the alcove until the last possible moment.

With a hiss of air brakes, the truck stopped at the curb. Abraham waited for its occupants to make the first move, but the doors of the cabin remained closed.

"Dammit," he muttered.

He popped open his compact umbrella and walked around to the driver's door. The man behind the wheel stared at him through the rain-dappled window and then pointed at the cargo area.

Because of Carter's no-questions mandate, Abraham had no idea how large a package he was picking up. He'd assumed it would be small enough to carry, so the fact that it was in the back instead of the cab troubled him.

A rod-and-latch system held the rear doors in place. Abraham boosted himself up onto the bumper, grabbed the handle, and opened one of the doors.

"Whoa," he said, raising the hand that held the umbrella.

Three men were inside, two aiming rifles at Abraham. Abraham's first thought was that the mission had been a lie, that its real purpose had been his elimination. It happened now and then, an operative needing to be taken out for any number of reasons. And though he couldn't immediately come up with anything he'd done or witnessed that would necessitate his termination, he thought his time had come.

For a moment he considered jumping down and running, but then the unarmed man in the middle said, "You a sci-fi fan?"

The authentication code, Abraham realized. "I've been known to dabble," he recited his line.

"James White—ever heard of him?"

"One of my favorites. *All Judgment Fled* is a forgotten classic."

"Stand down," the man said.

The armed men lowered their weapons to their sides.

So maybe this wasn't Abraham's last day on earth after all.

He started to pull himself inside but the main guy said, "Stay there."

"It's a little wet," Abraham said.

"You won't be here long enough to dry off."

The man walked to the far end of the enclosed space and knelt down. Abraham tried to see what he was doing but the interior light was too dim. When the guy headed back, he was carrying something in his arms. It was about three feet long, maybe six or seven inches thick, and wrapped in some kind of material. To Abraham, it looked like a gigantic loaf of bread.

As the man transferred the package to him, he said, "Good luck."

The first thing Abraham noticed was that it was warm. And the second—

"What the hell?" he said as the package moved in his arms.

"The sedative will keep her out for another four or five hours at least," the man said. "Now get the hell out of here."

He grabbed the door and started to pull it closed. When Abraham didn't immediately jump out of the way, the man said, "Do your job."

A million questions raced through Abraham's mind, but he knew the man would give him no answers.

I need someone to do the task and not ask any questions.

"Dammit," Abraham muttered as he stepped off the bumper.

The door shut with a slam, and before Abraham could snap out of his shock, the truck pulled away.

As he blinked, his gaze strayed down to the package. The material was a blanket, he realized. A suddenly very wet blanket. That was enough to get him hurrying over to the building and down the narrow alley to the back. Not sure how fast a getaway he'd need to make, he'd left the driver's door unlocked. Unfortunately, he hadn't done the same with those in back. He awkwardly worked the front door open and then punched the button unlocking the rest.

As quickly as he could, he maneuvered the bundle onto the backseat. He then started to climb back out but stopped himself. He touched the end of the blanket closest to him and felt legs and feet, so he leaned in and pulled the other side open, exposing a small, slack face.

A girl, maybe three or four or maybe even five. He wasn't good with the ages of kids that small.

Her skin was pale, but that could have been partly due to the cold, so it wasn't a clear indication of her background. She could have been Caucasian or Asian or Latin or Arab. If he could see her eyes, that might help, but closed like they were, they looked…well, like a kid's eyes. A few loose strands of hair peeked out from under the stocking cap she was wearing, but it was too dark to tell their color—some shade of brown or maybe black.

You're wasting time, he told himself.

He worked the wet blanket off of her and dumped it in the footwell. Since he didn't have another to replace it, he pulled off his jacket and draped it over her. As soon as he was behind the wheel and had the engine going, he flipped the heater to high.

The plan was to head west to Kurashiki, where he was to take a boat to Saijo on Shikoku Island. Carter had made the arrangements for this initial leg, so Abraham assumed the boat crew was aware there'd be two passengers, not one.

Driving out of town, his gaze constantly flicked back and forth between the road and his rearview mirror. At any moment, he expected to see flashing lights racing up behind him. It was irrational, he knew. There was no way anyone would suspect he had the girl, whoever the hell she was. But that didn't stop him from feeling like he was on the verge of being caught.

As he neared Himeji, he finally began to feel like he was no longer in imminent danger and allowed himself to retrieve his phone.

The line rang four times before Carter picked up. "You are *not* supposed to be calling me," Abraham's employer said. "I know I made that clear."

"What have you gotten me into?" Abraham asked.

"Is there something wrong? You received the package, didn't you?"

"You mean the *kid*? Yeah, I got her."

A pause. "Is she all right?"

Despite his anger, Abraham shot a quick look into the backseat. "She's asleep, so as far as I know, she's fine."

"Okay. Good, good," Carter said, relieved. "Abraham, I know you're pissed, but I'm sure you understand I had to do it this way. You wouldn't have taken the job if I'd told you."

"Damn right, I wouldn't have!" His voice rose higher than he wanted it to. Worried he might have woken the child, he glanced back again but the girl hadn't moved.

"Then I did the right thing," Carter said.

"What do you—"

"I needed you to do this. I can't tell you how important this is. I needed a break in the transportation line. Someone might be able to trace her to the people who handed her off to you, but you're undocumented. No one will ever know you were involved. The trail ended when you took possession. I just need you to get her to the drop-off, healthy and in one piece." He paused. "I wasn't lying when I said you were the only one I trusted enough to do this."

"Who is she?"

"You don't want to know that."

Abraham pressed his lips together, his eyes narrowing. "Then at least tell me if someone's going to be looking for her."

A pause before Carter said, "If things go as planned, no one's ever going to know she's missing."

"You're lying."

"I'm not. The interested party should be convinced that she's dead."

"And if they're not?"

"Like I said, no one knows about you."

Abraham stared at the road, processing what Carter had revealed.

"Are you still there?" Carter asked.

"I'm changing things up," Abraham said.

"What do you mean?"

"I'll get her there, but the old route's out."

"Why?"

"Because I'm off the books, remember? If you don't know where I am, no one will."

"Hold on, Abraham. Just tell me—"

Abraham disconnected the call and immediately removed the cell's battery and SIM card. After checking around to make sure no other cars were nearby, he rolled the window down enough to toss out the phone and the battery. The SIM card he snapped in half before sending each piece flying into the rain.

It was only then he realized he should've asked a few more questions. Questions like: How old is she? What do I feed her? Does she speak English? And, perhaps most important, what's her name?

He looked in the rearview mirror again. While the girl's eyes were still closed, she had turned on her side and pulled his jacket all the way up to her cheek. She looked blissfully unaware that anything was wrong.

He focused back on the road.

"Damn. It."

THE RAIN BEGAN to ease a couple dozen kilometers east of Hiroshima. By the time Abraham and his package had crossed over to the island of Kyushu, it had stopped altogether, and the clouds had begun to break apart enough so that he could see pale patches of early morning sky.

The girl, however, didn't begin to stir until they were in the mountains south of Yatsushiro. Abraham pulled into a wide spot at the side of the road, half hidden by pine trees, climbed out of the car, and opened the back passenger door. Crouching just outside so he wouldn't scare her too much, he waited.

Nearly three minutes passed before her eyelashes fluttered, and her lids opened on eyes that were not quite Western, not quite Asian, not quite any ethnicity in particular. She lay still for a moment, and then twisted to the side so she could look into the front of the car. Not seeing anyone, she pushed up and leaned between the two front seats.

"Mommy?"

Abraham's heart clenched.

The girl stayed where she was for several more seconds, as if her mother would suddenly appear. When she pulled back and saw Abraham, her breath caught in her throat.

"It's okay," he said in English, hoping he'd correctly guessed her native language based on the single word she'd spoken. "I was just waiting for you to wake up."

She scooted away from him several inches and hugged her arms around her chest. "Where's Mommy?" she asked. Still not a lot to go by, but her accent sounded North American.

"I don't know," he said, deciding the honest approach would be best. "She wasn't with you when we met."

She looked at him, her eyes guarded. "I don't know you."

"No. You were asleep."

"Asleep?"

He nodded. "Some people brought you to me. They thought I could help you."

"I want Mommy. Where's Mommy?"

"I wish I could tell you, but I don't know."

The muscles around her mouth began to tremble, and he

was pretty sure she was about to cry.

"Why don't you tell me your name?" he said.

She stared at him, silent.

"It's okay. I'm only here to help you. What's your name?"

It took a moment before she said, "Tessa."

"Hi, Tessa. You can call me Abraham."

"Abram?"

He smiled at her attempt. "I tell you what, if it's easier, just call me Abe." He never let anyone call him Abe, but under the circumstances, he was willing to make an exception. "Better?"

"Abe," she said, trying it out.

"Are you hungry, Tessa?"

A nod.

"How about we get something to eat? Can you buckle up?"

She looked around. "Where's my seat?"

"Either one is fine," he said.

"But...but..."

It took him a second before it dawned on him why she was so confused. She needed a child's car seat.

Wonderful, he thought, hoping the lack of one wouldn't get him pulled over.

"Just sit here," he said, patting the seat kitty-corner to the driver's, so he'd be able to see her without much trouble. "We'll get you a real seat later, okay?"

She hesitated before finally moving over. Abraham pulled out the seat belt and buckled her into place. The shoulder strap was a problem. It cut right across the side of her neck and could easily choke her.

"Lean forward a bit," he said, and then moved the strap behind her. "Perfect."

The lap belt would have to do for now

As he started to close the door, she said, "Are the other people helping Mommy?"

"Other people?"

"They came right after Mommy got hurt and fell down." The girl touched the center of her forehead. "They told me to wait in the kitchen. I go and…and…" Her brow was furrowed in deep thought for a second before she looked at him again. "And then I see you."

Dear God, Abraham thought. He had no trouble picturing what had happened. The termination of the girl's mother, a bullet to the head right in front of Tessa.

What the hell was going on?

It took all his will to smile and say, "Let's go get that food, huh?"

THEY HID OUT in the small, isolated house in the hills above Miyazaki. Abraham had arranged for its use through a friend in the business who was not connected to Carter, so he and Tessa would have a place to stay while false documents were created by a woman he trusted in Seoul, South Korea.

Due to a concerted effort on his part to make Tessa feel safe, her fear of him soon began to fade. The food helped, as did finally getting out of the car and moving into the house. In one of the closets, he discovered an old checkers set. The game was missing several pieces, but a few stones from outside worked as acceptable replacements.

He had worried that Tessa might be too young to play— she said she was four—but she quickly picked up the concept, and they passed the rest of that initial day and nearly all of the second in an almost endless tournament.

At least once an hour, she would ask about her mother. Abraham would either tell her he didn't know or try to distract her with the game. No matter what he did, though, he could feel his own sense of guilt building. Of course he couldn't be sure the woman was dead, but he'd been in the business too long to ignore his intuition.

He couldn't help but wonder what had triggered the events that now had him playing babysitter. At first, he thought Tessa might've been a pawn in some kind of high-powered custody struggle. Maybe her father had been in a position to use resources most people didn't even know existed to retrieve his daughter and eliminate her mother. But Abraham quickly dismissed that theory when he remembered Carter saying the interested party would think Tessa was dead.

Perhaps, then, the girl had just been a byproduct of an ordered termination. Her mother damned for whatever reason, and the transporting of the girl was a mission to return her to where she belonged, minus one parent. Or had this been a purposeful kidnapping? Maybe the girl would now be used to influence a relative in some important position. Maybe the mother wasn't meant to be killed but had gotten in the way, or maybe Abraham had incorrectly interpreted Tessa's description of what had happened and the girl's mother was still alive.

Stop it, he told himself.

No matter how distasteful the events that had brought him and the girl together, he couldn't let himself get involved. He had a job to do. That was all.

I really am getting too old for this.

"Your turn, Abe," Tessa said after she jumped one of his game pieces, tilting the balance in her favor.

"You are a tricky one, aren't you?" he said as he studied the board.

She smiled. "Go, go, go."

"Give me a moment."

He picked up one of his pieces, knowing his intended move would open him up to losing in another three turns, but he wanted to see what she would do.

As he set the piece down again, she clapped and said, "Ha, ha," and he knew she'd seen it, too.

Tessa was a smart girl.

A minute later, as she was making her winning move, the disposable phone Abraham had picked up before they'd arrived at the house began to ring.

"*Moshi moshi*," he said, answering.

"Is this Mr. Black?" a male voice asked in Japanese.

"It is."

"There is a package waiting here for you."

The man didn't need to say more than that. The package would contain the documents and Abraham knew exactly where to pick them up. "Thank you. I'll be there soon."

As he hung up the phone, he saw that Tessa had set up the board again.

"Me first," she said, then moved one of the pieces.

"Okay. But we need to leave after this game."

She looked at him, disappointed. "No. Not yet."

"I'll tell you what—we can take the game with us. How about that?"

She lit up. "Really?"

"Really." He looked at the board and made a move. "Your turn."

CHAPTER
TWO

ABRAHAM ARRANGED FOR a private plane to fly them from Miyazaki to Busan, South Korea. Tessa was fine on the drive to the airport, but once she saw the plane, she pulled to a stop.

It took Abraham another couple steps before he realized she was no longer beside him. He walked back and crouched down in front of her.

"You've been on an airplane before, right?" he said, keeping his tone light.

She hesitated before nodding.

"This one's just a little smaller than those big jets you're probably used to." He held out his hand. "I'll be right there with you the whole time."

She didn't move.

"Tessa, it'll be fine."

"Where are we going?"

"Someplace safe," he said.

Her cheeks pinched up the way they did before she was about to cry. "Will...will Mommy be there?"

Hold it together, he told himself.

"Your mommy wants you to be somewhere safe. That's why I'm here, to make sure nothing happens to you."

Though it wasn't an answer to her question, it seemed to keep her tears in check. She put her hand in his. The gesture was a simple one, but he could feel the weight of the trust behind it. Instead of making her walk beside him, he picked her up and carried her on board.

The flight took only an hour. Through the whole trip, Tessa squeezed herself against the edge of her seat, as close to Abraham as she could get. She did the same when they first boarded the train from Busan to Seoul. An older woman in the seat across the aisle finally teased the girl out of her shell. She smiled at Tessa and offered her a piece of fruit from a bag. After some prodding from Abraham, Tessa took it.

"Thank you," Tessa said, her voice almost a whisper.

The woman replied in Korean and laughed good-naturedly.

Tessa was initially taken aback by the response, but soon she was smiling and laughing, too. Within minutes, she was sitting next to the woman, playing a game with a deck of cards the woman had brought.

Abraham took advantage of the situation to move to an empty area near the doors, where he could still see Tessa, and pulled out his phone. He hesitantly stared at the screen for several seconds. Since not long after Tessa had been put in his arms, he'd been telling himself he was a disinterested courier simply doing a job, but the fissures in his attempt at self-delusion had grown too wide to close. He wanted to know what had happened to the girl's mother—*needed* to know. Because maybe then he could be sure he was helping Tessa, not hurting her.

Though 525—Gavin Carter's organization—had a good reputation, there were plenty of similar agencies becoming unintentionally entwined in something they shouldn't have been involved with. Abraham had no proof that was the case here, but it sure felt like it. Then again, the girl could be messing him up. There was no question she had affected him. If the package had been inanimate as he'd expected, everything would have been fine. Hell, if Tessa had been an adult, he could have handled the situation without forming any emotional attachments.

But she was a little kid. A trusting, good little kid.

And he could no longer deny he was in it deep.

He checked to make sure Tessa was still okay and then dialed a number he had long ago memorized.

"Hello?" a familiar female voice said.

"It's Abraham."

"Abraham?" A short pause. "What are you doing in...South Korea?"

Of course Orlando would know that. She had been his best apprentice, and had turned out to be an even better tech specialist than he'd ever been.

"Well, I'm not on vacation," he said.

"That thought never crossed my mind. Just checking in?"

He called her once or twice a month to see how she was doing, more often when things weren't going well for her, like when Durrie had died. She was his special one, the closest he'd ever come to having a daughter.

"Actually, I need an assist," he told her.

Her tone turned serious. "Problems?"

"No, just...well, I had to destroy my phone and haven't had time to redownload my address book. Hoping you can connect a call for me."

"Consider me your personal switchboard," she said. "Who are we calling?"

"Langley."

"You doing a job for the Agency?"

"There's someone there I need to talk to."

"I'll need a name."

"Actually hoping you can get me in the back door. I can find my way from there."

"You do realize that it's two a.m. in DC, right?"

"I do."

"Okay. Hold on."

The line sounded like it went dead but he knew better than to hang up. After several seconds of silence, there was a series of beeps. These were followed by another moment of dead air, and then a long tone.

As soon as the tone ended, Abraham punched in the number for the office he was trying to reach. The line rang three times, then—

"Becker," a male voice said.

"Good morning, Eli. It's Abraham."

"You're up late."

"Where I am, the sun's been up for some time."

"And where would that be?"

Though Abraham had no doubt one of the CIA's computers had already determined his location, Eli probably didn't have access to that info yet.

"Asia," Abraham said, not feeling the need to get too specific.

"You on something for us?"

"Not at the moment," Abraham replied, though he had no idea who had hired 525.

"Then why—"

"I'm hoping you can do a little digging for me."

"Depends, I guess."

Abraham had met Eli a few years earlier during a briefing for an Agency job. Eli was one of those intelligence wonks who balanced a superior analytical ability with substandard social skills. In other words, a smart guy with few friends. Somehow he had developed the idea that one of those friends would be Abraham. Having an analyst contact inside the CIA was something Abraham could not pass up on, but as it turned out, he really liked Eli, and would get together with him whenever Abraham was in the DC area, whether or not he needed a favor.

"Looking for some information on a job."

"So you *are* working for us."

Abraham hesitated the appropriate amount of time before saying, "For 525." Most of the work 525 did was subbed out from the Agency, though Abraham had no idea if this was one of those.

"Operation title?"

"Overtake."

"What exactly am I looking for?"

"There was a termination—a woman, I believe. In Japan. Probably in or near Osaka. Three, maybe four days ago. I want to know who she was and, if possible, why she was taken out."

"If you were meant to know that, don't you think you would have been told?" Leave it to Eli not to beat around the bush.

"Which is why I'm calling you and not my contact."

"What are you going to use the information for?"

"Not important."

"Yes, it is. I can't give you something that you might use to cause problems."

"I'm not going to cause any problems. I just…I just need to know."

"Curiosity killed the cat."

The line was delivered so close to monotone that Abraham nearly laughed. "I'll keep that in mind," he said. "Can you help me?"

"Maybe. This number you're using, is it the correct number for calling you back?"

"Will be for another few hours."

The line clicked dead.

Abraham was tempted to figure out if there was anyone else he could ask for help, but decided it was probably best to limit his inquiries. If Eli came up empty, then Abraham could try a different route.

He slipped the phone back into his pocket and returned to his seat.

"Whatcha you got there?" he asked Tessa.

"Candy!" she said excitedly, holding out a wrapper-covered treat. "For you."

"For me? I don't want to take your candy."

"For you." The look she gave him made him feel like her whole world would dissolve if he didn't take it. He was fairly sure her world already had, though she wasn't aware of it yet.

He lifted the candy out of her hand. "Thank you."

In a way only kids seemed to do, she jumped up next to him and gave him a tight hug. Then, just as quickly, she returned to the old woman.

"Can I have another?" she asked, holding out her hand.

ELI CALLED BACK as Abraham and Tessa were waiting at Incheon International Airport for a flight to Shanghai.

"There's not much I can tell you," he said. "Access to information on Overtake is tightly controlled. I assumed you wouldn't want me setting off any red flags."

Abraham couldn't help but feel disappointed. "No. Of course not. It was worth a try, I guess."

"I said there's not much I can tell you. I didn't say there was nothing."

"I'll happily take whatever you have."

"There was indeed a termination in Osaka three days ago."

"And it was part of Overtake?"

"Yes."

Abraham's shoulders sagged. While Eli's news did not definitively mean it was Tessa's mother who had been killed, who else could it be?

"Do you know the target's name?"

"I do not. But the subject *was* a woman, apparently in her twenties."

"Anything else?"

"The initial order was apparently for two targets, but was changed to one at the last minute."

"Who was the other target?" he asked, knowing full well the answer was sitting next to him.

"No information on that."

"Is that it?"

"That's all I've found," Eli said. "I could keep looking, I guess, but I do have other things I need to do."

"No, it's fine. You've done more than enough. Thanks, Eli. I'll call you next time I'm in town." This time, Abraham was the first to hang up.

He looked over at Tessa. She was curled up in a ball on the seat next to him, asleep. If her name had been on the termination list, why had it been removed?

The overhead speaker came to life, Korean first, then: "Ladies and gentlemen, we are about to begin pre-boarding for Korean Air Flight 895 to Shanghai. Please remain seated until your row is called. We now ask that those passengers needing extra time and those traveling with infants and small children to approach the gate. Thank you."

FROM SHANGHAI THEY flew to Dubai, and then Dubai to Nairobi, and Nairobi north to Europe. By the time Abraham and Tessa arrived in Nice, France, they had missed the preferred package delivery time by over twenty-four hours, no doubt sending Carter into a panic.

There was, however, a safety built into the schedule, an additional forty-eight-hour window that Abraham was to use if he felt it necessary. When this was explained to him at the beginning of the project, he had laughed. Having a delivery window of a few hours was not unusual, but one that was two days long definitely was. Now he understood why.

The handoff to the pickup team was to take place in Amsterdam, so Abraham and Tessa took a train to Paris, where they caught another to Brussels, Belgium. There, Abraham arranged for a car and drove the rest of the way, entering Amsterdam a mere ninety minutes before the final deadline.

He ditched the car not far inside the city limits and took Tessa onto a tram. The particular line they were using passed very near the transfer point. Abraham, however, had them exit four stops early and walk the remaining distance.

The air was brisk but not unpleasant, so the coats he'd purchased for them in France were more than up to the task of keeping them warm. And while he had also picked up some gloves, he wasn't wearing his, preferring to hold Tessa's hand without them.

"Abe," the girl said.

"Yes?"

"I'm thirsty."

"It won't be long now."

She looked at him, confused. "What won't be long now?"

He had yet to figure out how to tell her he would be

giving her to someone else, so he said nothing, knowing from their all-too-short time together that her attention would soon move on to something else.

She began to slow. He looked back at her and saw she was looking across the street at a coffee shop.

"Hot chocolate?" she asked, her eyes wide in hope.

He checked his watch. Twenty minutes to go. "Sure," he said. If they were late, so be it.

He led her over to the shop. As they entered, they were engulfed by a cloud of warmth that smelled of coffee and chocolate and cinnamon. After they got their drinks, they found a quiet table in the back.

"Careful," he said as Tessa's mouth approached the rim of her overly filled cup. "It's hot."

She took a tentative sip and pulled back, her lips pursed.

"Are you okay?" he asked.

She patted her lips with the tips of her fingers. "Hot," she said.

"I told you. Here." He handed her a spoon. "Stir it with this. That'll cool it down. But slowly. You don't want to spill any."

Like she was a surgeon performing a very delicate task, she gently lowered the spoon into her cup and began to stir, releasing wafts of steam into the air.

"I can see it," she exclaimed, smiling broadly.

Seeing the wonder in her eyes and hearing the excitement in her voice, Abraham couldn't help but smile, too.

Reluctantly, he looked at his watch again. No way they'd make it on time.

From his wallet he removed a piece of paper with the emergency number Carter had given him, written in a code only Abraham could read. Not wanting to do it but knowing he had no choice, he entered it into his phone.

"Quiet now," he told Tessa. "I have to make a call, okay?"

Without looking away from her spoon, she nodded.

His call was answered by an artificially modified voice.

"Identify."

"W7NJ8," Abraham said, using his call sign for the job.

The next voice that came on was not modified.

"Abraham?" Carter said, his tone strained.

"I'm here."

"Here where?"

"Transfer."

"Bullshit. I've got my team on the other line, and you most definitely are *not* at the transfer point!"

Abraham looked at Tessa. She was attempting another sip. Though she didn't jump back this time, she did start stirring again.

"Thirty minutes out," he said into the phone. "That's why I called."

"We'll pick you up. Where are you?"

"Thirty minutes out," Abraham repeated. "Tell your people to wait. We'll be there."

"I've been trying to reach you for days. What the hell?"

A beat. "My phone was damaged, had to ditch it."

"You could have called this number."

"One-time use. You told me yourself. In my book, that meant saving it for when I would really need it."

A tense moment of silence before Carter growled, "Get her here. Fast!"

"Hold on," Abraham said. "I didn't just call to tell you we were going to be late. I also have a question."

"A question?"

"Your answer will determine how smoothly things go from here."

"Is this some kind of joke?"

"No joke."

"Bring the girl *in*. That's what you were hired for. Not to ask any questions, remember?"

Abraham turned his back to Tessa and said in a low voice, "What are you going to do with her?"

"None of your fucking business."

"You made it my business when you decided it was okay

for me to transport human cargo without checking with me first. I need to know I'm not delivering her into something bad, and that she's going to be fine. So what are you going to do with her?"

"She'll be fine, okay? She's going to live the life of a princess. That satisfy you?"

"Not in the slightest."

"Bring her in!"

"I don't think you want word to get around that you've been dealing in child trafficking, now do you?"

"Oh, you bastard. You are *never* going to work again, for *anyone*."

Abraham said nothing. Carter was right. He was never going to work in the business again. But it was his choice. He knew no matter what the plans were for Tessa, this job was going to eat away at him every damn day. Better that happened when he didn't have another mission requiring his attention.

This was it. He was done.

Carter finally broke the silence, his voice calmer than it was before. "I get it. You're concerned. But believe me, we are not trafficking children. Hell, we *saved* the girl. The initial plan had been to kill both her and her mother."

So Tessa *had* been a target.

"But none of us wanted that," Carter went on. "Because of certain circumstances, though, it has to seem like the girl is dead."

"Jesus," Abraham said.

Tessa had her cup in her hands now and was taking a nice, big gulp.

"We've arranged for her to be taken care of. That's all I can tell you. No one can know any of this, understand?"

Carter could have easily been feeding him a story, but Abraham sensed the man was telling the truth.

"I get it."

"Will you bring her in now?"

"Thirty minutes," Abraham said and disconnected the call.

Like he'd done back in Japan, he removed the battery and SIM card, snapping the latter in half.

"Why'd you do that?" Tessa asked.

"Wasn't working right," he said. "How's your chocolate?"

"Good," she said, a bit of foam on the tip of her nose.

He saw that her mug was almost empty. "You want another?"

"I can have more?"

"We have time."

"Yes, please!"

ABRAHAM CARRIED TESSA into Rembrandtplein—Rembrandt Square—and headed toward the café where the transfer was to take place.

His original instructions had been to take a seat inside and he would be contacted, but before he was even close to the café, three men and a woman broke from a crowd of tourists and started walking toward him. He had seen them all before on other jobs but knew only the name of the woman—Desirae Rosette.

He stopped on the sidewalk a good thirty meters from the café and waited. When the group reached him, Abraham couldn't help but notice that all the guys had hands in pockets that were probably each gripping a pistol.

"Good to see you again," Desirae said, her subtle French accent always making her English sound lyrical. What was lacking, though, was sentiment. As with the handoff team back in Japan, her words were scripted.

"Long time," Abraham said. "Did you ever check out that book I recommended?"

"The Scalzi?"

"Yeah. *The Android's Dream*."

"A bit of a twist, but I enjoyed it."

They all relaxed a little as the prearranged banter came to an end.

"I assume you ran into some problems," Desirae said.

"Not really," Abraham replied.

"Can we get this over with?" one of the guys said. "It's too damn cold out here."

Desirae held out her hands. "I'll take her."

Tessa cried as she buried her face against Abraham's chest and clutched him tightly.

He so wanted to walk away while the girl was still in his grasp. He rubbed her back and then asked the others, "Where's your vehicle?"

"That's not your concern," another guy said.

"All I'm saying is that it might be easier..." He trailed off, hoping they'd get what he was implying.

Desirae got the message. "Of course. It's this way."

She headed toward the small street that ran beside the restaurant, while the others seemed content to wait for Abraham to follow her.

"You first," he said.

The guy who'd complained about the cold glared at him, but then he and his friends headed after Desirae. Abraham gave them a head start before following.

Their vehicle was a minibus, the back section rising high off the ground to make room for a luggage area underneath. The windows were tinted, and as if that weren't enough, they were also covered by curtains.

After the door was opened, Desirae and the men entered.

"No," Tessa whispered as Abraham neared the vehicle. "I don't want to go in."

His steps faltered. "It's okay," he said. "There's nothing to worry about." Not a lie, per se, more a hope. Still, the words made him feel like he was as guilty as those who had killed her mother.

He climbed into the van and paused when he reached the central aisle, unsure what he should do next.

Tessa shook in his arms. He could feel her staccato breaths, ragged and scared. He ran a hand over her hair, trying to calm her, but he couldn't hide his own unease. Quietly, she began crying against his shoulder, as if she was afraid if someone heard her, something worse would happen.

And, of course, it did.

Desirae, standing next to the driver's seat, motioned toward a row in the middle of the bus. "You can put her there."

Tessa dug her fingers into Abraham's arms.

Out of all the things he'd done over his decades in the business, walking down that aisle was the hardest. When he reached the seat, he crouched down and pulled Tessa away from him enough so that he could look her in the eyes.

Her cheeks were soaked with tears, her mouth a trembling frown.

He had to believe that no one would harm a girl so young, that Carter hadn't been lying, and wouldn't have had Abraham bring her this far just to eliminate her when that could have happened back in Osaka.

He brushed a hair away from her forehead. "It's going to be fine," he said. "Remember, this is all about keeping you safe. My friends here are going to help with that."

"No," she whispered.

"You remember when you first saw me?"

A hesitant nod.

"You didn't know who I was, but I turned out okay, didn't I?"

Another pause, another nod.

"My friends are okay, too."

Her expression darkened again.

"You'll see." He forced a smile on his face. When he could hold it no longer, he lifted her away from him and set her on the seat. "Nice and cushy, huh?"

She held her arms out to him, her chest heaving with rapid breaths.

"Hey now," he said, gently pushing her arms down. "I need you to be a good girl for me. Can you do that?"

"Stay with me."

"I wish I could, but I can't. I have some other things I need to do." He could feel his own eyes start to water as words became harder and harder to speak.

A throat cleared behind him. He wiped his tears before looking back.

Desirae, her face tense, said, "We're on a schedule."

"Back off," he mouthed, and then turned to Tessa.

"Don't leave," the girl said.

He touched her cheek. "You're going to be fine, Tessa. You're a strong girl. I've seen it. I want you to be strong for me again, okay?"

"No."

"Please."

No, again, but silent.

"I know you can do it. Be a strong girl."

She sniffled and finally whispered, "Okay."

Abraham rose to his feet. "It's all going to be fine."

He turned and started back down the aisle.

"Abe," Tessa called.

He kept walking.

"Abe!"

He closed his eyes as he halted, took a deep breath, and looked over his shoulder. "Yes?"

"When will you come back?" Tessa said.

He stared at her. There had been things he'd said to her he wasn't sure were true, but he had never said anything he knew was a lie. Until now. "Someday," he told her.

When he reached Desirae, he paused again. "If I ever find out someone has hurt her or treated her badly, I will hunt them down. Understood?"

"Relax," Desirae said. "No one's going to do anything to her."

He held her gaze and asked, "Where are you taking her?"

"You know I can't tell you that."

He continued to stare at her for another moment, and then slipped his bag off his shoulder. From inside he pulled out the box they had taken from the house in Japan. "She likes checkers."

He forced the box into Desirae's hands and exited the bus.

Standard procedure dictated that he immediately leave

the area, but he was no longer working from the book of standard procedure. He located a taxi a block away and had the driver wait until the minibus passed by.

"Follow it," Abraham said in Dutch.

The minibus worked its way south through town, and then turned onto a back road to Schiphol, Amsterdam's international airport. Long before it reached the public terminals, the bus entered the airport through a restricted gate.

"Do you have a pass to get in there?" the cab driver asked before they reached the turnoff.

"Just drop me at the side of the road," Abraham told him.

"I cannot stop here. There is no place."

Abraham threw three times the fare into the front seat and said, "Stop the damn car or I'll jump out!"

Flustered, the driver took his foot off the accelerator, slowing the vehicle enough for Abraham to hop out.

He had to wait for two other cars to go by before he raced across the asphalt to the airport side. There he stopped and looked toward the gate the bus had used.

"What the hell am I doing?" he whispered.

The bus was behind the fence, so unless he was thinking about sneaking into an international airport, Tessa and her escorts were already all but gone. Even if he were able to get beyond the barrier, what would that accomplish? They were likely leaving in a private aircraft, and while he might've been able to identify the plane, there was no chance he would learn its destination. Whatever paperwork they filed would've been falsified to cover their tracks.

All he really wanted to know was that Tessa would be all right. But how do you know the unknowable?

Abraham could hear his late friend Durrie's voice in his head. "Always remember the number one rule for surviving in this business: Never make it personal."

Too late for that.

Far, far too late.

CHAPTER
THREE

WASHINGTON, DC

"WAS I RIGHT?" the client asked, her frustration coming through loud and clear over the phone line.

Ethan Boyer, vice president of special operations at McCrillis International, paused for what he considered an appropriate amount of time before saying, "I can't help but wish you had come to us in the first place. If the project had been ours, you would have had no lingering doubts."

"Was I *right*?" she asked again.

"To be concerned? Absolutely."

"So you did find proof."

"We found indications."

"What's that supposed to mean?"

"It means those we've questioned so far weren't interested in cooperating, which leads me to believe they were hiding something."

"*Were*?"

He hesitated, confused. "You did order a full wipe-down."

Her instructions had been clear. Find out if the operation she'd contracted another organization to perform had been carried out as planned, as the company claimed, or if she hadn't gotten the whole truth, like she'd begun to suspect. In the process, the McCrillis team was to eliminate everyone associated with the operation so that no one would be left to divulge what had occurred. Which was exactly what Boyer's specialists were doing.

"Jesus, Ethan. I know exactly what I ordered. I just want to make sure you're getting everything out of these sons of bitches before you eliminate them."

"We're dealing with professionals here, so our usual means of information extraction aren't always as successful. But rest assured, we will find out the truth out of those we're still processing. That's why you came to us. Here at McCrillis, client satisfaction is everything."

"Can the PR speech. Just find out if they really got rid of the girl or not."

"That is our top priority." He paused. "We have yet to discuss what happens if we find out she's still alive."

"What's there to discuss? If she is, then I need your people to finish the goddamn job."

"It may take some time before we know the truth," he said, salivating at how lucrative this job could turn out. "Months, maybe more."

"I don't care how long it takes. Find out if I've been screwed, and if I have, rectify the situation. Can I be any clearer than that?"

He smiled. "No, ma'am. Your wishes are fully understood."

CHAPTER
FOUR

"AND WE SAID yes to this job because…?" Nate asked.

Quinn didn't bother answering. He'd been asking himself the same question and had yet to come up with a decent answer.

Four times in the last nineteen hours, they had been ordered to move into position, and, as of thirty seconds ago, four times they had been told to stand down.

"Please tell me we're not going back to the hotel again," Daeng said.

"No," Quinn said.

There was no sense in it. With their luck, they'd barely walk into their suite and Winston—the op leader—would call them back.

"Then I assume neither of you will mind if I stretch out on the floor," the Thai man said.

"Oh, by all means," Nate told him. "Make yourself comfortable. If you'd like, I could grab something for you. A coffee? A stuffed croissant?"

"A beer would be nice."

"Wouldn't it, though?"

Quinn pushed himself away from the wall and headed for the door.

"Where you going?" Nate asked.

"I'll be back."

"Hey, if you're actually going for coffee, wouldn't mind a cup myself."

Quinn glanced at him, not amused, before stepping into the hallway.

The building they were waiting in was being renovated, all the floors ripped apart and at various stages of being put back together again. Their floor, the second, was full of half-finished walls and bare concrete.

He walked all the way to the large room at the south end of the building and called Orlando back in San Francisco.

"Guess what?" he said when she answered.

She groaned. "Are you kidding me?"

"Nope."

"What the hell's wrong with these people?"

"I was kind of hoping you could tell me that. Did you get ahold of Helen?"

"I tried," Orlando said. "She hasn't called back."

Helen Cho was the head of the organization that had hired Quinn's team for the job.

"You think she's avoiding you?" he asked.

"I'm beginning to."

"This is ridiculous." He paused, considering their options. "All right. If we get jerked around one more time, we're out of here."

"I'm surprised you've lasted this long."

So was Quinn, but Helen was, in essence, a new client. And he often gave new clients more leeway than he usually would. "If she calls back, let me know," he said and hung up.

He should have known this was a bad idea from the beginning. It wasn't that Helen ran a shoddy shop—far from it. His few dealings with her so far had shown she was pretty buttoned up. But this was a sub-job, something she'd inherited from another agency that had overextended itself.

"I'm stuck with the team they already have in place," she had told Quinn and Orlando during the briefing. "That's why

I want you there. I know I can trust you to make sure things go right."

"We're not fixers," Orlando reminded her. "My people won't be picking up the pieces if yours screw up."

"I understand that," Helen said. "I'm sure everything will go fine. But I'll be able to sleep a lot better if I know at least one aspect of this project is handled by someone *I* trust."

It was far too early in their still-budding working relationship for a do-me-a-favor assignment, but Quinn and Orlando had decided to go ahead with it. If nothing else, it was a little chit they'd have in their pocket if they ever needed one in the future.

But now it was getting to the point of the absurd, and budding relationship or not, these continued delays were increasing the risk of danger to Quinn and his team. That was unacceptable.

Outside, the glow of central Copenhagen blotted out the stars in the northern sky. The operation was taking place just south of the city, in a business district in the suburb of Albertslund. From his vantage point, Quinn could see several of the other warehouses and outlets and office buildings that made up the area, but could not see the actual op location. It was in the structure directly behind the one Quinn and his team were waiting in. When they receive the go signal, they would head outside and pass between the properties via a hole Nate had cut in the fence separating them.

The roads in this part of town were quiet, the lights in most buildings off. He thought there couldn't have been more than a couple dozen people spread throughout the whole area, a situation that would change dramatically come the morning.

As the wind rumbled against the window, frigid air seeped into the unheated interior of the building, forcing Quinn to pull his coat tight and think about heading back to the relatively balmy room where the others were waiting. Before he could take a step, his phone rang.

The number on his screen was Winston's. "Yes?" he answered.

"How quickly can you get back?" Winston asked.

"We never left."

"Oh, excellent," Winston said. "We're a go."

"You mean stand by."

"No. Go. This is it."

"Are you sure?"

"Positive. He's driving up now. ID confirmed."

Quinn looked back outside. He couldn't see any headlights, but the target was likely approaching from the other direction.

"We'll call when we're ready for you," Winston told him. "Figure fifteen minutes."

WINSTON'S FIFTEEN MINUTES stretched to twenty-two. But at least when he called again, it wasn't another "stand down."

"All yours," the op leader said. "Not quite where we had planned, but—"

"What do you mean?" Quinn said, his annoyance returning.

"Still on the second floor. It's just that…well, you won't miss it. We're out of here."

The line clicked off.

Quinn tried calling back, but was greeted with a message in Danish that he took to mean Winston's phone had been turned off.

"Son of a bitch," he said.

"Problems?" Nate asked.

"Undoubtedly."

Clean kits on their backs, the three men headed out one building and into the other. There they took the stairs up to the second floor—or, as the Europeans counted them, the first.

Quinn opened the stairwell door, not sure what to expect. The corridor immediately outside looked unchanged from the walk-through he and his team had done a day earlier: standard white walls and several closed office doors.

The designated op room was down an intersecting hallway near the middle of the building. Quinn led the way, passing more offices and conference rooms and storage closets. As they turned into the new hallway, all three men came to a sudden halt.

"Well, that's different," Daeng said.

"What the hell?" Nate asked.

Quinn narrowed his eyes, his lips pressing together.

There were two bodies, not one—the target and a man dressed in a security guard uniform. A gun lay near the guard's body, meaning he'd had enough time to pull it out before being hit.

Per the mission brief, no guards should have been on duty in the building. Quinn was pretty damn sure that, despite Winston's obvious deficiencies, the op leader would have notified him if that had changed. So had Winston been so clueless he'd been unaware the guard was around, or had this guy come with the target?

While Quinn couldn't help but wonder what the answer was, ultimately it didn't matter. The resultant mess was now in his team's hands. As cleaners, it was their job to make the body—or bodies—disappear, and "clean" the scene so no one would know what had happened. The first task was the easier of the two. The bodies would be wrapped in plastic and carried out for disposal elsewhere. It was the second task that always proved more difficult, especially when a termination had not been carried out as planned.

"What were they thinking?" Nate said. "I count..." He paused. "Fourteen bullet holes. It was a damn shoot-out."

"Carpet's done for," Daeng said, kneeling next to the bodies.

Quinn could see pools of blood stretching out from under each corpse.

This was why they always designated an operations zone where the situation could be contained and controlled—in this case, an unused office Quinn and his team had covered in a triple layer of plastic. If the job had been carried out correctly, a single bullet would have done the trick, dropping the target onto the plastic.

Simple. Sweet. No mess.

Instead, Quinn and his colleagues were left with a disaster—bullet holes in the walls, ruined carpet for which they had no replacement, and more blood splatter than they had paint to cover.

A good cleaner had hundreds of tricks he could use, ways of either making things look like nothing happened or diverting attention to some other catastrophe, such as a staged act of vandalism. The elite cleaners, of which Quinn was one and Nate was quickly becoming, had thousands. But there were those rare situations where no matter what level of abilities a cleaner had, only one possible solution existed.

Quinn looked at Nate and could see his former apprentice had reached the same conclusion.

"You want to do the bodies or would you like me?" Nate asked.

"You and Daeng handle them. I'll get things set up here."

While Nate and Daeng wrapped the body of the security guard with plastic from the unused op room, Quinn removed his pack and began pulling out the items he would need.

Over the years, he'd had to invoke this nuclear option less than a dozen times. It wasn't a decision he ever arrived at lightly. Implementing it would often adversely impact people who had no connection to the target or anything the target had been associated with. But sometimes there was no choice.

Quinn grabbed the bottles of accelerant and doused the area around each bullet hole before doing the same to the bloodstains on the carpet. Once those areas were dealt with, he sloshed more along the hallway, down to the room where the op was supposed to have taken place. He then splashed liquid through each of the open doorways, emptying the first bottle and part of the second.

By the time he made his way back, Nate and Daeng were tapping closed the plastic holding the original target. Quinn retrieved three timer-based igniters that were standard clean-kit equipment. Each was constructed mostly of cardboard with a few small plastic pieces, all sturdy enough to do the job but put together in a way that ensured the whole device would burn completely, leaving no evidence of its existence.

After they had all donned their packs and the wrapped corpses were lifted—one over Nate's shoulder and the other over Daeng's—Quinn placed one of the igniters directly over a patch of accelerant next to the largest of the bloodstains, and moved the switch into the ON position, giving them three minutes to exit the building.

As they moved down the hall, Quinn placed another igniter where the hallways intersected, and the final one halfway back to the stairwell. It was a shame they had to burn the whole building, but he couldn't take the chance that the fire department would arrive in time to put out the blaze before all the evidence had been destroyed. A large fire would keep the crews from reaching the back of the building until it was too late.

Quinn, Nate, and Daeng had just passed through the hole in the fence when they heard a distant whoosh as the first igniter engaged, and by the time they were driving away in their van, Quinn knew the hallway was totally engulfed in flames.

Despite the fact they had to deal with two bodies instead of one, the disposal went exactly as planned. A forty-five-minute boat trip out to sea, weights securely wrapped and tied around each body, and slits cut into the plastic so that water and sea life could easily get inside. Then it was a simple matter of up and over.

As they motored back to shore, Quinn pulled out his phone and called Orlando again.

"Done," he said when she answered.

"Done as in you bailed? Or done as in job completed?"

"Job completed."

"Glad to hear it. Everything go smoothly?"

"Only if you consider a total burn-down smooth."

She was silent for a moment. "Well, then, I guess I'll set up a meeting for when you get back."

"First thing."

CHAPTER
FIVE

TAMPA BAY, FLORIDA

ELI BECKER WOULD have never answered the call if he had checked his calendar ahead of time.

Same day every year.

"Have you heard anything?" Abraham had asked.

Of course Eli hadn't, mainly because he couldn't even remember the last time he'd poked around for any news.

There had never been any news. Not a squeak, not a peep. Nothing.

"No," he had replied. "And I won't. You know I won't."

He could hear the man's breaths over the line, every exhale a near sigh. A dozen seconds or so of this, and then, like always, a whispered "Thank you" and a click as the call went dead.

Eli tried to refocus on his job. As an analyst for the CIA, his workload was never ending, but every time he received this particular call, his mind would wander afterward. There was guilt for not having checked like he long ago promised he would, anger that the calls had not stopped, and, as much as he hated to admit it, curiosity. Why had he been unable to learn anything? Of all the people in the world, he was one of those best placed to uncover any information he might want.

He'd known before he pushed back from his desk that he would give it another go.

Just one more time, he'd told himself. *I owe him that much.*

Now, forty-eight hours later, he wished he'd left it alone. The unfamiliar woman's voice on the phone moments before had said they knew what he'd been looking into and would come after him. She said she could buy him a little time, an hour or two at most, but if he valued his life, he had to leave as soon as he could. She didn't have to tell him who "they" were. He may not have known their names, but he knew what they were capable of. He believed the woman, and had never been so scared in his life.

The photograph he'd been looking at when she called was still on his screen. He stared at it, knowing he should purge it from his system, burn his hard drive, and dump the ashes in the Chesapeake Bay, but he couldn't. Despite the trouble he was now in, he had made a promise.

So instead, he spent ten minutes recording a video message and then copied the pic, the message, and the other information he had discovered onto a micro disk. Once that was done, he stashed his computer in its hidey-hole, made a quick call to his office to say he wouldn't be in that evening, and took a shuttle bus to Dulles International Airport.

There, he rented a car using a false ID and a valid but equally bogus credit card, and headed into the streets of Herndon around the airport, turning randomly left and right until he was sure no one was following him. At a convenience store just off the tollway, he purchased a disposable phone and a twenty-five-dollar phone card, then continued east to the Tyson Galleria at Tysons Corner, where he parked in a lower level of the garage, tucked the keys under the rental's front seat, and got out.

The mall was busy but not packed, so he was able to make his way across it to the attached Ritz-Carlton Hotel without any problems. At the concierge desk, he arranged for a 2:00 p.m. cab to the airport, and then used a computer in the business center to purchase a ticket on the 3:50 p.m. flight to Tampa for Charles Young, the name on the false ID he was carrying.

With twenty minutes to wait until the cab arrived, he found a chair in a quiet corner of the lobby and nervously pulled out the new phone.

The line rang four times before—

"Hello?"

"It's…it's Eli."

Nothing, not even the sound of breathing. Finally, Abraham said, "You *have* heard something."

A voice in the back of Eli's mind screamed *Hang up now!* but he ignored it and said, "Yes, I have."

CHAPTER
SIX

SAN FRANCISCO, CALIFORNIA

QUINN, NATE, AND Daeng flew from Copenhagen to London, where Quinn caught the next flight to San Francisco and his two friends headed to Dallas for their next job.

At SFO, he made his way through passport control, cleared Customs, and found Orlando waiting in his BMW at the curb outside the terminal.

"Welcome home," she said.

He leaned across the center console and kissed her. "Remind me again why we do this?" he said when he finally pulled away.

"Because desk jobs don't suit us."

It was true. There was a definite rush in doing the job of a cleaner, a living on the edge that could never be reached sitting in a fourteenth-floor management meeting. But Quinn had never been in it solely for that reason, or, for that matter, the money, which was generous to say the least. He'd excelled at being a cleaner because no other profession utilized his abilities more thoroughly and filled the place inside him that kept him grounded to the world, that made him forget, if only for a little while, how out of place he often felt with the rest of humanity. Well, most of it, anyway.

Orlando understood him. Nate did, too, usually. And Daeng. And—something he never anticipated—so did his sister, Liz. There was a handful of others in the business he also got along with well, but beyond that, he felt like he never quite belonged.

"So when's our appointment with Helen?" he asked as they headed north into the city.

"I was told she wouldn't be able to fit us in until early next week."

"Next week? I don't think so."

"Good, then we're in sync," she said. "I thought maybe we could just drop in."

"Right now?"

"Why not?"

He smiled. "Have I told you lately how much I love you?"

ONE OF THE things that had troubled Quinn about a potential working relationship with Helen Cho had been the fact she was based in San Francisco, the same city where Orlando and, for all intents and purposes these days, Quinn lived.

It felt too close, too accessible. His previous main employer—the now defunct Office—had been located in Washington, DC, providing a nice little three-thousand-mile buffer. Quinn had never had to worry about going out for a cup of coffee and running into Peter, the man who had run the organization. While that hadn't happened yet in San Francisco with Helen, he suspected it was only a matter of time.

On this particular day, though, her proximity was an advantage.

The building Helen's organization was located in was a five-story structure near the bay. It had but a single street-side entrance—a plain door easily missed by most passersby.

Quinn did the honors of pressing the intercom button.

"Yes," a male voice answered.

"We're here to see Helen," Quinn said.

"I'm sorry. Helen?"

The long flight had sapped much of Quinn's patience, so it took a good deal of effort not to bite the guy's head off.

"Tell her Quinn and Orlando are here."

"I'm sorry, sir, but even if a Helen did work here, if you're not on the schedule, you're not getting in."

"I'm going to assume you're new, or so low ranking you haven't learned how to get out of your own way, so do yourself a favor—pass the message on to Helen and open the damn door."

"Sir, I would rather not have to send security out there."

Quinn stared at the camera, the look on his face deadly serious. "Please, by all means. Send them out."

There was no immediate response.

After two minutes, Orlando whispered, "I knew I should have stopped to pick up a coffee first."

"Why aren't you as angry about this as I am?"

"I am. I'm just cold."

Another minute.

"We could try shooting out the lock," she suggested.

"I don't have my gun."

"I'm sure there's something in the trunk that'll work."

"We'll give it another few minutes, then maybe."

Thirty more seconds.

"We could call the fire department," she said. "Say we smelled smoke coming from inside. That should get us in."

Before Quinn could respond, the door opened, and standing on the other side was Helen Cho.

"Quinn. Orlando. So sorry to have kept you waiting. Please come in."

She moved out of the way so they could enter the building.

"Shall we go up to my office?" she suggested.

"That's probably a good idea," Quinn said.

They took the elevator up to the fifth floor and walked to the corner office. A white fabric couch and matching chairs were at one end, while an oversized desk and black executive chair were at the other.

"Would either of you like something to drink?" Helen offered.

"I'm fine," Quinn said.

"Coffee would be great," Orlando answered.

Helen turned to her assistant standing in the doorway. "Two coffees, David, if you will."

"Yes, ma'am."

David closed the door as he left.

Helen gestured for them to take a seat on the couch, then settled into the chair across the coffee table. "So, how long have you been back?"

"An hour," Quinn said, his lips barely moving.

Helen raised a defensive hand. "Before you say anything, I get it. You're upset."

"Upset? Why would we be upset that you dodge Orlando's calls and refuse to see us until—when was it—next week?"

"I've been in wall-to-wall meetings all week. There is a whole realignment going on and this office is going to be a central player. So I'm sorry I wasn't able to get back to you right away, but there are other things that take my time."

"Like assigning us to work with amateurs?"

"Now hold on. I know things didn't go like clockwork, but—"

"Oh, not even close."

"We all know not every job goes like we'd hope, so I'm sure we can move past that."

"Stop right there," Quinn said. "Do you think this is the first time I've ever been in the field? Do you think this is the only job I've been on where something's gone wrong?"

"No. That's not what I meant."

"It sure as hell sounded like that was where you were going."

"I didn't mean to give you—"

"Helen, your ops team was a joke! We were lucky the only collateral damage was a security guard. It could have easily been me or one of my people."

"Wait," Helen said. "What security guard?"

For a second, Quinn was unsure whether to believe her or not, but her confusion appeared genuine. "Winston didn't tell you, did he?"

"The report I received was that the target had been eliminated and the scene turned over to you."

"That's it?" he said.

"That's it."

Quinn stared at her in disbelief. "If these are the type of people you hire, clearly our relationship isn't going to work out." He put his hand on the couch, intending to stand up, but Orlando stopped him with a touch to his thigh.

"Easy," she whispered. She turned to Helen. "You had mentioned that this was an op started by another organization before being forced on you. What we need to know is if this will be a normal occurrence or not."

"Of course not," Helen said.

There was a knock on the door.

"Yes?" Helen said.

David entered carrying a tray holding the coffee, some sugar, and cream. If he sensed the tension in the room, he showed no sign of it as he set the tray on the table and left.

Orlando dumped a little cream in her cup, and in a calm tone devoid of accusation, said, "You act like we should already know this kind of thing isn't normal, but this is the first official project we've worked on together. So, based on our limited information, we can only assume this happens often."

Helen looked as if she were going to snap off another quick response, but she stopped herself and leaned back, looking suddenly exhausted. "I'm sorry. You're right. This was a catastrophe from the beginning."

Quinn snorted, drawing the immediate response of Orlando's fingers digging into his leg.

"To answer your question," Helen went on, "since we're still a relatively new agency, we occasionally have to take on some, shall we say, less than desirable work. I'm trying to limit that as much as I can. And so far, the Copenhagen project is the only one I haven't been in the position of fully controlling who was hired."

In the pause that followed, Quinn was going to say

something, but once more Orlando made it clear he should keep his mouth shut.

"Perhaps it wasn't a good idea bringing you on board for this one, especially since it *was* our first." She looked right at Quinn. "But I would do it again. And if our roles were reversed, you would have done the same thing."

Orlando's thigh-piercing grip eased a bit.

"You could have been a bit more forthcoming," Quinn said. "Let us know exactly what we were in for."

"You're right, but unfortunately I didn't know." Helen held up a hand again to hold off a response. "I was assured that Winston and his people were a top ops team. That's not an excuse. I'm just telling you what happened. I should have had my people dig deeper, but I didn't. That is my failure. One that I will not repeat." She grimaced. "I understand your anger and frustration. Throw in some guilt and regret and that's what I'm feeling right now. If you want to walk out and never work with us again, I completely understand. But I hope that's not the case."

While Quinn couldn't completely let go of his anger yet, most of it had ebbed. He wasn't sure how to respond and was glad when Orlando did it for them.

"We appreciate that," she said. "Thank you. I hope you understand that we're going to have to talk things over before we get back to you."

Helen nodded. "That's more than fair." For the first time, she picked up her coffee. "I do have a favor to ask, though."

"And what would that be?" Quinn asked.

"I'd like you to tell me exactly what happened."

"I'M NOT SURE I appreciate you shutting me down like that," Quinn said once he and Orlando were back in the car, heading toward her house.

"Oh, really? So you're the only one calling the shots now?"

"That's not what I mean," he said. "It's just—"

"It's just what? You're pissed off because the job didn't

go the way you thought it should? Helen represents a lot of potential work for us. That means for you and me and Nate and Daeng and anyone else we might need to hire. This was one project. A completely screwed-up one, but only one. She's helped us in the past so I think we owe her the benefit of the doubt, don't you?" She paused. "What I was doing in there when I 'shut you down' was refocusing the discussion so that we wouldn't burn any bridges we didn't need to. Unless you'd prefer to handle everything yourself again."

"Of course not." He rubbed his eyes and leaned back in his seat. He knew she was right. "Sorry."

She grunted.

"Is that an I-forgive-you?" he asked. "Or a you're-an-idiot?"

"Both, but just so I'm clear, more the latter than the former."

"God help us if we're not clear."

They drove on in silence for another several minutes before Orlando said, "If I'm really going to handle the administrative end of things, then it might be best in the future—if you're not of sound mind—that I go into meetings like this alone."

"Since when am I not of sound mind?"

"You don't want me to answer that."

He raised his hands in surrender. "Whatever you say, boss."

After all that had gone down on Duran Island—Peter dying, and Orlando nearly so—and the subsequent rooting out of those responsible, some decisions had to be made. The first concerned Quinn's status. For a while, when he was in Thailand recuperating from injuries received during the Mila Voss incident, he'd considered retirement. Some days he'd leaned heavily toward it, while others found him unsure what to do.

All the crap that had gone down since then, however, made it hard for him to deny he was good at what he did. Very good. And as tempting as sitting on a beach doing nothing was, his taste for the job had been reignited. There was another reason, too, one deep down inside he had no intention of sharing with anyone: the thought that if he didn't stay in the game, he wouldn't be able to properly react if someone threatened his friends or family again. He had to stay in the secret world. He had to remain sharp. He had to protect those he cared about.

The next decisions after the Duran Island debacle had been about the business itself. There was Nate, of course. Quinn's former apprentice had been keeping things going while Quinn was away, even using Quinn's name to maintain appearances. They could have parted ways like Quinn had done with Durrie not long after he completed his own apprenticeship, but Quinn offered Nate an equal partnership and Nate had accepted.

"For now, anyway," Nate had said. "We'll see how things go."

The partnership Quinn proposed wasn't just for the two of them. Orlando would make them a trio. Her role in their new configuration was the final decision that needed resolution. Her injuries were still a long way from being completely healed, and while she insisted she would be fine in the field, she had not put up much of an argument when Quinn proposed she take on the role of manager, handling such things as job requests and overall logistics, which she'd always taken care of anyway.

The Copenhagen job was the first under the new structure. Not exactly an auspicious beginning, but their portion of the project had gone off without a hitch.

Orlando found a parking spot almost directly in front of her house. As they climbed out, she pulled her phone from her pocket, checked the screen, and held the device up to her ear. Quinn moved ahead of her and started up the stairs to the front door. When he reached the porch, he looked back, expecting her to be right behind him, but she had stopped on the sidewalk, still listening to the phone.

As she lowered it a few seconds later, she looked surprised and a bit confused.

"What?" he asked.

She didn't answer. Didn't even look at him.

"Orlando."

She blinked and turned in his direction.

"What's up?" he asked.

"A voice mail," she said. "From Abraham."

CHAPTER
SEVEN

TAMPA, FLORIDA

IT TOOK EVERYTHING Abraham had to keep the rental car at the pace of the traffic around him. As much as he would have liked to press the accelerator to the floor, he knew that would only draw attention, something he had to avoid at all costs.

God, he couldn't remember the last time he had felt this nervous.

"Yes, I have," Eli had said when he'd called Abraham back.

The admission had so stunned Abraham he was barely able to speak. "What…?"

"I think it's best if we meet," Eli said.

Abraham struggled through the shock. "Of course. Um, I can come to you. Should be able to get to DC in—"

"Not DC."

"You're not there?"

"I soon won't be."

For the first time, Abraham could hear fear in his friend's voice. "What's wrong? Did something happen?"

"Might be nothing," Eli said. "I'm probably overreacting." A short pause. "Look, can you get to Tampa by tomorrow?"

"Florida?"

"Yes."

"I can probably get there by tonight," Abraham said. If the San Diego airport didn't have any direct flights, he could hop up to LAX in Los Angeles, which had one.

"Tomorrow. Eleven a.m. Azure Waves Hotel. Ask for Charles Young."

"Okay. I'll be there."

"Don't tell *anyone*."

Abraham had been right about being able to get there that night, but just barely. Because of flight schedules and the time difference with the East Coast, he'd arrived in Tampa not long before midnight. When he got to his hotel, he had tried to sleep, but because he was so wired, he only picked up an hour here and there.

Seven years earlier, after he had left the girl named Tessa with the pickup team in Amsterdam, he had left the espionage life and traded his townhome in eastern San Diego for a small bungalow in the Pacific Beach area. He had planned on leading a quiet life—jogging along the beach, reading books, and drinking more than his fair share of wine. He'd even thought he could volunteer some of his time at the tutoring center where he'd first spotted Orlando before taking her on as an apprentice. And while he ended up doing all of those things, none could push away the memories of Tessa.

"Abe!" she called to him. "Abe! Abe! Abe!"

Whether he was asleep or awake, it didn't matter. She called.

"Don't leave."

But he had, and it had been the worst decision of his life.

Six months into his retirement, he had called Eli.

"I need to know what happened to her," he'd told his friend. "I need to know she's all right."

Eli had been hesitant, but said he would do what he could.

For a while, Abraham checked in with him every week, but the analyst would always tell him he had found nothing new. Operation Overtake was sealed tight. To keep from annoying his friend too much, Abraham cut his calls down to once a month, and then once a year on the anniversary of when he'd last seen Tessa.

With the years stacking up, he had come to believe Eli would never find anything. But finally his old friend had, and Abraham could barely keep his hands from shaking at the prospect of learning what it was.

He found the Azure Waves Hotel a few blocks from the beach and pulled into the lot. It was a decent-sized place, with a trio of buildings surrounding what he figured was a pool area. And while it was no Four Seasons, it seemed like a nice old resort, someplace where families on a budget would be more than content to stay.

Abraham climbed out of the car and headed over to the lobby entrance.

The interior sported a retro 1960s décor, complete with a few scattered lava lamps and three plastic egg chairs. A few guests were gathered around a display of brochures, and some kids were sitting on a couch staring down at game consoles in their hands.

"Welcome to the Azure Waves Hotel. How can I help you?" the male receptionist asked when Abraham approached. The receptionist's name tag identified him as Devon.

"Good morning," Abraham said. "I'm meeting a friend of mine. I believe he's staying here."

Devon smiled. "Your friend's name?"

"Charles Young."

The receptionist typed it into his computer and looked at the screen. After a moment, his helpful expression turned into a puzzled one.

"Everything all right?" Abraham asked.

Devon donned a quick smile. "One moment," he said, and then stepped through a doorway along the back wall.

Abraham did not like the look of this. He plopped his arms on the counter as if bored, and sneaked a look at the computer screen. The name Charles Young was there, with the room number 721 beside it. There was some text in a box lower on the screen, but the font size was too small for him to read.

Soon, the receptionist reappeared, bringing with him an older blonde woman in a business suit.

"Good morning, sir," the woman said. "I'm Keri, the assistant manager. I understand you were looking for one of our guests."

"Yeah. Charles Young. I'm supposed to meet him here. Is there a problem?"

"Are you a friend of Mr. Young's?"

"A good friend. What's going on?"

"I'm sorry, Mr...." She paused, looking at Abraham.

"Durrie," he said, his old partner's name the first that came to mind.

"I'm sorry, Mr. Durrie. Mr. Young was taken to the hospital last night."

Abraham inwardly tensed. "Why?"

"From what I understand, it was a heart attack."

Heart attack? Though heart attacks *could* strike a thirtysomething person like Eli, the timing seemed extremely suspicious.

"Do you know what hospital he was taken to?" he asked.

"I would think Tampa General, but..." The woman looked at the computer. "Huh, there's no mention here, but Tampa General is closest."

"Who found him?"

"Actually, he was very lucky. Someone was visiting when it occurred and called an ambulance right away."

"So your staff didn't call the ambulance."

"No, sir."

"Do you have the name of the person who was visiting him?"

She hesitated, then said, "I'm not sure I should be giving that information out."

"Mr. Young is my friend," Abraham said. "Chances are, I know his visitor, too. And if Charles isn't at Tampa General, then this person will probably know where he is."

She thought about it for a moment before glancing back at the monitor. "Tina Dotson," she said.

"Thank you," he said. "I appreciate the help. Could you

give me directions to the hospital?"

Her look of discomfort shifted back to one of sympathy. "Of course."

ABRAHAM SPOTTED THE watcher as he made his way back to his car. A young guy, sitting in a sedan parked in a spot that gave him a clear view of the hotel entrance. Abraham caught the faint glint of a camera lens a second before the man lowered the device into his lap.

Had the guy snapped a shot of Abraham, or had he decided it wasn't worth it?

Abraham was confident he looked sufficiently old enough that even if a picture had been taken, the watcher wouldn't consider him much of a threat. Just to be safe, though, Abraham drove out of the lot at the expected slow speed for someone his age, and turned in the opposite direction of the hospital. For good measure, he left his blinker on far longer than necessary.

Three blocks away, when he could no longer see the resort, he worked his way over to a parallel road and drove to Tampa General as fast as caution would allow. Instead of heading inside, though, he parked in the lot and retrieved his laptop from the overnight bag in the passenger seat.

"All right," he said after the computer had booted up. "Let's see if you're here or not."

He hacked into the hospital administration's wireless network and navigated his way into the patient database, where he searched for patients named Charles Young. He wasn't surprised to find there was no one by that name.

He contemplated searching again, this time using Eli's real name, but decided it would be better not to have it noted by the system. He couldn't chance activating a digital tripwire that would let someone know of his attempt.

Minimizing the hospital's interface, he opened a new window and used Tampa General's network to connect to the Internet. From there, he made his way to the website for Azure Waves. As he had hoped, there was both a public section and an employee-only area. Though he'd been out of the business for seven years, he had done his best to keep up with the latest innovations in hardware and software, so breaking through the firewall into the private area was like walking through air.

Once there, it took him less than thirty seconds to find the incident report for Eli's "heart attack." According to the night manager, Charles Young had been taken from the hotel at approximately 11:20 p.m.

Abraham was about to close the window when he noticed that the manager had also entered the name of the ambulance company. An unexpected bonus. Abraham copied the name—Tobin Ambulance Services—and pasted it into a holding file, then returned to the hospital database.

A trip to Tampa General in an emergency vehicle with siren and lights blazing would have taken no more than five minutes. To give himself a cushion in case the time in the hotel report wasn't accurate, Abraham examined the emergency room admittance records from 10:40 p.m. until 12:30 a.m.

Plenty of people had come in, but none were heart-attack victims matching Eli's description. Though Abraham was pretty sure of what he'd find, he accessed the admittance records of other hospitals in Tampa and neighboring St. Petersburg. Eli was at none of them.

Yesterday, when Eli had called, he'd seemed scared. Had someone come for him?

Need to get a look through his hotel room, Abraham thought. *See if there are signs of a struggle or worse.*

First, though, he copied the name of the ambulance company into Google's search box and located the company's website. Unfortunately, unlike the hotel's, this company's business records were not kept on the same server. He entered the company's address into his GPS, and seventeen minutes later was parked at the curb right in front of the Tobin Ambulance Services facility.

Sure enough, the company's records were kept on an internal system Abraham was able to access through the company's "secure" Wi-Fi network. Tobin's schedule showed no mentions of any trips to Azure Waves Hotel, but there was an entry for a long-distance hire earlier that evening. Under the notes was a mention that the vehicle in question—ambulance 072—would be gone for up to twenty-four hours, and that it was a vehicle-only hire, with crew supplied by the client.

That had to be it.

He found the vehicle database and clicked on AMBULANCE 072. There were maintenance records, supply requests, and—as he'd hoped to find—a list of vehicle equipment. Like many companies these days, Tobin Ambulance Services had installed transponders in their ambulances to keep track of each vehicle's whereabouts. An unintended benefit was that the transponder would also allow someone to track where a particular ambulance had gone within the last twenty-four hours.

While Abraham could accomplish quite a bit on his laptop, this was not something for which he had the appropriate software. He would need help, and there was really only one person he could ask.

The line rang a single time before being answered by a short message.

As soon as the beep sounded, he said, "Orlando, it's me."

GLORIA CLARK—KNOWN as Tina Dotson to the Azure Waves night manager—reached for her phone. A moment earlier, it had buzzed twice fast, once slow. A text, but not just any text. The message on the screen read:

TG C.Y. fl trp 11:26 a

It was the digital flag she'd buried in the Tampa General Hospital database to notify her if anyone performed a search for a Charles Young, the name Eli Becker had been using at the Azure Waves. Apparently, three minutes earlier, someone had done just that. Which meant the surveillance she'd set up outside the hotel had been a waste of time. Those interested in the CIA analyst had somehow learned about Becker's supposed heart attack and were checking area hospitals remotely.

She had thought that might happen, but had hoped it would take at least a couple of days, if not a week, before someone came looking for Becker. Instead, only twelve hours had passed. An uncomfortable cushion at best.

She frowned, knowing they would have to move again soon, likely delaying their progress. The client wouldn't be particularly happy, but she'd waited this long, so what was a few more hours?

But leaving soon was not the same as leaving right away. Gloria retrieved the special bag and went into the other room, where King and Nolan were waiting.

"Call Andres," she said to King. "Tell him I don't need him in Tampa anymore and to get his ass up here." She looked at Nolan. "You're with me."

Together they headed toward the back room where Becker was locked away. It was time to find out what the son of a bitch knew.

CHAPTER
EIGHT

ORLANDO'S SON, GARRETT, was still at school, so the only people home when she and Quinn entered were Mr. and Mrs. Vu, the Vietnamese couple who took care of the household and watched Garrett when Orlando was away.

"Welcome home, Jonathan," Mr. Vu said.

"You look hungry," the man's wife noted. "I make pho special for you. Come, come." She motioned for Quinn and Orlando to follow her to the kitchen.

"Maybe later," Orlando told her. "We have some work we need to do so we'll be up in the office."

"But he just fly a long trip," Mrs. Vu said.

"No problem," Mr. Vu told his wife. "You can bring to them."

While Mrs. Vu looked annoyed, she made no further argument and headed toward the back of the house, her husband following.

Quinn and Orlando went upstairs to the room Orlando used as an office at the front of the shotgun house. Where one desk had once been, there were now two. Quinn pulled his chair close to Orlando's as she set down her phone and played the message through the speaker.

"Orlando, it's me," Abraham said. Though he was trying to sound calm, there was an urgency in his voice. "I need your help. Just a little research so it should be easy. It's time sensitive, though. I really need you to call me back as soon as you get this. Thanks. I'll talk to you soon."

Quinn frowned. "He didn't come out of retirement, did he?"

"Not that I'm aware of."

She tapped CALL BACK. The first ring didn't even finish before Abraham answered. "Hello?"

"You called?" she said.

"Thank God. I was starting to think that maybe you didn't get my message."

"I've got Quinn here with me."

A beat. "Johnny?"

Only two people had ever called Quinn that. The other was dead. But while his mentor Durrie usually had a sneer in his voice when he'd said it, Abraham had always used the name with respect.

"Hello, Abraham," Quinn said.

"What's this about needing some help?" Orlando asked.

"I, um, well, I'm not sure if, um…" Abraham's voice trailed off.

"Why don't you just tell me what's going on?"

"I was kind of thinking I could talk to you alone."

"Alone?" she said. "You know I'll tell Quinn whatever you tell me."

"Even if I ask that you keep it to yourself?"

"Yes," she said without hesitating.

"It's okay," Quinn said, rising from his chair. "I don't want to make you uncomfortable. I'll step out for a minute."

"If she's going to tell you anyway, don't bother," Abraham grumbled.

Quinn exchanged a look with Orlando. Abraham didn't usually get upset easily.

"Seriously," Quinn said, "if it's going to be a problem, then we can—"

"No, no, it's fine." Abraham paused and took a deep breath. "Really, it's fine. I just…" He fell silent again.

"Abraham?" Orlando said.

Nothing for a moment, then, "I need a little help tracking a vehicle."

"Please tell me you haven't taken on a job," she said.

"Of course not."

"So you want me to track this car down for fun?"

"I want you to track it down because I need to know where it went."

"Why?"

He didn't answer.

"Okay," she said. "I guess I could look it up. Do you have a plate number?"

"I could look up a plate number myself. What I need to figure out is what route it took last night."

"Took, as in past tense?"

"Yes."

Looking more confused than ever, she said, "I'm not sure how you're expecting me to do that. If you're thinking satellite footage, that's going to be time consuming and possibly fruitless."

"No, I don't mean satellite footage," Abraham said, his exasperation leaking through again. "The vehicle I'm interested in has a transponder."

"Oh," she said. "Sure, if it has a transponder, that's different. Are we talking a big rig?"

"It is *not* a big rig."

"Then what?"

"A vehicle I'm trying to find."

Orlando glanced at Quinn, silently asking, "What the hell?" Since he was thinking the same thing, all he could do was shrug.

"Do you at least have the transponder ID?" she asked.

"Of course I do." He read off a number. "Can you track it?"

"It would help if I knew where I'm supposed to be looking, and, if possible, a more precise time frame than just last night."

"Tampa, Florida, eleven twenty p.m. onward."

"Is that where you are? Tampa?"

No response.

She frowned. "Abraham, what's going on?

"Nothing. This is a small matter, that's all. Something for a friend."

"So you *are* working a job."

"A favor only. Listen, if you don't want—"

"Relax," she said. "Why don't you let me look into this and call you back, okay?"

"You won't be long, will you?" he asked. "I need to know right away."

"I'll call you as soon as I can."

Orlando hung up and stared out the window, lost in thought.

Quinn was considering breaking the silence when a knock on the door did it for him.

Orlando made no indication she'd respond, so he said, "Yes?"

"May we come in?" Mr. Vu asked.

"Please."

Mrs. Vu came first, carrying a tray holding two steaming bowls of pho, and her husband was right behind her with glasses of her homemade lemonade.

"Thank you," Quinn told them as they set the meal on the desk.

"If you want more, let us know. We bring up," Mrs. Vu said.

With that, the couple left and pulled the door closed behind them.

Whether it was the click of the lock or the aroma of the pho, Orlando finally pulled herself from her trance. Without a word, she woke up her computer and began working. Knowing it was best not to disturb her, Quinn started in on his soup. It was as delicious as ever. Mrs. Vu had even added the exact amount of Sriracha sauce he liked.

"Well, this is not what I expected," she said several moments later. "Turns out Abraham's mysterious vehicle is an ambulance."

Being in mid-bite, Quinn could only respond with a grunt.

She opened another program and plugged in the

transponder number. The computer took nearly fifteen seconds to gather the data and display it in list form. After studying the results, Orlando clicked on one of the addresses and a map opened. She nodded to herself, then performed the task again with a different address.

"Huh," she said.

"What?" Quinn asked.

"Looks like this ambulance only went on one trip last night, starting at a place called the Azure Waves Hotel."

"Where did it go?" he asked.

She motioned for him to be quiet, so he dipped his chopsticks back into the pho, this time coming up with a tasty-looking piece of beef.

Finally, Orlando leaned back. "Well, they didn't stay in town."

"Where did they go?" he asked between chews.

"Mississippi."

Quinn raised an eyebrow. "That's a long way from Tampa."

"It is," she agreed. "Looks like they stopped at a private home in a town called Moss Point."

Quinn leaned over so he could see the map. There were only four states in the US he had never been to. Mississippi was one of them. According to the map, Moss Point was in the narrow tab of land that touched the Gulf of Mexico at the southern end of the state, only a few miles from Alabama.

Orlando switched from the overhead satellite shot to a street-level angle of the house in question. It was a brick one-story, with a gray roof and wide lawn. Nothing special about the place. Just an average house on an average street.

She opened another window and entered the address into a search engine.

"Oh," she said in surprise. "Says here the house is currently on the market. And...it looks like it's been for sale for nearly a year." She clicked through the photos. "If these shots are accurate, then no one's currently living there."

"Are you sure it was the ambulance's final destination?"

Quinn asked. "Maybe they just made a stop there for some reason."

"This is as far as they went." She checked the screen again. "The vehicle sat there for thirty-four minutes, then headed back to Florida. Enough time to unload someone and stretch their legs."

"Maybe the listing's out of date," he suggested. "Could be the place was recently purchased and someone who needed an ambulance to get there is moving in."

She picked up her phone. "One way to know for sure." She pulled up the real estate agencies information and dialed the number. "Yes, good afternoon. How y'all doin'?" she said, affecting a very passable Southern accent. "Thank you. I'm fine, too. The reason I'm calling is because my husband and I are moving to the area soon. We've been looking at different houses on the Internet—....Oh, sorry, yes, I'm Mary, Mary Hanson....Good to meet you, Debbie. See, we saw a place online that I believe you are the agent for." Orlando gave the woman the address of the house the ambulance had visited, then listened for several seconds. "I see....Now that's interesting....How large are the bedrooms?...Oh, is that right? Well, to be honest, I'm not sure that would work for us, then. Guess we'll have to keep looking....I'll check out what else you have to offer. We'll be sure to stop by your office when we get to town....Yes, yes. Thank you again." She hung up.

"I'd like it very much if you'd use that accent from now on," Quinn said. "Will that be a problem?"

"Troll," she scoffed, her voice back to normal. "The house is still for sale, but it's under a short-term rental."

"How short?"

"A week."

"So an ambulance takes someone to a house that until a day ago was empty, and will be again in a few more days," he said. "Why would they do that?"

Orlando stared at Quinn's half-empty bowl of pho before twisting back to her computer and tapping on the keyboard again. He leaned in behind her so he could see what she was doing. She had the website to Azure Waves Hotel on the screen and was using it to work her way into the company's system.

"There's an incident report here," she said. "One of the guests apparently had a heart attack last night. A guy by the name of Charles Young. Sound familiar?"

Quinn shook his head. "Sounds generic, if you ask me."

Though she didn't say it, he knew she was thinking the same thing.

"There was a woman with him when it happened," she said, still looking at the screen. "Tina Dotson."

That didn't sound quite so generic, but he'd still never heard the name before.

"According to the report, she's the one who called for the ambulance," Orlando went on. "Get this—at eleven twenty p.m. It came from a place called Tobin Ambulance Services, which happens to own the vehicle the transponder number belongs to."

"So instead of taking this Mr. Young to a hospital," Quinn said, "they took a man who'd just had a heart attack to...Mississippi? I don't think I like where this is going."

Orlando frowned, her eyes staring once more out the window. "Neither do I."

CHAPTER
NINE

MOSS POINT, MISSISSIPPI

THE MOMENT ELI heard the doorknob turn he closed his eyes, hoping his captors would leave him alone if they thought he was asleep.

The slap to his face told him otherwise.

"Mr. Becker. Your attention, please."

He recognized the voice as belonging to the woman who had called herself Tina, though he now doubted that was her real name. She'd followed him off the elevator at the Azure Waves Hotel when he was returning from his errand. She'd acted drunk at first, but once the doors had closed after the other riders got off, she had sobered up in a hurry and shoved a gun into his side, telling him to take her to his room.

Once inside, he'd felt the sting of a needle, and the next thing he knew, he was here—wherever here was—strapped to a gurney and wearing only his underwear.

The woman slapped him again. "Mr. Becker, I know you're not asleep."

As he reluctantly opened his eyes, she grabbed his chin and tilted his head up so she could lock her gaze onto his. "Are you listening?"

He nodded.

"Good," she said. "Overtake. The name familiar?"

Eli tried, really tried, to keep his face blank, but his eyes couldn't hide the truth.

"So that's a yes," she said. She let go of his chin and straightened up. "Here is what's going to happen now. You will tell me everything you know about Overtake. After you do, you can go home. Nod again if you understand."

As he nodded, he whispered, "I don't really know anything."

She smiled. "We both know that's not true."

"I swear, I don't. I've heard the name, yes, but that's all."

She leaned forward again, not stopping until her face was a few inches from his. "You *will* tell me everything I want to know," she said. "The more you cooperate, the less painful it will be for you. So, Overtake."

She stared at him, waiting for a response. When he said nothing, she shrugged. "Very well," she said, turning for the exit. "I'll be right back. Just need to fetch one of my colleagues. We'll see how long you can hold out once he starts in on you."

His eyes stayed on the door as it closed.

He knew that no matter what he said, she would never let him go.

So say nothing, Abraham's voice whispered in Eli's head.

If only it were that easy, he thought.

What does easy have to do with it?

He had no answer for that.

TAMPA, FLORIDA

WHILE WAITING FOR Orlando to call back, Abraham returned to the Azure Waves Hotel and made his way up to room 721.

According to the hotel registry, Eli had booked the room for three nights, meaning it was possible it had not yet been cleaned and given to someone else. Abraham listened at the door and heard only the quiet of an empty room. Working not quite as quickly as he had before he retired, he disabled the lock and let himself in.

In the bathroom he found a used towel dumped on the floor, dry to the touch. It had been there since at least early that morning, long before any new guests would have been assigned the room. Therefore, Eli must have dropped it there the night before.

Abraham moved into the bedroom. The only evidence that anyone had been there was the rumpled cover on the bed. If his friend had come with any luggage, it was gone. About the only good news was that Abraham saw no signs of a struggle or any bloodstains.

His phone vibrated. He yanked it out and raised it to his ear. "Orlando?"

"You expecting someone else?" she asked.

"Were you able to figure out where it went?"

"I was."

"Well?"

"Abraham, I'm going to ask you again. What's going on?"

"I told you, it's…a favor."

"A favor," she repeated, not sounding convinced.

His jaw tensed. "Are you going to give me the information or not?"

"I want to know what you're getting yourself into. You're too old to be messing around in anything dangerous."

"What I'm up to is not your business. If you don't want to help me, that's fine. I'll find someone else who will."

"Abraham, you know you can tell me anything," she said.

He tried to rein in his frustration. "I know that. And I realize you're only trying to do what you think is best for me." He paused, knowing this was getting him nowhere. "I apologize. I…I shouldn't have involved you."

Before she could say anything, he hung up.

He squeezed his eyes shut. "Dammit, dammit, dammit."

A second later Orlando called again. He sent her to voice mail.

It didn't matter that she *was* right and he was too old to

be messing around. He had no choice. He had involved Eli in the search for information about Tessa and now Eli was in trouble because of that.

The phone vibrated again, and once more he rejected the call.

With his former apprentice no longer an option, who else could he ask? He stared across the room, thinking. The vast majority of his contacts weren't working anymore. They were either dead or living out what time they had left in peace and quiet. Anyone still in the business would likely barely remember him.

There has to be someone.

His phone beeped. Not a call this time—a text.

Of course it was from Orlando. What was unexpected, though, was the content of the text—an address in Moss Point, Mississippi. As he was reading it, a second message came in.

Be careful

He sent her a reply.

Thank you.

SAN FRANCISCO, CALIFORNIA

ORLANDO READ THE text from Abraham.

"Well?" Quinn asked.

She turned the phone so he could see.

"He's going there, you know," he said.

"I know."

"Maybe this Charles Young guy is just an old friend he's trying to track down."

Her look indicated she didn't believe that for a second. Neither did Quinn, for that matter. If it were that simple, Abraham would have told them what was going on instead of going all George Smiley.

"How involved do you want to get?" he asked.

"It's Abraham," she replied.

Of course it was. Abraham had brought her into the business, helped her become who she was. Which meant Quinn owed him a huge debt, too, because if Abraham hadn't given her a chance, Quinn and Orlando would have never met.

"Do we know anyone in the area?" he asked.

"Winger was working out of New Orleans last I checked," she said.

"Right. Marguerite Caron might be there, too, if she's not on a job."

"I'll call them. See if one of them is free."

Quinn put his hand on her back. "See if they're both free. While you do that, I'll check on flights for us."

She kissed him hard. "Thank you."

CHAPTER
TEN

MOSS POINT, MISSISSIPPI

BY THE TIME Abraham flew out of Tampa, it was already mid-afternoon.

The closest airport to Moss Point, Mississippi, was in Mobile, Alabama, but the earliest flight headed there was booked, so it was faster for him to fly into Pensacola, Florida, and then drive the ninety-five miles in a rental. By the time he turned off I-10, the sun was nearing the horizon, triggering the automatic headlights to flick on.

The road led over a bridge and onto a spit of land that took Abraham into Moss Point. Using the car's built-in GPS, he navigated through the area until he found himself on a wide residential street lined by trees and brush and well-manicured lawns.

He slowed so he could read the numbers printed on the mailboxes at the end of each driveway. When he reached the one corresponding to the address Orlando had given him, he drove on without looking directly at the house. The most he could gather from the corner of his eye was that it had a brick façade, a For Sale sign stuck in the front yard, and no cars parked in the driveway.

He continued on until he reached the end of the block, where he turned and found a place to park. This being a small town, he knew a stranger would be noticed so he let the evening grow a bit darker before he finally climbed out of his car.

When he reached the intersection, he paused next to some trees and studied the street where the target house was. While there were no streetlights, several of the homes had powerful porch lights and flood lamps mounted to garages that could, if he wasn't cautious, expose his presence. The right side of the road, the side opposite the house, seemed the darkest, so that was the one he used.

He was only a couple houses shy of being directly across from his target when he heard a car engine start. He dropped to a crouch and shuffled off the shoulder into a clump of bushes. Back the way he'd come, headlight beams fell across the road from one of the driveways. A moment later, a truck rolled into view. It sat at the meeting point of driveway and road for several seconds before it turned onto the street and drove right past him without slowing.

Abraham waited until the taillights disappeared in the distance before he continued on. Once he had an unhindered view of the brick house, he paused again. Though the driveway was still empty, he noted that its garage was large enough to easily accommodate three cars. The house itself was a decent-sized one-story structure. Three bedrooms would be his guess, more if the house extended farther back than he could see. Like the other homes in the neighborhood, this one had no fence, only hedges and trees that seemed to mark the boundary between properties.

He'd expected to see lights in at least some of the windows, but the place was dark. Perhaps the people who had arrived in the ambulance were sticking to the rooms at the back of the house. If they were holding Eli against his will, that was certainly a possibility.

He continued down the edge of the road opposite the house, going a hundred feet past the driveway entrance before deciding it was safe enough to cross to the other side. He then made his way back to the edge of the target property and scanned the tall hedge dividing its lot from the one he was standing in front of. The hedge was fairly thick most of the way back, but not thick enough to prevent him from angling his way between bushes. He checked the neighbor's house—a few lights on and the telltale flicker of a television.

Dog? he thought.

Probably. But he hadn't heard any barks yet, so if there was one, hopefully it was inside.

He took a tentative step onto the target property. When no one yelled at him and no dog barked, he took another and another and another. When he was level with the garage, Abraham squeezed slowly through the bushes, a task that was not as easy as it was in theory. He'd put on a little weight since he'd retired, so his stomach rubbed against branches it would have never touched when he was active.

Once he was on the other side, he moved up tight against the garage wall and worked his way to the back corner. He listened before he peered around and found that the rear of the place was as dark as the front.

His confusion growing, he snuck over to the house. No voices, no sounds of plumbing, no television. Nothing.

There were several windows across the back and an elevated wooden deck with a set of French doors leading into the house. In a crouch, he moved over to the nearest window and rose just enough to peek inside, but it was a wasted effort. The window was covered with a shade and he could see nothing.

No shade on the next window, but beyond was only a bare room.

He headed over to the short staircase leading up to the deck. No shades or curtains over the French doors, only the same empty darkness he'd seen in the bedroom. He stopped a tread shy of the deck and stared inside the house, looking for the slightest hint of movement.

"No one's home."

Abraham nearly jumped out of his skin. He twisted around, his hands moving up, ready for a fight.

The voice belonged to a tall woman with wavy dark hair. She was standing on the grass by the base of the stairs, holding a sound-suppressed GLOCK 9mm at her side.

"We already checked," she said. "Whoever was here is long gone."

Abraham was weaponless, but he wasn't about to let himself be taken prisoner by whoever these people were. When she opened her mouth to speak again, he rushed down the steps and slammed his shoulder into her chest, sending them both to the ground.

Just because he was getting old didn't mean he'd forgotten his moves. It did, however, mean some of those moves came with greater consequences. As he pushed himself back to his feet, there wasn't a joint in his body that wasn't screaming in pain. He tried sprinting around the side of the house to get away, but what he accomplished was more of a fast walk.

"Hey!" the woman yelled. "What the hell?"

Expecting a bullet to pierce his back at any second, he kept going, grabbing the corner of the house as he reached it and using the redirection of his momentum to propel him toward the street. But he'd barely reached the front yard when a man raced out from God only knew where and grabbed him around the arms. The shoulder Abraham had slammed into the woman felt like it was on fire. He stifled the scream but could not keep the pain from his face.

The man released him and said, "Dude, are you all right?"

Before Abraham could answer, the woman ran up, fire in her eyes. "I do *not* appreciate getting pushed to the ground." When she noticed his discomfort, some of the anger left her face. "What's wrong with you?"

Abraham took a couple of deep breaths, forcing the pain down. "Whatever you want, there's nothing I can tell you," he said. "I don't know anything."

"Uh, sure. Whatever," the guy said. "We don't actually need anything from you. We're only here—"

"Then you won't mind if I leave," Abraham said, taking a backward step away from them.

"Mr. Delger, we're here to help you, not hurt you."

"Speak for yourself," the woman said as she rubbed her chest. "I might want to do a little hurting."

Abraham stared back and forth between them. "How do you know my name?"

"What do you mean, how do we know your name? Orlando told us," the guy said.

Abraham cocked his head. "Orlando?"

"Yeah. She's the one who sent us." The man studied Abraham for a second. "I take it she didn't let you know that."

Abraham shook his head.

"That explains a lot, doesn't it?" The guy held out his hand. "Dylan Winger."

Cradling his right arm to keep the pain in check, Abraham said, "You'll understand if I don't shake."

"Oh, sure. Sorry." Winger dropped his hand and asked, "What happened?"

"He rammed his shoulder into my chest is what happened," the woman said.

"Then you've already met Marguerite," Winger said.

Abraham and the woman glanced at each other but made no other acknowledgment.

"Why would Orlando send you?" Abraham asked.

"Oh, I don't know," Marguerite said. "Maybe because she thought you'd do something foolish like walk up to a house that might have been occupied with people who would not have been as friendly as us? Think that might be it?"

"You already told me the house is empty."

"*You* didn't know that."

"I suspected it."

"At what point? Before you snuck up on the house? Or after you looked through the windows?"

Abraham glared at her, more because she'd hit too close to the truth than anything else. As he broke eye contact, another wave of pain shot up his shoulder, causing him to wince and suck in air.

"Maybe I should take a look at that," Winger said, taking a step toward him.

"I'm fine," Abraham told him.

"Clearly you're not."

Reluctantly, Abraham let Winger approach. The man gently probed his shoulder.

"The good news is, it's not dislocated. Just bruised, I think. You might want to take it easy on who you tackle over the next few days."

"Gee, thanks," Abraham said.

"Always happy to help."

Abraham looked back at the house. "You're sure it's empty?"

"If it weren't, don't you think someone would have come out by now to ask what we're doing on their lawn?" Marguerite said.

Abraham turned to Winger, "You've been inside?"

"Marguerite was first on scene. She did a quick look around."

Abraham glanced at her again but said nothing.

She grunted and rolled her eyes. "Come on. You'll want to look anyway."

She led the two men back around the house and through the French doors.

"Ruts," she said, pointing at the depressions in the carpet leading from the foyer and into the hall to the bedrooms. The ruts were parallel, a couple feet apart.

Marguerite, Abraham, and Winger followed them down the hallway and into the bedroom, where the shade had been pulled down. Unlike every other room Abraham had seen in the house, this one was not empty. Near the door were a couple bags of trash, and against the wall a cheap plastic outdoor chair.

The carpet marks led right into the middle of the room and then stopped. Marguerite knelt down.

"See these?" She nodded at the end of the depressions, where an inch-long stretch had sunk deeper into the carpet than the tracks in general. "And there." She pointed to a spot several feet back down the trail, where two identical marks had been left.

There was no need to explain what they were. Abraham had recognized them as the points where wheels had stopped. He could surmise three things from this. One, by the length between the sets of wheels, the object attached to them was long, like a table or a bed. Since Eli had apparently been taken away in an ambulance, it wasn't much of a leap to guess the marks had been made by a gurney. Two, by the depth of the four indentations, the gurney had remained in position for at least an hour, probably more. And three, the depth also meant the gurney had been carrying something heavy. Like a body.

He walked over to the bags of trash. Mostly they contained fast-food cartons and empty cups and dirty napkins, but there were also some wadded tissues, a few cotton balls, and a few empty bandage wrappers.

"How long ago did you get here?" he asked Marguerite.

She stared at him blankly.

With a sigh, he said, "Look, I'm sorry I hit you, but you would have done the same in my circumstances."

"I would have knocked you out," she said.

"So you're mad at me because I didn't knock you out?"

She groaned. "I got here about two hours ago."

"And they were already gone?"

"Yes," she said, disinterested.

"Did you find anything else?"

"What, like a note with a forwarding address?"

Matching her tone, he said, "Well, if you did, that would be helpful, wouldn't it?"

She stewed for a moment before saying, "No. I didn't find anything else."

Abraham headed for the bedroom door.

"Where are you going?" Winger asked.

"To look around," Abraham said. "I assume that's all right."

He searched the rest of the house, carefully checking for anything that might have been left behind, but there was nothing else, so he headed out the French doors, intending to return to his car and get the hell out of there. As he stepped outside, he found Marguerite and Winger on the deck, leaning against the railing.

"All done?" Winger asked.

"Yeah," Abraham said. "Uh, thanks, I guess, for...I don't know. Whatever reason you were supposed to be here."

He headed for the stairs.

"Mr. Delger, please. Not so fast," Winger said.

"I've got things to do," Abraham said, not stopping. "So if you'll excuse me—"

"Actually, our instructions were to stick with you."

That stopped Abraham. He turned back around. "What? Why?"

That's when he realized Winger and Marguerite weren't the only ones who'd been waiting on the deck. There were two others near the house.

"Because that's what I told them to do," Orlando said.

CHAPTER
ELEVEN

DALLAS, TEXAS

THE DALLAS AREA was experiencing a cold snap. According to the weather forecast, there was a small chance of snow in the next forty-eight hours.

Nate didn't hate the cold like Quinn did, but he didn't like when it interfered with his work. In preplanning his and Daeng's current assignment, he had decided on a course that involved a remote burial and the use of their standard chemical mix that would reduce a body to sludge before anyone could discover the grave and dig up the remains.

Unfortunately, the cold was causing two problems. The lesser issue was the ground freezing, making it harder to dig out a final resting place. The larger one concerned the chemical stew itself. It didn't work very well when used at temperatures under forty degrees. The projected average Dallas temperature for the next seven days was thirty-one degrees. And tomorrow evening, the night of the op, the temperature was predicted to dip to as low as nineteen degrees, throwing Nate's intended strategy out the window.

"May I make a suggestion?" Daeng asked.

"By all means," Nate told him.

They were in Nate's hotel room and had just confirmed the latest weather data.

"It's very simple. In the future we don't take work so far

from a large body of water we can use to dump the remains."

"Funny," Nate said, not laughing. "But I'm not worried about the future at the moment. I'm worried about what we do now."

"Naturally," Daeng said. "That's why I'm thinking of the bigger picture."

"You do realize you're not helping, right?"

"That is a matter of perspective."

"And you realize saying *that* also doesn't help?"

"What? Is my suggestion not a good one?"

"Your suggestion is impractical in the 'bigger picture' and unhelpful in the here and now."

"But you already know what we're going to do in the here and now."

"Uh, no, I don't. That's what I'm trying to figure out."

"You know it. You just don't realize it yet."

"That philosophical crap is going to eventually result in either Quinn or me killing you. You've been warned."

"If it is my time to go, then so be it. I will gladly accept whatever is—"

"Oh, for the love of God!"

Daeng tried to hold a straight face, but only lasted a few seconds before he began to laugh. Nate frowned, but soon joined in. When they finally calmed down, they were both out of breath and smiling.

"Fine," Nate said. "Basement protocol."

"See, I told you that you already knew what to do."

The basement protocol was nearly the same as the grave option Nate had originally planned. The only difference was the use of a basement floor, typically inside a business facility, and preferably a new one where concrete hadn't been poured but soon would be. While basements might be cool, they seldom ever dipped below forty degrees. It wasn't Nate's favorite option. He thought the idea of burying a corpse underneath a building people would be spending their days in was kind of creepy.

Unfortunately, it didn't look like they had a choice.

"Since you're obviously the smarter of the two of us

tonight," Nate said, "I'm going to let you find our location."

"That honor should go to you," Daeng said.

"Uh-uh. You're not talking your way out of this one."

"But—"

Nate held up a hand. "It's all you, brother." He stood up and patted Daeng on the back. "I'm sure there are plenty of new buildings going up not too far away."

Before Daeng could argue again, Nate walked into the suite's bedroom and shut the door. He checked the time and added seven hours. Early, but not too early.

He pulled out his phone, and a few seconds later, Liz's sleepy voice traveled under the Atlantic Ocean and halfway across North America before slipping into his ear. "Hello?"

"Don't you have class this morning?"

"Hi," she said, a smile in her voice. "My early class got canceled so I don't have anything until ten."

After missing most of her classes in the fall due to what happened on Isla de Cervantes and the events that sprang from it, Quinn's sister had finally returned to Paris to continue work on her master's degree in art history at the Sorbonne.

"Sorry," Nate said. "I'll let you go back to sleep."

"No. Don't you dare hang up yet."

"At least tell me you slept well."

"I dreamt about you so it wasn't too bad, I guess."

"Look out your window. What's it like there today?"

He heard the covers of her bed move. "Wet and cold. How about there?"

"Cold and dry."

"In L.A.?"

"Texas."

"Work?"

"Well, I didn't come here to watch the Cowboys play."

"Are you being careful?"

"I'm thinking about it."

"Think harder."

The line went quiet for a moment.

"I miss you," she said.

"What, with all those French guys around? I doubt it."

"Don't joke. I do. I mean, these French guys are fine for sex and all, but it's always you I think about."

"Do I need to come over there?"

"Absolutely."

A beat. "I miss you, too," he said. "Every minute."

"Come see me."

"What about the French guys?"

"They'll understand."

MISSISSIPPI

"PLEASE TELL ME you realize how dumb coming here on your own was," Orlando said.

They had taken rooms at a motel in Pascagoula, just south of Moss Point. While Marguerite and Winger had gone off to get some sleep, Quinn and Orlando had hauled Abraham into their room.

"Apparently I *didn't* come here on my own," Abraham told her.

"You know what I mean."

"I'm not an amateur," he shot back. "I've done much more dangerous things on my own. This was nothing."

"Really?" Orlando said. "And when was the last time—"

Taking a page out of Orlando's book, Quinn put a hand on her shoulder to calm her down. He said to Abraham, "Why don't you tell us what you expected to find here?"

"What I expected to find is none of your business. If I'd known you were going to meddle, I would have never called in the first place."

Quinn could feel Orlando tense again under his palm, so he squeezed a little, hoping it would be enough to keep her in check.

"We're not meddling," he said. "We're concerned, that's all. You've been out of the field for a while now, and let's face it, you're not exactly young anymore."

"Are you trying to win points here?" Abraham asked.

"I'm trying to have an honest conversation."

Abraham grunted derisively.

"If you don't want our help," Quinn said, "we understand. But before you make that decision, think first. Who better to share what's going on with than us? We can help you."

Quinn waited, hoping Abraham would realize he was right, but the older man kept his mouth shut.

Orlando fidgeted in her seat. Quinn squeezed again and received a quick sideways glare.

"Could you at least give us some idea of what this is about?" Quinn asked Abraham. "That would ease our concerns. Did you hire on for a project?"

Abraham hesitated. "I told you before it's a favor. It's personal."

"Okay. Still doesn't mean you need to take it all on yourself."

Abraham sighed and pushed himself to his feet. "Thank you for your concern, but I don't need any help." He headed across the room.

Quinn jumped up. "Wait. We're your friends, Abraham. Helping is what friends do."

Pausing at the door, Abraham said, "I realize that. As your friend, I'm telling you, please, leave me alone."

He pulled the door open and left.

"Wow," Orlando said as she rose to her feet. "Nice job."

"Yeah, well, if you'd kept it up, he would have left even sooner."

She hurried over to the dresser where she'd left her backpack, unzipped one of the sections, and began rummaging through it. A few seconds later, she pulled out a small plastic box and removed something from inside. She threw the box back in the bag and ran to the door.

"Where are you going?" Quinn asked, heading after her.

"No. Stay here. I'll be right back."

With that, she was out the door and gone.

ABRAHAM WAS IN the parking lot, his key fob in hand, when

93

he heard footsteps racing out of the hotel.

Without looking back, he unlocked the door of his rental car.

"Abraham," Orlando called from behind him.

He stopped, one hand on the door, then turned. "I told you, I don't need any help."

"I know," she said, slowing as she reached him. "I...I didn't want to leave things like that. Look, I'm sorry. I can't help but worry about you."

He relaxed a little. "You don't have to worry about me. You know that. I've always been able to take care of myself."

"Yeah, you have. It's just hard for me to turn off."

He touched her arm and smiled. "Orlando, always taking care of everyone else. I'll be fine. There is *nothing* to worry about."

She looked him in the eye, as if trying to read his soul. "You promise?"

"I promise," he lied.

Her grin was one of resignation. She nodded and put her arms around him. "Whatever you're doing, just be careful, okay?"

"Always," he said, holding her tight.

"And if you need anything—*anything*—call me. I'll do what I can, and I won't ask any more questions."

As much as he would've liked to believe that, he knew that given the opportunity, she wouldn't be able to keep herself from getting involved. But this was his mess, and he didn't want anyone else put in danger because of him.

"I appreciate that," he said.

She pulled back enough so that she could look at him, her hands clasping his shoulders. "But you're not going to, are you?"

He let his smile be his answer.

"Promise me you'll at least let me know when everything's all right," she said, grabbing the collar of his suit coat on either side of his neck and giving it a gentle tug.

"I promise," he said.

Her eyes narrowed as she studied him some more, then

94

she finally let go of his jacket and stepped back.

"So where are you going now?" she asked.

"Ha. Nice try," he said. He opened the door, climbed in, and looked back at her. "It's good to see you."

"Now I know you're lying," she said.

He laughed as he pulled the door closed and started the car.

QUINN WAS SURFING through the limited options on the TV, trying to occupy his mind, when Orlando rushed back in.

"Is he gone?" he asked.

"Yes," she said, heading straight for her backpack.

This time, she opened the large rear section and removed her laptop. Sitting at the desk, she turned the computer on and hacked into the hotel's wireless system.

Quinn moved in behind her. On the screen was a map of Pascagoula, with a green glowing blip moving steadily away from their location.

"You tagged him," he said.

"Of course I did," Orlando replied.

"He'll find it."

"Maybe. But he hasn't yet." She looked back at him. "You think Marguerite and Winger are up for a little tailing job?"

"I'll let you wake them up and ask."

CHAPTER
TWELVE

LOUISIANA

BECKER HAD NOT left DC as cleanly as he'd thought. Gloria and her team, after finally connecting his name to the person who had been looking into Operation Overtake, had rushed to his home after learning he'd not gone to work. Unfortunately, he was gone by then.

Gloria figured he must've been making a run for it, so she ordered facial recognition checks to be done at all area airports and train stations. They got a hit at Dulles, but weren't able to determine he was traveling under the name Charles Young until after his plane had left. That led them to the Tampa flight, and then to a reservation at the Azure Waves Hotel.

A McCrillis company jet rushed Gloria and her men to Florida, where, after reaching the Azure Waves, she had played the part of the drunk riding up the elevator until it was time to slip the muzzle of her gun into Becker's side. After they stepped into his room, she'd administered a sedative via syringe and guided him into a chair as he lost consciousness. Ten minutes later he was transported down to the ambulance, and Gloria and her team were on the road.

A textbook acquisition.

She had hoped their stay at the Moss Point house would last longer than eighteen hours. But the fact that someone was looking for Becker meant relocation had to come sooner than planned.

She was prepared, though. On the flight from DC, she had arranged for the use of half a dozen places throughout the southeast, in anticipation of a situation such as this.

Their new location was a farm twenty miles west of Baton Rouge, Louisiana.

A corporation controlled the land around the place, while the old farmhouse and barn and the few acres immediately surrounding them were still in private hands. As with many places like it, after the owner passed away, the heirs had decided to sell it. The farmhouse had been on the market for nearly six months, so it had been easy to obtain as another short-term rental.

Upon arrival, they put Becker in a small bedroom at the end of the hall. It was so small that it had barely enough space for the gurney, a chair, and the table where Gloria left the bag of tools she would use to continue extracting information from Becker.

In the limited time they'd had back in Mississippi, she had tried to get Becker to talk by having one of her men rough him up. Usually, a physical approach was all that was needed for those who had never been trained to withstand interrogation. Becker, however, proved to be more stubborn than she'd expected, and ended up passing out without divulging anything.

Anxious to get him to talk, and knowing they would soon need to leave Moss Point, she had decided to forgo another beating and try the drug route. But instead of turning him into a blathering idiot like it should have, the drug, combined with his deteriorating physical condition, plunged him into a deep state of unconsciousness he'd remained in throughout the drive to Louisiana and the transfer to his new room.

Once her men were on watch around the farm, she returned to Becker's room, not wanting to delay the interrogation any longer. She wasn't surprised to find his eyes were still closed, and his breathing as steady and deep as it had been when they brought him in.

But enough was enough.

"Mr. Becker," she said, slapping his face. "Mr. Becker, time to wake up." When he didn't respond, she slapped him again. "Mr. Becker, open your eyes."

Nothing.

Very well, then. She walked over to the table and opened her bag. From inside, she removed two boxes, one that contained her syringes, and another that contained her drugs. She selected a stimulant, drew the appropriate dose into the syringe, and returned to the bed.

"Last chance," she said.

No movement.

She stuck the needle into his arm and depressed the plunger. Though his appearance remained unchanged, she knew it would be only a matter of minutes before he was wide awake.

She set the empty syringe on the table and decided to visit the toilet while she waited, to make sure nothing interfered with her work once she got started.

ELI HAD WOKEN as the vehicle he was in pulled to a stop. Hoping to stave off another beating for as long as he could, he'd kept his eyes closed and his breathing slow and deep so no one would know he'd regained consciousness.

Doors were opened and fresh air rushed inside as his abductors climbed out. A few minutes passed before another door opened and his gurney jerked left and right before being pulled outside. As his bed rolled over rough ground, he heard the men around him tell each other to "watch it" and "go left" and "not so fast." Finally, the rolling smoothed out, and Eli knew from the echo they'd entered a building.

When the gurney stopped, he heard the others walk off and a door shut. Then silence.

He remained motionless for several minutes before he allowed himself to crack open an eyelid. He was in a small room, with cream-colored walls and a window covered by linen curtains. The door was on the other side, by the foot of the bed. He could see the edge of a table in that direction, too, and a black, thick-sided duffel bag sitting on top of it.

Very carefully, he lifted each of his hands, checking to make sure there had been no adjustments to the leather cuffs that tethered them to the sides of the bed. The one on the right was tight as ever, but there was still play in the one on the left. That was the cuff he'd been working on right before his captors had come in and beat the crap out of him at the last location. Thankfully, they either hadn't noticed or hadn't thought it important enough to check.

He started rotating his hand back and forth again, hoping to expand the cuff enough so that he could slip it off. He could tell he was close; maybe another quarter inch would do it. What he wouldn't have given at that moment to be one of those people who could dislocate their thumbs at will.

As he twisted again, he heard someone right outside the door. Immediately, he dropped his hand to the side and closed his eyes. The door opened, and from the sound of the steps, he knew it was the woman. She had a different way of walking from the men, less labored and random, as if every step was calculated to land at a specific angle and pace—confident, assured.

"Mr. Becker." As soon as the words were out of her mouth, Eli felt the sting of her hand against his cheek.

He almost opened his eyes, came so damn close. If she'd hit any harder, he would have.

She told him to wake up and slapped him again. Again, he simply rolled with it, playing the part of the unconscious prisoner. It wasn't that hard. The drug they had given him wasn't completely out of his system yet and helped suppress his response.

"Mr. Becker, open your eyes."

After a few seconds of silence, he heard her walk to the table at the foot of the bed and begin rummaging through the bag.

When she returned, she said, "Last chance."

If he wasn't afraid before, he was now. It took

everything he had not to open his eyes to see what she was planning. His imagination was more than willing to fill in the details, picturing an array of torture devices from knives to Tasers to pliers and things he didn't even know the names of. When the needle pricked his skin, it was almost a relief.

As she walked back to the table, he felt only a slight burning sensation at the point of injection, but a moment later, before she had even left the room, the burn began to spread.

Like a jolt of liquid electricity, the drug raced through his body, cycling up his heart, making it pound so rapidly it felt like it was going to burst out of his chest. His lids shot open wide, his whole face tensing at the sudden surge of energy.

His breaths came hard and fast as his muscles began to contract.

Stop!

Involuntarily, his fingers curled in toward his palms and his feet yanked at the cuffs holding them to the bed.

Stop!

He gritted his teeth, trying to regain control.

Stop it!

One by one his muscles began to relax, until he was finally able to breathe almost normally again. But then he caught sight of the door.

She's coming back, and when she does...

With renewed purpose, he began twisting his left hand against its cuff again, his gaze switching back and forth from the restraint to the door.

He felt his hand slip a little, so he pressed his thumb as tight as he could to his palm and pulled. Resistance at first, but it lasted only a second before his hand popped free.

He immediately reached over and undid the cuff on his right wrist, then sat up and leaned toward the restraints holding his ankles. That's when he heard her steps in the hallway.

Close.

Too close.

No way he could free both feet before she got there.

His gaze fell on the black duffel back. Without a second

thought, he scooted down as best he could, stuck a hand inside the bag, and grabbed whatever was in reach. Just as quickly he lay back down and covered his hands with the sheet.

Blindly, he tried to identify what he had grabbed. A plastic case a bit longer and thicker than a cigarette box, something that felt like a wooden chopstick, and a metal instrument with a palm-length handle at one end and a blade at the other. A scalpel?

As the door opened, he flattened his hand but didn't bother closing his eyes.

The woman smiled as she entered the room. "Mr. Becker, nice to see you awake again."

"Where are we?" he asked.

"No place important."

Her hand was on the bag now. He could let her look inside.

"I want to go home. Please. Let me go home."

She looked over. "All you have to do is cooperate and you can go anywhere you want."

"I'll...I'll cooperate," he said, sounding defeated. "I'll tell you whatever I know. I just want to go home."

She lifted her hand from the bag and took a step toward the bed. "I'm pleased to hear that. It'll save us both a lot of trouble. Why don't we start at the beginning? Tell me why you were looking into Operation Overtake."

Another step. At his hip now. Not close enough yet.

"You promise not to hurt me again?"

"If you truly cooperate, there will be no reason to hurt you."

He'd have only one shot at this, so he waited.

One more step. "Mr. Becker?"

He nodded as if he'd come to a decision. "Overtake. I...I was looking..."

"Looking for what?"

A little closer, dammit!

"For...for..." he said, hoping to draw her in closer.

Instead, she turned back toward her bag.

"For the girl," he blurted out. "I was looking for the girl."

The woman turned back around and moved in close. "The girl? But the girl is dead. She is dead, isn't she?"

"Well, um, you see, I was hired to…"

When he was sure her gaze was locked onto his, he gripped the knife and worked his right hand out from under the sheet.

"Hired to what? Find the girl?" the woman demanded. "Tell me! Is she alive?"

"Okay. Okay. I'll tell you." His voice weakened with every word, so she leaned in close to hear him.

"What happened to her?" she asked. "She *is* alive, isn't she?"

"She is…none of your business!"

In a burst of speed, he swung his arm around her and jammed the knife into her back.

NOLAN WAS STATIONED closest to the farmhouse and was the first to react to the gunshot. He raced across the parking area, fumbled momentarily with the front door, and rushed inside.

He paused in the living room, trying to figure out where the noise had come from. He had just taken a step toward the kitchen when he heard a door in the hallway fly open, followed by a thud of something striking a wall.

His pistol in his hand, he ran over to the hallway entrance.

Someone was near the other end, writhing on the ground.

"Identify yourself," he said, moving slowly forward.

The person rolled over, cursing painfully.

"Ms. Clark?" Nolan asked, lowering his pistol. "Jesus, what happened?" He hurried down the all and crouched beside her. "Are you all right?"

"No, I'm not fucking all right," she spat.

She was trying to reach behind her back for something. As she did, she turned, and he could see a piece of metal sticking out between her shoulder blades near her spine.

"Let me," he said.

He grabbed the handle and tugged the implement free. Nearly the entire length of the blade had been buried in her back.

"Who did this?" he asked.

"The fucking prisoner."

He jumped up and approached Becker's room, his gun raised. Behind him, his boss said something, but he was focused on the door that had swung almost all the way closed. All he could hear was silence from inside as he shoved it open with the barrel of his pistol.

"Hands where I can see them!" he shouted as he stepped through the doorway.

The command was unnecessary.

He lowered his gun and said, "Shit."

CHAPTER
THIRTEEN

NEW ORLEANS, LOUISIANA

ABRAHAM SAT NEAR the gate, waiting for his flight to DC.

From the moment he'd purchased the ticket, he'd felt guilty. He wanted to be out looking for Eli, but who knew where his friend had been taken by now? The only thing he could think of doing was to go to Eli's apartment near Washington, DC, to see if he could track down any hint of the information Eli had wanted to give him. Maybe if Abraham knew what it was, he could figure out what had happened to Eli.

It was a long shot, but at the moment his only shot.

The other seats began filling up around him but he barely noticed. All he could think about was how he'd failed his friend.

MISSISSIPPI

SHORTLY AFTER SEVEN a.m., Orlando and Quinn returned to the neighborhood where the Moss Point house was located.

"Which one first?" Quinn asked as they climbed out of the car.

Orlando looked around before pointing at a two-story house to the left of the one where Eli Becker had been taken. "They have the best view," she said.

She and Quinn had dressed in business suits that morning, knowing the importance of looking the part they were playing. As they neared the front door, they could hear the sounds of a family getting ready for the day—a TV, someone running around, dishes clattering.

Quinn pushed the doorbell button.

A distant, "Ronny, get that. If it's Mrs. Fuller, tell her you need a few more minutes."

A set of small feet across a room, followed by the door squeaking open. A skinny boy of around eight stared out at them, then said over his shoulder, "It's not Mrs. Fuller, Mom."

"Who is it?"

"I don't know."

Orlando said, "We'd like to speak to your parents, please."

"They want to talk to you," the boy said, his eyes still on Orlando and Quinn.

A deep sigh preceded heavier steps moving toward the door. A woman appeared, wearing a long faded pink robe and hair that looked like it had been brushed back in a hurry.

"Can I help you?" she asked, not doing a great job of concealing her impatience.

"Ma'am, I'm Agent Sax, and this is Agent Mullins," Orlando said, flashing the fake FBI badge that was part of her kit. "Wondering if we could ask you a couple questions?"

The woman touched her son's shoulder. "Ronny, go finish your breakfast."

"I'm already done," he argued.

"Then go finish getting ready. Mrs. Fuller will be here soon."

He left reluctantly.

When they were alone, the woman asked, "What kind of questions?"

"About the house next door," Orlando said.

"Next door? It's empty."

"We believe someone may have been using it in the last

thirty-six hours," Quinn said. "Did you see anyone?"

She shook her head. "Sorry."

"Maybe someone else in your family saw someone?"

"We were at a marching band competition for the last couple of days. Got back last night."

They thanked the woman and then tried the house to the right, where an older man named Harold Purdue greeted them in jeans and a tan work shirt. When they asked their question, he said, "Sure, I saw them. Came in night before last. Pretty much stayed inside the whole time until they left yesterday. I called the police because I thought maybe they were breaking in or something, and the cops checked with the Realtor." He nodded out at the sign in front of the other house. "Apparently all was on the up and up."

"Do you know what time they left?" Orlando asked.

"Well, I can't say for sure. They arrived in an ambulance, you know, but it left right after they got there. Yesterday morning there was a van parked out front. Not sure when that showed up. Went out for my afternoon walk. When I came back, the van was gone."

"And you're sure they weren't still in the house?" Quinn asked.

"We watch out for each other here. The Saunders, they own that house—they're good people. So I figured it was my duty to go on over and say hello. You know, get a good look and make sure they're not doing anything illegal like. I headed over after the walk but the place was empty and locked up."

"Two more questions, if you don't mind," Orlando said.

"No problem."

"What time did you take your walk yesterday?"

"Same time I take it every day. Start out at three fifteen and get back here just a hair after four o'clock."

"And the van—could you give us a description?"

"I could, but I'm guessin' a picture would suit you better."

"You have a picture?" Orlando asked.

Purdue smiled. "That's three questions. But yes, I do.

When strangers show up, I like to make sure they're not going to be a problem. I told you we take care of each other here."

PURDUE'S PICTURE WAS a bit blurry, but Orlando was able to clean it up enough to determine the vehicle was a white Ford E250 cargo van. She couldn't improve the resolution enough to read the back license plate, but the vehicle had a few telltale markings they could hopefully use to ID it.

Satellite footage was out. From the research she'd done the night before, she knew two satellites had passed over the Moss Point area the previous afternoon. Unfortunately the timing of their crossings did not coincide with the 3:15-to-4:00 p.m. window Mr. Purdue's walk had established.

That meant Orlando and Quinn would have to rely on traffic cameras. They concentrated their efforts on the I-10 since it was the only highway out of the area. Any other route and Eli Becker's abductors would have risked getting stuck in stop-and-go traffic.

Orlando concentrated on the closest eastbound cam to the on-ramp the van would have taken to enter the freeway, while Quinn did the same for the westbound one, each focusing on archived footage from a two-hour window starting at 3:15 p.m.

Ten minutes into their search, Quinn said, "I think I have it."

Orlando paused the footage on her screen and looked over at his. He pressed PLAY and the cars he'd been looking at started moving again.

After a moment, he said, "Here it comes."

Right on cue, a white van drove into the frame from the bottom of the screen. He let it play until the vehicle disappeared, and then reversed the footage and paused on the best shot of the vehicle.

"There," Quinn said, pointing at a dark line along the back fender. "And there." A dent on the roof line.

Both points of damage matched those on the van in Purdue's picture.

"Yeah, that's it," she said.

Leapfrogging west, camera to camera, they followed the van across the state line into Louisiana. There it transitioned to the I-12 and continued west past Baton Rouge.

"We should have seen it by now," Quinn said a few minutes later.

Orlando increased the speed of the footage they were looking at, and watched long enough to account for any fuel or food breaks the people in the van might have taken. No sign of the vehicle. They did a quick check to see if it had circled back in the other direction but it made no reappearance, which meant it had left the highway.

She consulted the map. The area looked sparsely populated, no real towns, just farm country. Even better, it had only three potential exits.

A Realtor had been used for the house in Moss Point, so Orlando guessed one was also employed for this next location. A quick search brought up all the real estate companies working in a ten-mile circle—about two dozen.

She and Quinn split the list and began making inquires about houses that might be available for a short lease. The final tally was four.

It was time to head west.

LOUISIANA

MARGUERITE SAT AT the airport bar, drinking water and keeping a watchful eye on the departure area for the flight to Washington, DC. The plane had arrived at the gate ten minutes earlier, and while its passengers were still making their way off, those waiting to board began to stir, several even getting in line.

Abraham, on the other hand, hadn't moved an inch, his gaze still on the far wall. She figured he was thinking about his missing friend. She couldn't help but feel sorry for him. He looked almost lost.

Her phone vibrated on the bar.

She picked it up and said, "Yes?"

ABRAHAM WASN'T THINKING about Eli. Earlier he had been, but those thoughts had led him to ones about the girl.

Tessa.

She would be eleven now, and likely didn't even remember him. They'd been together for only a few days, and that was more than half her lifetime ago.

He, of course, could never forget her.

He found himself falling into the familiar game of guessing who she was and why she was so important. He could make up a million answers, but had no idea if any of them were even close to the truth.

I should have never left her.

He hadn't heard the person take the seat next to him, so he jerked in surprise when she said, "You sure you want to go to DC this time of year? It's kind of cold."

His face hardened when he realized who it was.

"Well, look at us," Marguerite said, "running into each other for a second time in two days."

"What do you want?" he asked.

"Relax," she said. "I'm just passing on a message."

"What message?"

"Orlando says you'll want to stay."

"Why?"

"She said to tell you she thinks she found Eli."

THEY MET AT a Love's Truck Stop just west of the Mississippi River. Having traveled farther, Quinn and Orlando were the last to arrive, finding Marguerite, Winger, and Abraham inside the restaurant.

The moment Abraham spotted them, he pushed out of his seat.

"How do you know his name?"

Orlando raised an eyebrow. "Really? You don't think I could figure that out?"

"Then where is he?"

"Close to here."

"You're not lying, are you? This isn't some trick to keep tabs on me?"

She fingered the collar of his jacket and removed the tracking chip. "I've already been keeping tabs on you," she said, showing it to him. "But no, it's not a trick."

"Why don't we all sit and we can fill you in," Quinn suggested.

Begrudgingly, Abraham returned to his chair while Quinn and Orlando took the empty ones to his side.

Orlando explained how they had tracked the van and narrowed the possible destinations down to four. "It's not a guarantee," she said. "They might not be at any of these places, or they may have already moved on, but it's better than nothing."

Abraham was quiet for a moment, and then said, "You didn't have to do this. You could have gone home."

Orlando put a hand on his. "Of course we had to do this. That's what I've been trying to tell you. It's what friends do, what *family* does."

He hesitated, then clapped his other hand over hers.

SINCE THE IDENTITIES of the people who'd taken Eli were still unknown, splitting up so they could check the houses faster was not an option Quinn would even entertain. They headed out together in the sedan Quinn and Orlando were using, leaving Winger's and Marguerite's cars at the truck stop.

The first two houses they visited were being used by families who looked like they'd been there more than a day or two. The third had clearly been occupied sometime in the last several days, but from the abundance of cigarette butts and the piles of empty beer cans, Quinn thought it likely the place was being used as a hangout for local teens.

That left them with one final option.

Like the others, it was a farmhouse, in this case set off the road several hundred feet, with a faded white barn in back and a few shade trees in the yard. They couldn't see, however, any vehicles or signs of life from the main road.

They drove past the long driveway to the end of the field,

where a ditch about four feet deep ran all the way back to a small, wild grove about fifty yards beyond the house. Quinn parked their car where it couldn't be seen from the property, then they all piled out and began working their way down the trench.

Every fifty feet or so, Quinn would pause and check the house. There were still no signs of movement, no light coming from inside. He had hoped to spot the van parked behind the home, but as the back area came into view, all he could see were more grass and bushes and trees.

He gathered everyone together and said, "Orlando and I are going to go over and check." He could see Abraham opening his mouth to protest so he pointed at him. "You are going to stay here. No argument. You come with us and we'd spend all our time worrying about you."

Abraham looked none too happy.

"Permission to shoot him if he tries to follow you," Marguerite said.

"Permission granted," Orlando replied.

"I'll stay, okay?" Abraham said.

Quinn and Orlando continued down the ditch until they reached the grove at the back of the field. They moved through the trees until the barn was between them and the house, and then sprinted across the open ground.

Quinn peered through the barn's partially open door. It was a big, wide, open space holding nothing but dust. They moved to the east side, where the shadows were already deep and black, and headed to the front end. There they stopped and got their first good look at the house.

"Window, second from the right," Orlando whispered.

Quinn looked where she indicated. It was curtained like the other windows along the back, but the rod holding the drape in place was askew, as if something had bumped it.

"See any movement?" he asked.

"No."

Staying low, they traversed the ground between the barn and the house, crouched next to the back-door steps, and waited there for some kind of response. When none came, Quinn eased up the stairs and peered through the window in the door.

The room beyond was a kitchen with nothing on the countertops, and no table or chairs in the breakfast nook. The door was locked, so he pulled out his set of picks and remedied the situation in seconds.

He pushed the door open an inch and listened for sounds from inside. After hearing nothing, he opened the door wide enough for them to enter.

A fine layer of dust covered the counters and sink. Their information indicated the house had been rented in the last forty-eight hours, but the occupants had apparently not made use of the kitchen.

Odd.

There were two doors out of the room—one to the left leading into a small laundry area, and one straight ahead that accessed the rest of the house. They moved toward the latter, stopping again to listen.

Quiet came in many forms. The peaceful quiet of people sleeping. The tense quiet of someone lying in wait. The hollow quiet of empty space. Quinn was familiar with all. This quiet was the last. But while he was sure no one else was in the house, there had been those rare times when his senses were wrong, so he kept alert as he eased into the living room, scanning for danger.

Orlando touched his arm and pointed at several places on the floor in front of them. The hardwood planks had received their fair share of dust, too, but in a large section the dust had been disturbed. Someone had been here recently.

There was something else, a smell in the air Quinn recognized immediately. Tangy and metallic.

Blood. And not just a drop or two.

He looked at Orlando again and saw she'd also registered it.

They moved into the dining area and through an opening into a hallway that contained several open doors. The smell was considerably stronger here. Not only that, they could hear something now, low and constant. Almost a hum.

Like the smell, it was a sound Quinn knew.

Slowly, they moved down the darkened hall, checking the first room, then the second, before approaching the last door. As they neared, Quinn noticed something on the hallway wall opposite the room. A dark spot, runny, like someone had dribbled paint against it.

He moved up to the door, checked to make sure Orlando was ready behind him, and then swung into the opening, moving his gun back and forth as he looked for targets.

If dealing with the dead hadn't been his profession, the smell would have overwhelmed him. The body was crumpled across a gurney that took up the majority of the room. The smell was more blood than rot, which meant the victim hadn't been dead that long. By the growing swarm of buzzing flies, though, he knew it had been at least a few hours.

He moved to the side so Orlando could take a look.

The dead man couldn't have been more than forty years old. He was clothed only in a pair of underwear, and while his hands were free, his ankles were strapped to the gurney with leather restraints. He had bruises on his face, shoulders, and legs, all of which looked no more than a day or two old. What had killed him, though, was a gunshot to the forehead.

"Fits the description," he said.

"Yeah," Orlando agreed. "Dammit."

She moved in for a closer look.

"Needle marks," she said, nodding at the man's upper arm.

They saw at least four insertion points. Quinn had no doubt something had been pumped into the guy's system to get him to talk.

"Abraham?" he asked.

Orlando was quiet for a second before she sighed and said, "I'll get him."

QUINN HEARD THE back door slam open, and then hurried steps moving through the kitchen and living room.

"Where?" Abraham said outside the hallway.

"Down there," Orlando replied. "Last door on the left."

A moment later, Abraham appeared in the doorway.

"Oh, my God," he said.

As he moved over to the gurney, Orlando entered the room behind him.

"It's him, isn't it?" Quinn asked.

Abraham dipped his head, covering his eyes with his hand. "Yes," he whispered. "It's Eli."

Quinn put a hand on Abraham's back. "I'm so sorry."

"It's my fault. It's my fucking fault."

"Of course it isn't," Orlando said. "You couldn't have stopped them."

"You don't understand," he said, but didn't elaborate.

"If it helps at all," Quinn said, "I think he went down fighting."

Abraham looked at him, brow furrowed.

Quinn gently lifted Eli Becker's left forearm. "Look at his wrist. It's all cut up and some of the skin is missing right where the cuff would be." He set the arm down and lifted the cuff as far as it would go. "See, it's still closed, but it looks stretched. The other cuff is open. I think he worked the first one free and then undid the buckle on the other."

"A lot of good it did him," Abraham said.

"True, but I have a feeling he did a little damage. There's a large bloodstain on the hallway wall. Fresh. Too far away to be his."

Abraham glanced back at the hallway before returning his gaze to his dead friend.

"Don't you see?" Orlando asked. "The way he was killed was reactionary. If it had been planned out, they would have gone with a considerably less messy method and dumped his body someplace it would never be found. If you ask me, they weren't ready to get rid of him yet. Which means they probably didn't get out of him whatever it was they were trying to learn."

"He's still dead, though," Abraham said.

No one had a response for that.

Abraham took a deep breath. "We can't leave him here."

"No," Quinn said. "I'll take care of it."

DALLAS, TEXAS

DAENG HAD CHOSEN well.

Instead of finding a building that was part of a new construction project, he'd located a secluded tavern outside the city that was in the process of being totally refurbished. In addition to the interior being gutted, the renovations seemingly included replacing all plumbing and sewer lines, necessitating the removal of large chunks of concrete from the basement floor. The kicker was that the place sat in the center of three acres of tree-filled land, giving Nate and Daeng more than adequate privacy.

As soon as the construction crew had cleared out that afternoon, Nate and Daeng had moved in. Nate selected the largest of the temporary basement trenches, and they began by digging sideways under the remaining concrete floor. After that was braced with two-by-four supports, they started digging a grave that would be at a lower level than the new plumbing.

They had been digging only a few minutes when Nate's phone rang. While he hopped out to take the call, Daeng continued digging.

"Hello?" Daeng heard Nate say. "Oh, hey....Good. Just doing some prep work. Termination's scheduled for eleven p.m. We should be done and on our way back by morning....What?....Um, had to improvise a little....Ground and chemical—why?....Excuse me?....Well, I guess. That's kind of....No, no. It's okay....I'll text you the address."

A few moments later, Nate hopped down into the trench again.

"That was Quinn," he said. "We'll have to dig a little deeper."

Daeng dumped a shovelful of dirt on the pile. "Why?"

"Apparently we're going to have an extra body."

CHAPTER
FOURTEEN

LOUISIANA

TAKING WINGER WITH him, Quinn returned to Baton Rouge, where he ditched the car he and Orlando had arrived in and procured a crew-cab pickup, complete with a cover over the back. After stopping at a Home Depot for supplies, they swung by the Love's Truck Stop so Winger could pick up his sedan and then returned to the farm.

Abraham insisted on helping wrap Eli in the newly purchased plastic. After they were done, Quinn secured it with duct tape, and with Winger and Marguerite's help, carried Eli to the truck and placed him in the bed.

"You two are officially released," Orlando told the two freelancers after everything was closed up. "I'll wire your payments to your accounts."

"Not necessary," Marguerite said. "We take care of our own, you know?"

"Yeah," Winger agreed. "No charge."

"That wasn't our deal."

"Keep it. We'll just send it back," Marguerite said. She looked at Abraham. "Think twice next time you try to run away from a pretty woman."

Abraham could barely manage a smile. "Thank you for your help."

"You all take care," Winger said.

He and Marguerite walked over to his car and left.

"Let's get going," Quinn said. "It's already going to be late by the time we get there."

He climbed behind the wheel while the other two entered the passenger side, Orlando insisting her old mentor ride up front. No one said a word as they made their way through the parish roads back to the interstate.

After they'd been cruising along the highway for several minutes, Orlando said, "Why did they kill him, Abraham?"

Abraham stared out the window before saying, "Quinn's probably right. He was trying to get away."

"That's not what I mean and you know it." She waited, but he said nothing. "Why did you say it was your fault?"

"Because it is."

Quinn could have felt the tension between them from a mile away.

"Need I remind you that we're transporting a body for you across state lines?" Orlando said. "Perhaps it was none of our business at first, but now we are in this. Thick. So, what is going on?"

More silence. Quinn shot a quick glance at Abraham, thinking the old tech was going to stonewall again, but the look on the man's face told a different story, one of pain and confusion and need.

"Seven years ago," Abraham finally began, "I was hired for a job. My last one, though I didn't realize it until the end."

A pause.

"What was the job?" Orlando prodded him.

"I...I was to pick up a package in Osaka and take it to Amsterdam."

"You were a courier?" Orlando said.

"There comes a point as you get older when the jobs you were once offered don't come your way nearly as often. Sometimes you end up having to take something...less."

Quinn heard not only sadness in the words but a loss of self-respect. It was so seldom anyone ever lasted in the business as long as Abraham had that it'd never occurred to

Quinn what the older man had gone through at the end of his career.

This time Orlando waited out Abraham's silence.

When he spoke again, he said, "I expected the package to be something I could put in my pocket, or at the very worst, in my bag. What I didn't expect was a four-year-old girl."

"A child?" Orlando asked.

"Tessa," Abraham said. "That's her name."

Quinn said, "Maybe you should tell us about this mission."

Abraham told them what he knew about Operation Overtake and the days he spent escorting Tessa from Japan to a team in Amsterdam.

"And you have no idea where they took her?" Orlando asked when he finished.

"My job was done. I wasn't supposed to know." He turned his head away, facing the side window. "I should have insisted on going with them. At least then it would have been easier for her."

"You know they would've never let that happen," Quinn said. "That's not how these things work."

"I know, but...I didn't even try."

"I still don't understand how Eli Becker works into this," Orlando said.

"Eli was a contact of mine, a friend." He paused. "I just wanted to make sure Tessa was all right. Since Eli worked for the CIA, I thought there might be a chance he could get access to information about her that I never could. He came up dry, but I asked him if he could keep checking now and then for me, in case something surfaced. Every time I called him, he'd tell me the same thing—sorry, no news. I know he was annoyed with me, but he never shut me down. Just said he'd continue looking. The last time I called to check was a few days ago. Like usual, he had no news. But then *he* called me the day before yesterday. Said he found something, but didn't want to tell me over the phone. Asked me to meet him at the Azure Waves Hotel in Tampa. When I got there, they told me he'd had a heart attack the night before and was at the hospital. Well, you basically know the rest. So you see, it *is* my fault this happened to him. If he hadn't been looking into Tessa for me, no one would have come after him."

"Who do you think these people are?" Quinn asked.

Abraham shook his head. "I've been trying to figure that out since I realized Eli had been taken. My best guess is that they're connected to whoever has Tessa now. Maybe Eli was getting too close to the truth and they wanted to shut him down."

While Quinn knew it wasn't the only possibility, it was a good guess given what little they knew.

"You have no idea who Tessa is?" Orlando asked.

"No, but not from lack of trying. After leaving her like I did, it seemed as good a time as any to retire, so I ended up with a lot of time on my hands. For the first several months, I was on the Internet for hours, researching missing kids, looking for a death I might be able to connect to the murder of her mother, just trying to find anything that would hint at who she was or where she'd come from." He grimaced. "I don't search as much as I used to. Just a couple hours."

"A couple hours what?" she asked.

He hesitated. "A day."

Seven years on and Abraham was still looking for the girl every single day. Quinn didn't know what to think about that. His own mentor, Durrie, had always stressed that one should never become personally involved in a job. Quinn couldn't claim to have always lived up to that rule, but a job had never turned into an obsession for him like this one had for Abraham.

"So the only thing Eli told you was that he'd found something," Quinn said.

"Yeah."

"No hint what it was?" Orlando asked.

"Nothing."

"Was he the kind of person who would have put together a backup plan in case something happened to him?" Quinn asked.

119

"He wasn't a field op but he did work for the Agency, so…maybe."

"I'm going to ask you a question," Orlando said, "and I need you to answer honestly. Given what's happened, are you giving up your search? Or do you still want to find out about Tessa?"

"I don't think I can give up."

"Even if it gets you killed?" Quinn asked.

Abraham shrugged. "Even then."

"All right," Orlando said. "Then one more question. Will you accept our help?"

The hum of the tires filled the silence that followed.

"Yes," Abraham finally said. "Please."

DALLAS, TEXAS

IT WAS NEARLY one a.m. when Quinn pulled the truck into the empty strip mall parking lot on the edge of Dallas. He texted Nate:

We're here

Eight minutes later, a van sporting an advertisement for a plumbing company entered the lot, Daeng behind the wheel. They followed the van into a less densely populated area with a few scattered businesses and homes on wide lots. Three miles in, the van turned off its lights so Quinn did the same. A little farther down, they turned onto a gravel driveway next to a sign that read:

RICH & DAWN'S
BBQ RANCH

Tacked to the bottom of this was a smaller sign.

GRAND REOPENING IN APRIL!

The driveway went on for about half the length of a

football field before ending in a large parking area. While no other vehicles were present, a corner of the lot was filled with building supplies and equipment.

Quinn pulled in right behind the van and killed the engine.

"Welcome to Texas," Daeng said as Quinn climbed out.

After they shook hands, Daeng greeted Orlando with a hug and introduced himself to Abraham.

"Where's Nate?" Quinn asked.

"Inside. Let's get your body and I'll show you the way."

They retrieved Eli's body and carried it down the stairs to the basement. Nate was standing waist deep in a channel that had been cut out of the concrete. On the floor next to the opening was a body wrapped very much like Eli was.

"This our extra guest?" Nate said.

"He's not a guest," Abraham snapped.

Nate looked surprised by the reaction. "Sorry. I didn't mean anything by it."

"You should be careful what you say."

"You're right. No excuse."

Abraham frowned but said nothing more.

"Where do you want him?" Quinn asked.

"Next to this one would be great."

Quinn and Daeng gently set Eli down.

Quinn asked, "How's this going to work?"

"You checking up on me, boss?" Nate asked.

"Only if you think I should."

Nate smirked. "We bring them into the trench one at a time. Chem prep, then slide them under here…" He patted the floor next to where the bodies were lying. "And lower them into the hole. Fill everything back in and we're done."

"All right. You ready to go?"

"Just waiting for you."

"Let's start with Eli."

Daeng jumped into the trench with Nate while Quinn scooted Abraham's friend right to the edge. Once Eli was lying on the dirt in the channel, Nate cut slits into the plastic,

121

exposing the body. He dumped liberal amounts of their dissolving chemical through each of the slits. When finished, he and Daeng maneuvered the body into its grave.

The other body went through the same process, and soon they were filling the hole with a mixture of the dirt they'd removed and a binding material that would hold it all in place for a long time, ensuring that no one would ever know anything had been added to the construction.

When everything was done, and the tools and two-by-four supports cleared away, Quinn held out his hand and helped first Daeng and then Nate hop out.

"About earlier," Abraham said to Nate. "I may have…reacted poorly."

"Not at all," Nate said. "Working around the dead all the time sometimes makes me forget they were real people. It was a good reminder."

An awkward silence fell between them.

"You guys are more than welcome to stay there all night," Orlando announced, "but I'm beat. So, if you don't mind, I'm going to have Daeng drive me somewhere where I can get some sleep."

CHAPTER
FIFTEEN

GLORIA OPENED HER eyes and reached for her phone. Her hand didn't make it very far before a stab of pain reminded her about the wound on her back.

After the incident with Eli Becker, she and her team had left the scene in a hurry, not really caring who might find the body. Gloria's main focus had been getting to a doctor. Nolan had called their point person back at McCrillis headquarters, who had arranged for them to meet up with a discreet physician in Lake Charles, Louisiana.

While the wound had only needed three stitches to close, the puncture itself had been deep, damaging the muscle nearly all the way down to her ribcage. According to the doctor, if Becker had stabbed her a half inch to the right, the blade would have plunged into her spinal cord.

Once they'd finished with the doctor, they had driven to Houston and checked into a hotel near the airport, in anticipation of their 6:45 a.m. flight to DC.

Gloria reached her phone on the second try and checked the time—5:17 a.m.

Shit.

Gritting her teeth, she swung her legs off the bed and stumbled into the bathroom, where a hot but rushed shower helped ease some of the pain. After drying her hair and applying her usual scant amount of makeup, she donned her best blouse and suit jacket, headed over to the desk, and turned on her laptop.

At exactly 5:30 a.m., a chime announced the incoming video call. A moment later, the image of McCrillis's client—a woman with silver-streaked dark hair—filled the main part of Gloria's screen.

"Good morning, ma'am," Gloria said.

"Well?" the woman asked. "What has he told you?"

"Unfortunately, Eli Becker is dead."

A twitch of the woman's eyebrow. "And how did that happen?"

Gloria hated these calls. The woman's question was a perfect example of how counterproductive they were. But she was the client, and since things on this project had started heating up again over the last couple of months, the woman had insisted on these occasional briefings. Ethan Boyer—Gloria's boss—had acquiesced, with Gloria having no choice in the matter. It did not mean, however, she needed to go into detail about how things went down.

"It will be in the final report," she said, knowing that the document would reflect a more company-flattering version of events. "The reality is, he is no longer an asset."

The client glared from the monitor. "Were you able to get anything out of him? Is the girl alive or not? Please tell me he told you that much."

Gloria hesitated, then said matter-of-factly, "I'm not sure he knew."

"So that's a no."

Gloria felt no need to respond.

The woman sat back in her chair. "He didn't even know who he was working with? Or why he was looking for her?"

"No, ma'am. I was in the pro—"

"The girl!" the woman shouted. "I need to know!"

"We feel it's likely he left something behind. I'm going to have the items he had with him analyzed. In the meantime, my team and I are heading back to DC to search his place."

For several seconds, the woman looked as if she were on

the verge of another rant. Finally, teeth clenched, she said, "I expect better news the next time we talk."

The screen went blank.

CHAPTER
SIXTEEN

THEY CAUGHT A six a.m. flight out of Dallas to DC, Quinn promptly falling asleep before the plane even reached cruising altitude.

The night before, after they'd buried Eli, they had gone to the hotel Nate and Daeng had been using. Orlando and Daeng had been the only ones who'd tried to get some rest, achieving, at best, a ninety-minute nap prior to when they needed to leave for the airport. Quinn had spent the time filling Nate in on recent events, while Abraham had stood by the hotel window and stared out into the night.

"Sir, can I ask you to return your seat to its upright position, please?"

Quinn cracked open his eyelids. "No problem," he said as he pushed the button that returned his seat to the FAA-required uncomfortable position.

Beside him, Orlando was in the process of shutting down her laptop.

He leaned over and kissed her cheek. "Good morning."

"It was already morning when we left."

"Don't kill the mood."

She raised an eyebrow. "If it was mood fulfillment you were looking for, you shouldn't have waited until we were descending," she said, purring. "There was a good hour there when no one was in the restroom, and the flight attendants were busy doing their flight-attendant thing. Could have been fun."

"If you're trying to up my frustration level, mission accomplished."

She smiled as she slipped her computer back into her bag. She then leaned back and rubbed her eyes.

"Didn't you get any rest?" he asked.

"A little. But one of us had to figure out where we're going before we get there."

"And?"

"Eli has a townhouse in Bethesda."

"Can't imagine that took the whole flight to figure out."

She hesitated, then said, "Thought I'd do a little hunting for the girl."

"And?"

"Nothing."

After they arrived at Dulles International, they rented a Ford Explorer and made a quick stop in Reston to purchase heavier jackets and gloves before heading toward Maryland.

A layer of clouds filled the sky, dulling the light. Quinn hoped it wasn't some kind of precursor to a storm. The scattered patches of snow along their route were already pushing his annoyance level too high.

The townhouse was located about half a mile away from the Walter Reed military hospital, on a road that dead-ended at a park. A sign indicated the complex was called Warwick Mews. According to the information Orlando had dug up, it consisted of twenty-eight units, each with two stories up and a half-sunken basement down, and were divided into four rows of seven units each. The exteriors had been well maintained, but Quinn guessed the buildings had been built at least thirty years ago.

The Mews had driveway entrances at both ends that led into parking areas for visitors. Residents had garages at the back of their units that were accessed through the visitor parking area and then down the center between two of the rows.

"There," Orlando said. "Ninety-four-twenty-three."

She pointed at the third townhouse from the end. Like the others, it had steps leading up to a deck where the front door was located.

Quinn pulled to the curb and looked at the two units flanking Eli's. Since it was nearing ten thirty in the morning, he was hoping most people who lived in the complex would be at work. The townhouse to the left looked appropriately dark, but the one to the right looked like it could be a problem. He didn't see any movement through the half-covered windows, but a stroller was on the deck and a few toys were lying around, suitable for a child young enough to have not started school. Which meant the possibility of a parent or nanny being home.

He glanced back at Abraham. "How likely is it that Eli would have made friends with his neighbors?"

"Over time, maybe," Abraham said. "I don't know for sure, though."

"What about a wife? Girlfriend? Boyfriend? Roommates?"

Abraham shrugged. "He never talked about anyone but he was kind of awkward. I don't think romantic relationships would have come easily to him. But you never know."

As Quinn scanned Eli's place, he saw no obvious signs that someone was home.

"Okay," he said. "We can't all go walking up there. That'll draw too much attention. Nate, Daeng—"

"I know, I know," Nate said. "Stay in the car."

"Sorry."

"Someday maybe I'll make *you* stay in the car and see how you like it."

Quinn, Orlando, and Abraham climbed out and made their way up to Eli's porch. Quinn peered through the front window, saw a dark and quiet living room, and beyond it, an equally unoccupied kitchen.

"Alarm?" he whispered.

"I'd be surprised if there wasn't," Orlando said.

She dug into her bag and pulled out a device that looked like a beefed-up mobile phone. After tapping on the screen several times, she moved the box along the outside of the doorjamb. Given her barely five-foot height, she had to stretch to cross the top of the doorway. As she came down the other side, the device emitted a soft beep. She continued to the bottom, receiving a second beep six inches from the ground before she finally looked at the screen again.

"Not bad," she said. "He's using a Nevin D-60L."

The Nevin was not a top-of-the-line security system but pretty damn close. Way more sophisticated than what a normal townhome owner would have.

"Can you deactivate it?" Abraham asked.

"Please," she told him. "You didn't train me to be an amateur."

She had barely begun the process of turning off the alarm when the door to the home with the kid's stuff on its deck opened.

A woman in a bright red jacket and holding a bundled-up child hurried out and pulled the door closed behind her. She was nearly to the stairs before she realized Quinn and the others were next door.

"I don't think he's home," she said, continuing down the steps.

"Well, that explains why he's not answering," Quinn said lightly. "You don't know when he might be back, do you?"

"No idea. Didn't even know he was going away."

"Well, thank you anyway."

She reached the bottom of the steps and started to walk away but then looked back. "You friends of Mr. Becker's?"

"I'm his uncle," Abraham blurted out. "In town on business. Thought I'd stop by."

The woman seemed to relax. "I'm sorry you missed him. He'll be disappointed."

"Me, too. I guess I'll just leave him a note." He reached into his jacket like he was going to pull out a pad of paper and a pen. "Thanks for your time. Sorry if we held you up."

"When I see him again, I'll let him know we spoke."

"That would be very nice. Thanks."

Apparently satisfied they weren't up to anything, she hurried across the lawn and climbed into a Prius parked at the curb.

After she drove off, Quinn said, "Not bad for being a retiree."

"It hasn't been *that* long," Abraham said.

Before Quinn could point out exactly how long it had been, Orlando said, "Done."

From his wallet, Quinn removed a hard plastic card and punched out the pre-cut pieces of the metal-free lock-pick set it contained. He disengaged the locks in less than thirty seconds.

There was a double beep from somewhere inside as he opened the door, but no blaring alarm.

Stepping across the threshold, he said, "Hello? Anyone home?"

No sound.

In addition to the living room and kitchen he'd seen through the window, the main floor included a small bathroom, a staircase that went up to the second floor and down to the basement, and a rear door to the outside.

"Down or up?" he asked.

"Up first, I think," Orlando said.

The second floor held three bedrooms and two full bathrooms, one of which was part of a master suite. Quinn thought it was a lot of space for one guy, but when they looked through the bedrooms, he changed his mind.

Eli had apparently been a collector. Filling the two spare bedrooms were paperbacks and comics and graphic novels and movie posters and vintage toys, most with a sci-fi theme. Almost as fascinating was the fact that everything seemed to have its place. The rooms looked like a combination museum and library. Quinn wouldn't have been surprised if Eli had a detailed catalogue he could use to quickly locate each item.

"This stuff has got to be worth a mint," Orlando said.

"Look at this." She was in front of a vertical stack of posters individually wrapped in plastic sleeves and backed by cardboard. "I think this is an original, first-release *Star Wars*."

"I don't think that's what we're looking for," Quinn said.

"I know, but…what's going to happen to all this?"

"No idea."

"Down here!" Abraham called from somewhere outside the room.

They stepped back into the hall.

"Where are you?" Quinn asked.

"Master!"

They found him standing next to one of the nightstands, the drawer open.

"What is it?" Orlando asked.

He held up a stack of letters and then flipped through them so Quinn and Orlando could see that while the envelopes looked similar, each was addressed to someone different.

"One's for me," Abraham said.

He pulled out his and set the others on the bed.

A first-class stamp in the right corner, and in the return-address area a single word: BECKER. No number or street or city.

"Open it," Orlando said.

Abraham turned it over and worked the sealed flap free. He pulled out the folded piece of paper inside and opened it up so they could all three read it.

Abraham,

Your friendship has always meant a lot to me. A man in your position needn't have given me the time of day and yet you did. Life hasn't always been easy for me. People are always the hardest for me to understand. I never had that problem with you, though. You made it

131

so that I didn't have to try to understand you, that our friendship just was. I can't tell you how much I appreciated that.

My biggest regret is that I was unable to help you find your answers before I died.

Be well, Abraham. I wish I could still be there to answer your calls.

Eli

"I don't get it," Quinn said. "Did he know he was going to die?"

"I don't know," Abraham said, confused.

"I don't think so," Orlando said as she gently took the letter from her mentor and looked it over. She then picked up several of the envelopes and examined them. "I think these have been waiting here for a while. Just in case."

"Just in case he suddenly died?" Abraham said.

"Look, you've as much said it yourself. He was a bit odd. Maybe he thought because of his work, there was always the possibility he might not be around that long."

Abraham thought for a moment, then said, "Maybe, but who knows?"

"I do," she said. "Look at these envelopes." She held out the ones she'd been examining. "The edges are darker than the fronts and backs." She set them down and grabbed one of the others. "Except for the front of this one. It was the one at the front of the stack. It's darker, too." She rubbed her finger across it. "See? Dust. These have been here a while."

Abraham took the envelope and held it up for a closer look.

"Then there's this." She picked up the opened letter again and read, "'My biggest regret is that I was unable to help you find your answers before I died.'" She lowered it again. "He *did* find answers. That's why he wanted to meet you."

Abraham still looked confused, so Quinn put a hand on his shoulder and said, "Find anything else?"

"Uh, no. Not yet." Abraham dropped the envelope he was holding on the nightstand. "I don't even know if there's anything here that's going to help us."

"No sign of a computer?" Orlando asked.

"No," Abraham said.

That was the top item on their search list. Eli must've had one, and if any of the information he intended to give Abraham was on it, Orlando should be able to dig it out.

"We need to keep looking," Quinn said. "We don't want to be here when the neighbor gets back."

While Orlando helped Abraham search through the main part of the bedroom, Quinn checked out the walk-in closet. On one side was a large collection of T-shirts that spoke to Eli's passion for sci-fi, while on the other were the utilitarian suits and shirts and ties Quinn guessed he wore to his job. The shoes were also subdivided—five pairs of nice leather dress shoes in varying degrees of brown under the suits, and three pairs of broken-in sneakers under the T-shirts. Quinn ran his hands through all the clothes, feeling for anything unusual. He came across a comb and some change but nothing useful. He also checked behind the clothes along the wall for hidden compartments. If something was there, he didn't find it.

Above the clothes racks, running around the entire room, was a two-foot-wide shelf holding boxes and stacks of sweaters and a few other odds and ends. One by one, Quinn checked through the boxes. Most contained the junk people accumulate over the years—magazines and photographs and Christmas cards and the like.

It wasn't until he moved a pile of thick sweaters that he came across something unusual. It happened when the bottom sweater caught on something, causing the ones on top of it to tumble onto Quinn.

He gathered the sweaters and placed them on the ground,

out of the way. He then tried to free the remaining sweater from whatever it had snagged on. The shelf was too high for him to see over the top, so he moved his hand under the sweater and felt around. The yarn had hooked onto what he thought at first was a small knot of wood. But as he tried to free it, the knot clicked down.

He froze and listened, expecting to hear the sound of a latch releasing or a drawer opening, but there was nothing. Maybe the knot was just a knot. He pulled down one of the boxes stuffed full of papers and used it as a stepping stool so he could see for himself.

While it did look a bit like a knot, it most definitely wasn't. He pressed it again and the button popped back up. Still no responding sound, though.

"Anything happening out there?" he called toward the door.

Orlando stuck her head inside the closet. "What?"

"I found a button and pushed it a couple times, but nothing's happened in here. Thought perhaps it controlled something out there."

"Do it again," she said, and ducked back into the bedroom.

Quinn depressed the button. "Anything?"

For a few moments there was nothing, then she called, "In the bathroom."

When he entered, he found her kneeling near the toilet and Abraham standing a few feet behind her. In front of them, two of the large tiles that went up the side of the wall were now sticking out at an angle, creating an open wedge at the top. Visible behind the tiles was a metal door with a keypad and digital read.

Orlando looked at Quinn. "You are a genius."

"Hey, you can't say things like that unless I have a recorder on. But yes, I am a genius."

"You'd be more of a genius if you could get that safe open," Abraham said.

"That's *my* job," Orlando told him.

She moved the tiles until they were completely out of the

way, and then pulled out the same device she'd used on the alarm. After she'd navigated through several menus on the touch screen, she placed the box against the keypad and touched the screen one more time. Suddenly numbers began blinking on an off.

After approximately ten seconds, the number 6 appeared and stayed there. A beat later, the same number showed up on the safe's digital display. Next up was 1, and then 0, and 2, and finally 7. The display on the safe blinked on and off three times before they heard a loud *clunk*.

Orlando removed the box, slipped her fingers into the divot that served as the handle for the safe's door, and pulled.

"Hello there," she said.

Inside were two shelves. The top one held a few files and some closed envelopes, and the bottom the laptop she'd been hoping for.

As she started to pull the computer out, Quinn's phone vibrated. It was Nate.

"What's up?" he asked.

"Company, I think," Nate said.

"The neighbor's back already?"

"No. Not that kind of company. Sedan just pulled into one of the visitor spots. Three men, one woman, all suited. Walked fast into the garage area. They're out of sight now. Could be heading your way, could be going someplace else entirely. I didn't like the looks of them, though. Wherever they're going, they're bringing trouble."

Quinn touched Orlando on the shoulder. "Out. Now."

"What about the rest of the stuff?" Abraham asked.

"We'll bring it with us," Orlando said.

"Fast," Quinn told her.

As she began scooping out everything from inside the safe, Quinn hustled Abraham into the bedroom and said into the phone, "The front still clear?"

"Yeah, you're good there for now," Nate said.

"All right. We'll use the—"

A pop from downstairs. Not loud, but distinct. The

opening of a door a bit out of alignment with its frame.

"Check that," he whispered. "We may be coming out hot."

He hung up and glanced around. The master bedroom was at the back of the house. Not the way he wanted to leave.

He moved his mouth right up to Abraham's ear. "As quiet as you can, go to the front bedroom. I'm going to grab Orlando and we'll be right behind you."

Abraham nodded and headed out of the room.

Quinn moved back into the bathroom, stepping carefully so that none of the floorboards squeaked.

"They're inside," he whispered.

She shoved the tiles back into place, stuffed the computer and papers into her backpack, and jumped to her feet.

Quinn led her through the hall and to the front bedroom. As Orlando carefully closed the door, Quinn unlatched the window and gave it a test upward push. He breathed a sigh of relief as it slid easily along its frame. Because it was winter, Eli had removed his screens, so as soon as Quinn had the window all the way open, he stuck his head outside.

The roof that covered part of the entrance-level deck was only a few feet below the windowsill.

"Come on," he said. "Orlando first."

She crawled out the window.

"Abraham," Quinn said, holding out a hand to help the older man.

"It's okay. I can do it."

Abraham ducked through the frame and disappeared outside.

As Quinn lifted a leg over the sill, he heard a noise from the other side of the bedroom door that sounded very much like someone coming up the stairs. He hurried out and lowered the window, wishing he had a way to lock it.

He motioned for Orlando to head over to the deck roof of the townhouse that had looked unoccupied. Once there, he lowered himself and took a quick glance through the window, confirming no one was home.

"Abraham," he said.

The older man's legs appeared first. As he lowered himself, Quinn grabbed him just above the knee to help guide him. Without warning, his rate of descent increased. Quinn tried to catch him, but ended up becoming more of a landing pad as Abraham tumbled completely off the edge.

Quinn was sure the sound of the crash would draw the attention of the visitors next door.

"Move," he said to Abraham, pushing him off.

As soon as he was free, Quinn jumped to his feet and called to Orlando, "Come on."

She eased over the edge and didn't let go until Quinn had a good hold of her. Quickly, he set her down, his eyes darting over to Eli's deck. No one yet.

"You have any trackers with you?" he asked Orlando.

She shot a guilty glance at Abraham. "A couple."

"Give me one, then you two go to the car. I'll tag their vehicle and meet you a few blocks away."

She pulled out a plastic box and removed a tracker identical to the one she'd put on Abraham's collar. "Be careful," she said.

He kissed her. "I'll see you in a few minutes."

QUINN HAD TO assume the intruders were professionals, which meant at least one of them would have remained outside the townhome, covering the entrance they had used. But when he looked down the access road at the back of Eli's building, he could see no one.

He pulled out his phone, flipped up the collar of his jacket, and walked with purpose into the alley, pretending to scroll through e-mails. His eyes, however, were moving back and forth just enough so that he could take in both sides of the alley.

The backs of the units consisted of garages separated by narrow, fenced-off patios. Most people seemed to be using the extra space as storage areas for bikes and the like.

Eli's patio was empty, the back door the others had used

to get in, closed. Nowhere to hide there. So, was there a sentry or not? Or was someone waiting in the sedan Quinn planned on tagging? That would be a problem.

Quinn chuckled as if he'd read something amusing, then looked up, just a normal guy checking his progress.

There.

On a patio two homes ahead and on the right, where a permanent wooden shed had been built. Not big by any means, three foot wide at the most, and sticking out from the townhouse perhaps twice that distance. It was tall in comparison, seven feet with a sloping roof. There were two stacks of heavy-duty plastic storage containers, and another stack of outdoor chairs on the patio. A virtual fort someone could hide inside.

He tapped Orlando's number and raised the cell to his ear.

"Are you okay?" she asked.

"Yeah, sorry. I'm heading out now. Had to take care of a little thing here at home first," he said.

"Oh, we're playing that game, are we?"

"Yeah," he said, a quick laugh in his voice. "Something like that."

As he drew level with the shed, he kept his eyes forward and focused on his peripheral vision.

"Do you need help?" she asked.

"No, no. It's all good. I should be there on time."

A twist of a shadow. Simple. Subtle.

A civilian would have dismissed it as a trick of the eye, if the person would even notice it at all, but to Quinn it was proof he was right.

"If you could do me a favor and make sure everyone's ready to go when I get there," he said. "Better if we don't waste any time."

"South southeast of you," she said. "Battery Lane. There's a big ambulance dispatch station at the corner with Old Georgetown Road."

"Uh-huh," he said. He was past the shed now, only a unit away from the end of the alley.

"We're in the parking lot on the north side."

"That's great. Thanks. I'll see you soon."

He put the phone away and shoved his hands into his pockets, tensing his arms to ward off the cold—not something he needed to pretend to do. Keeping his pace unchanged, he turned left out of the alley, toward the main road. As soon as he was out of the sentry's line of sight, he angled over to the cars parked alongside the lot where the sedan was.

He pulled the tracker out of his pocket and dropped to a crouch. Using the other cars to shield his presence, he worked his way back to the sedan and slipped the tracker into its grill, jamming it into a niche so that even if the adhesive had trouble hanging on in the cold, the chip wouldn't go anywhere.

He grabbed his phone again and sent a quick text to Orlando.

Tracker in place

Her reply came moments later.

Active and working

CHAPTER
SEVENTEEN

THE FIRST SURPRISE came when Gloria and her team discovered the alarm to Becker's home was off. The analyst had left town in a hurry, but Gloria found it hard to believe he'd have gone without properly securing his place.

Unsure what they would find, she and two of her men proceeded inside with extreme caution. They did a thorough check of the main floor first and found that the front door was unlocked.

She was willing to admit there was a slight possibility Becker had fled without setting his alarm, but there was no way he would leave a door unlocked. Someone else had been here. Why and how long ago were the questions.

She tapped Nolan on the shoulder and motioned to the stairs. He headed over with King right behind him and Gloria bringing up the rear. Halfway up he paused, pointed at the floor above and then at his ear. Next he held his thumb and forefinger about a quarter inch apart, indicating he'd heard something but it had not been very loud.

"Go, go," she mouthed.

Once they reached the next floor, she silently asked which room the noise had come from, but he shook his head, unsure. The first door led into a master bedroom, while the second and third opened onto rooms crammed with shelves and boxes full of items she didn't take the time to ID. All three rooms were unoccupied.

"We're clear," Nolan said, no longer muting his voice.

"So what the hell did you hear, then?" she asked.

"I don't know. It was a short…whoosh, I guess. Like two things rubbing against each other. I guess it must have come from a neighbor's place."

"You're sure?"

"No, but there's nothing here."

She walked over to the window and looked out. They were on the side of the house facing the road. Nothing out there but cold air and a dead lawn.

"All right," she said, turning back to her men. "Let's tear this place apart."

"ANOTHER BLOCK AND a half down," Orlando said, checking the map on her phone. "It'll be on the right."

"Got it," Nate said.

She looked into the back where Quinn was sitting with Abraham and Daeng and held out her hand. "I need to set you up."

Quinn gave her his cell.

Quickly, she went through his apps until she found the one she wanted, and then input the information that would allow him to track the beacon he'd left on the sedan.

Half a minute later, Nate pulled the SUV into an open spot at the curb next to a Starbucks coffee shop.

"Let's go," Orlando said to Abraham.

Quinn climbed out of the car so Abraham could exit, and then switched to the front passenger seat where Orlando had been. "We'll come back for you in a while," he said.

"Try to make it back before they close," she told him. She swung her bag over her shoulder and looked at Abraham. "Come on. Let's see if we can find a table."

Quinn directed Nate to a street three blocks away from Eli's place, where they found a parking spot at the curb and settled in to wait. It was another twenty-two minutes before the tracking dot on the map began to move, bringing the total time the others had spent inside the townhome to around forty minutes.

As Nate started the SUV, Quinn watched the dot move down to Old Georgetown Road and then head southeast. The sedan's route would take it within a half block of their position in less than thirty seconds.

He watched the intersection, and as soon as he caught sight of the intruder's vehicle, he said, "Let's move, but slow. Give them a few blocks' lead."

Nate shifted into DRIVE and pulled into the road.

ALL THE TABLES were occupied when Orlando and Abraham entered the coffee shop.

"I've got this," Abraham said. "You get us something to drink. You know what I like."

While Orlando was in line, Abraham walked slowly toward the area where the majority of the tables were located, taking on a small but noticeable limp, and donning a friendly smile that turned into a cringe every time he put weight on his "bad" leg. When he got to the tables, he slowed as if confused and looked around. Several of the tables' occupants glanced at him then quickly looked away.

He shuffled forward a few feet, and stopped in front of a table where a young guy of about twenty sat in front of a pile of chemistry and math books.

"Excuse me," Abraham said in a tired old voice. The kid looked up. "You wouldn't happen to be leaving soon, would you?"

"Uh, oh, um, no," the guy said. "Sorry. I'm...I'm studying. Big test coming up."

"Of course. I understand." Abraham took a step back. "I hope you do well."

"T-thank you."

He gave the kid a smile, and then turned and looked around again. As he knew would happen, he caught several of the other customers looking at him again. While most immediately glanced away again, another guy about twenty years old didn't break his gaze soon enough and had no choice but to acknowledge Abraham's hopeful smile. The guy had a book bag at his feet that hinted at his own need to study, but there were no books on the table, only his hand holding the phone he'd been smirking at and typing on since Abraham had walked up.

"Are you leaving?" Abraham asked.

"Um…" The guy looked like he was trying to come up with any response that would allow him to stay, but finally his shoulders sagged. "Sure. Just…two seconds, huh?"

"Oh, wonderful. Take your time. And thank you."

As the kid returned his attention to his phone, Abraham moved to within a foot of the table and stared down. When the kid realized he was being scrutinized, he stuffed the phone in his pocket and stood up.

"All yours," he said.

"Thank you again," Abraham told him.

Orlando walked over a few minutes later with a couple cups of coffee. "Nice table."

"Just good timing," he said.

"Is that what you call it?"

She arranged her computer so that the screen faced the wall and only she and Abraham could see it. She then did the same with Eli's machine.

When his old friend's computer came to life, it asked for a password. Orlando reached over to pull the laptop in front of her but Abraham said, "I can get this."

She looked at him. "Are you sure? There've been a lot of advances in the decade you've been gone."

"First of all," he said, centering the computer in front of him, "it hasn't been a decade, and second, do you think I've just been sitting around doing nothing?"

"Oh, so they teach advanced hacking at the old folks' home nowadays, do they?"

"My fellow active seniors and I are insulted by your terminology. Now quit wasting time talking to me."

With a smirk, she turned her attention to her own screen.

Abraham couldn't help but smile himself. It felt good to be working with Orlando again. He'd had three different apprentices over the years, but she had been, by far, his favorite and best.

Whip smart. Funny. Perceptive.

And above all else, caring.

He had missed that. So much.

Focusing on the computer screen reminded him why she was sitting next to him, and it wiped the smile from his face.

Eli.

Dammit.

He closed his eyes for a moment and tried to set his feelings aside so he could work.

"Need a little help already?" Orlando asked.

He opened his eyes again. "Absolutely not."

Perhaps Orlando could have broken through the security screen faster, but Abraham was satisfied with getting past it in only a couple of minutes. "Done," he said, turning the screen so she could see.

"Nice. May I?"

"Have at it."

She leaned over and accessed the operating system. After a few moments of clicking and typing, she returned to her own laptop.

"Okay," she said. "I've got it slaved and am cloning the drive to my cloud. Should be done in a few minutes, then we start with some global searches."

"Sounds good," he told her.

She pulled her backpack onto her lap. "In the meantime, we should look through these," she said, removing the files and envelopes that had also been in the safe.

GLORIA WAS ON the phone the minute they climbed back into their car.

"We did a complete search," she told her boss, "but didn't find anything useful."

"No computer?" Boyer asked.

"No, but someone was in the house before us. They could have taken it."

"What?"

"The door was unlocked and the alarm was off."

"Did you see anyone?"

"Uh-uh. Don't know how long ago they broke in."

"Who do you think it was?"

"No clue yet."

"Well, then, what's your next move?"

"I have Becker's clothes and bag. Want to get them scanned in case he hid anything in them. Thought we'd swing by the office and drop them off. After that, I thought I'd look into some of his colleagues. If it seems like one of them might know what he was up to, I'll give them a visit."

"I'm at the Ritz-Carlton for the next hour," Boyer said. "You'll save a lot of time if you can get them to me."

McCrillis International's office was way on the other side of the Capitol building. At this time of day with traffic, it would take more than an hour of travel time. The Ritz-Carlton, while still in DC, was much closer to her current location.

"Thank you, sir. That would be very helpful."

"We'll meet in the courtyard." He gave her instructions on how to get in, then said, "Text me when you get there."

THE BLIP ON the tracking app headed south out of Bethesda on a direct course for Washington, DC. Once they were in the city, following the car at a distance would no longer be an option. Quinn and his team needed to be in sight of the car when it stopped so they could see where its occupants went.

"Let's move into point," Quinn said when they were still several miles outside the district.

With a nod, Nate depressed the accelerator and began closing the gap. "There it is," he said a minute later.

The sedan was three cars ahead in the same lane they were in. It took another mile and a half for Nate to maneuver past the car without drawing attention to their SUV. He then increased the separation to nearly a block, at which point he eased back on their speed and matched the flow of traffic. Now, thanks to the tracker, they were following the sedan from the front.

"Do we have any idea what the deal is with this Tessa?" Daeng asked from the backseat.

"I told you everything I know," Quinn said.

"Do you think Abraham is holding something back?"

"I doubt it."

"How well do you know him?"

"Very. He was Orlando's mentor."

No one said anything for a few moments.

"I'm not sure I like this," Nate said.

Quinn took a quick glance at his friend before looking back at the screen. "What do you mean?"

"The idea of anything having to do with kids. I just...I don't like it."

Quinn understood where he was coming from. The world they traveled in was full of pain and death. You could get immune to seeing the body of an adult who'd been terminated, but never that of a child. A few years earlier they'd been involved in an incident that had centered around the kidnapping of a busload of kids. There were moments in the months afterward when Quinn would catch Nate staring off into nothing, the potential of what could have happened undoubtedly still playing through his apprentice's head. Hell, the scenarios had played nonstop through his own mind for a while there.

"We're not dealing with any kids," Quinn said. "We're trying to make sure whoever killed Abraham's friend isn't going to come after him."

"Really? Seems to me we're trying to help him find out about her."

"All right, yeah. That, too. But just information. That's all."

Though Quinn couldn't see Nate's expression, he could feel the other cleaner's sideways glance and knew Nate was thinking, *Are you sure about that?*

According to the tracker, they were less than half a mile from Washington.

"Slow down," Quinn said. "Let them catch up."

THE FILES AND envelopes from Eli's safe turned out to contain only personal items pertaining to his bank accounts, his townhouse, and a place in Kansas he had apparently inherited from his parents. The general search of his computer was equally unrewarding, returning no hits on any of the keywords used.

The lack of easily accessible data didn't come as a shock, though. Eli wouldn't have been so careless as to leave in plain sight something that had spooked him enough to make him flee his home.

That, of course, didn't mean there was nothing to be found. Given Eli's position at the CIA, he would've had the resources to securely hide information from prying eyes. Most of them, anyway.

Using her digital arsenal, Orlando scanned the drive for encrypted files, sifted through operating system logs for anything out of place, and did a sector-by-sector search for ghost data. As the last of these was completed, a dialogue box popped open with text reading: XJ982323/ubr2.xuki.

"I don't recognize the extension," Abraham said.

Orlando frowned. "Neither do I."

A fact that troubled her.

She opened a program she'd dubbed Surgeon and used it to extract the file from its hiding place, and then copied it to an isolated partition on her own drive. Leaving the full file closed, she opened the metadata, but all she found was useless garbage.

What kind of file was a .xuki?

Not wanting to waste the time it would take to figure it out on her own, she opened her messaging program and sent a quick note to the Mole.

You there?

His answer came back within seconds.

Where else would I be?

She typed again.

.xuki—heard of it?

The Mole:

Seriously?

Orlando:

Seriously. Why?

Five seconds later, her phone rang. She donned her earpiece and answered, "Yes?"

"You've never heard...of it?" the Mole asked in his odd cadence, his voice electronically distorted into a metallic monotone as always.

"I wouldn't be asking if I had."

A pause. "You must have missed...it while you...were recovering."

"Missed what?"

"The dot-xuki virus." He pronounced the extension *zoo-key*.

Orlando frowned. While she had been out of the loop after she was shot, she had specifically worked hard to catch up on any important tech developments she might have missed.

"I've never heard of it."

"It was...hush-hush. Hit only...CIA data storage center outside Washington, DC....Inside source said only...three data banks...and their backups wiped."

"That's it? Just three data banks at one location? Didn't show up anywhere else?"

"Nowhere."

That was probably why she hadn't heard of it.

"Why...are you...asking?" he said.

She looked around the coffee shop, but Abraham was the

only one paying her any attention. "Found a dot-xuki file on a drive I'm looking through."

"What drive?"

"That's not something I'm prepared to share at the moment. Were the perpetrators caught?"

A hesitation, then, "Not...to my knowledge."

"So it's probably a good idea if I don't open the file."

"Can you...read me the...file name?"

She didn't see the harm in that, so she did.

The Mole said nothing for several seconds, then asked her to read it to him again. After she did, he said, "Is the file...isolated?"

"Yes."

"I have...a suggestion."

"What?"

"Hold." The pause that followed lasted half a minute. When he spoke again, he gave her a web location. "Go there. You will find...a conversion...program I would like...you to...try on the file."

"Converting it into what?"

"Download the program...please."

Once she had done so and opened it, she was presented with a screen containing two boxes and a button at the bottom marked ENTER. Written in light gray through the box on the left was SELECT FILE, while the box on the right held a pop-up list of three choices: EXECUTE, DOCUMENT, and IMAGE. She selected the .xuki file, but before clicking one of the options, she said, "Please tell me you wrote this program."

"I did," the Mole said.

"Which option should I try first?"

"I would only...caution that if...EXECUTE works, do not open...the file."

"Gee, thanks."

She decided to go ahead and try that one first, but the Mole's program kicked back an error message reading:

UNABLE TO CONVERT. FILE TYPE UNKNOWN.

With some relief, she tried DOCUMENT and received the same response. When she clicked on IMAGE, instead of receiving an immediate error message, her cursor began spinning as it processed the file.

After several seconds, a new window opened and a picture appeared.

"Oh, my God," Abraham said, staring at the screen.

The image was of a girl.

"Tessa?" Orlando asked.

"I think so. Yes…yes, it's got to be."

The girl in the picture was not the four-year-old he'd described. This one was older. If the picture was recent, she'd be eleven now. Her dark brown hair lay thick over her shoulders and down her back. Her eyes, also brown, were not looking at the camera but almost, as if someone standing near the photographer had called her name.

"Who…is Tessa?" the Mole asked.

"At the moment, it might be better if you don't remember that name."

A beat. "Understood. But I…take it that the conversion…worked."

"It did. Thank you. I appreciate it. What I don't understand, though, is why it was disguised with a dot-xuki extension."

"Perhaps it was…not disguised. I have a theory that…the dot-xuki virus…was designed to do…more than just wipe the servers. What if…the destruction was…merely a way to cover—"

"Their tracks," she said, seeing where he was going. "You're thinking they were stealing data, aren't you?"

"Yes…and did not want anyone…to know what they took. Once…they had the…wanted files, the drives were…wiped." A process that could have happened in a matter of seconds, from virus arrival to total destruction.

"So the file I have here—" she said.

"Is one…that was extracted from…the CIA," he finished for her.

"Thanks," she told him. "I appreciate the help."

"You know where...to find me...if you need more."

Orlando slipped her phone back into her pocket and turned to Abraham. "You're sure this is—" She stopped herself when she saw the streak of a tear across his cheek.

"I'm sure," he said.

"At least you know she's alive."

"Yes. She is, isn't she?" He continued to stare at the monitor.

Tentatively she asked, "Is knowing that enough for you?"

Even before he spoke, she could see in his eyes that it wasn't. "Something must be wrong. Why else would Eli have been killed? We need to make sure she's safe."

Orlando squeezed Abraham's shoulder. "Let's see if Eli left us anything else, huh?"

CHAPTER
EIGHTEEN

QUINN HAD THE compact zoom attached to his phone's camera before the sedan pulled past them a few short blocks before DC. He snapped pictures of each of the four occupants.

The results were far from stellar. The shots of the driver and the man sitting behind him were completely useless, only a hint of a face in each. The photos of the woman in the front passenger seat and the man behind her were profile shots and therefore better, but—due to motion blur and the reflections in the window—not by much. Still, he texted them to Orlando, hoping there was enough for her to get a hit on at least one person.

They continued following the sedan past Tenley Circle, McLean Gardens, and the US Naval Observatory. When they reached Dupont Circle, the others drove only two stops around the arc before turning onto New Hampshire Avenue NW. At M Street, they turned right again and continued two blocks to 23rd Street, where they turned left.

By the time Nate turned the Explorer around the last corner, the sedan was three-quarters of the way down the block and slowing.

"Pull to the curb," Quinn ordered.

Nate eased the truck to the side of the road.

As soon as the sedan came to a full stop, two of its doors

opened.

"Daeng, you're with me," Quinn said. "Nate, you know what to do."

"Stay in the car," Nate said, pretending to be annoyed. In truth, if the sedan went anywhere, his job would be to follow.

Quinn and Daeng exited and quickly moved over to the sidewalk. Casually, as if they passed this way every day, they walked toward the other end of the block. Only two people had emerged from the sedan—the woman and one of the men. While she was empty-handed, her companion was carrying a small suitcase.

The driver's window of the sedan was open and the woman was saying something to the men still inside. When she finished, the car pulled back into the street. Behind him, Quinn could hear Nate shift the SUV out of Park and take up pursuit.

"We're eyes only," Quinn told Daeng. "We find out where they're going, get a few pictures, then we're out."

"Sounds like fun," Daeng said.

Quinn had known Daeng long enough to realize his Thai friend wasn't being sarcastic. Daeng was usually up for almost anything.

The woman glanced their way as she moved onto the sidewalk, but she appeared not to give their presence any importance. With her colleague in tow, she walked over to the building that lined the block and entered through an unmarked door.

Quinn had hoped they'd stay out in the open a bit longer, giving him and Daeng more time to narrow the distance between them, but so much for that.

Picking up his pace, he made a quick study of the building. While there were businesses here and there along the ground floor, the nine floors above them appeared to be occupied by either offices or condos. Plenty of places for the man and woman to get lost in before Quinn and Daeng could get eyes on them again.

Daeng reached the door a half step ahead of Quinn and

tried the knob.

"Locked."

No keyhole in the door, only a security pad on the wall. Unfortunately, the device that could have circumvented the system was in Quinn's bag in the SUV.

He looked around. A dozen yards to his left was the main door to the building, probably with a receptionist or security guard waiting inside. To his right, a restaurant at the corner. More people, but…

"Come on," he said to Daeng and headed for the restaurant.

A hostess greeted them with a pleasant smile as they entered. "Welcome to Nic's. Just the two of you?"

"Yes," Quinn said.

"This way."

She turned and walked into the dining area.

"A table by the window okay for you?" she asked.

"Fine," Quinn told her. "Could you direct me to your restroom first?"

She stopped. "Oh, of course. Back there and to the right."

"I could probably use a stop, too," Daeng said. He smiled at the waitress. "Which table will be ours?"

She pointed toward the windows. "That one there. I'll have water waiting when you get back."

"Great."

The two men headed through the restaurant, bypassed the restroom entrance, and entered the kitchen.

Eight people were present—five cooks and three in the cleanup crew. The only ones who had so far noticed Quinn and Daeng were the two men washing dishes near the door. But both went right back to what they were doing without saying anything.

Along the back wall in the corner was a metal security door, clearly denoting where the restaurant ended and the rest of the building began. In other words, a rear exit.

Quinn and Daeng walked quickly toward the door, and were halfway there when a member of the cook staff said,

"Hey, what are you doing? You're not supposed to be back here."

"DC police," Quinn barked.

If the guy said anything in response, it was lost as Quinn and Daeng rushed through the rear exit into a long service corridor.

A bundle of pipes ran along the ceiling in one corner, while evenly spaced fluorescent lights hung in a line down the center. Quinn immediately ran to the left, mentally working out the distance between the restaurant and the doorway the others had entered. Exactly where he expected it was a short corridor that ran all the way back to the outside wall. No one was there.

He could feel the tick of every second as he scanned farther down the central hallway, trying to figure out where the man and woman might have gone. He spotted a door about fifty feet away to the right with a sign that read:

COURTYARD ENTRANCE

"This way," Quinn said to Daeng, hoping he was right.

He raced over and pushed the door open.

Bare trees and bushes lined a short, windy path that led from the door to a walkway. On the other side of the walkway was a tan block wall, high enough to conceal the rest of the courtyard from view. They followed the path up a series of steps until they could see over the top of the obstruction. The brick wall turned out to be supporting a central section where a few trees and grass probably grew in the summer.

To the left of this area, another set of stairs led up to a portion of the large courtyard that was raised even higher.

"I think someone's up there," Daeng said.

Quinn had heard the footsteps, too, clacking rhythmically on the stone path. He jogged up until he could just see over the top of the stairs, then stopped.

The woman and the man from the sedan were nearing a set of glass doors that led back into the building, their backs to Quinn and Daeng. At first Quinn thought they were going inside, but instead a pudgy man with salt and pepper hair stepped out and greeted them.

Crouching, Quinn moved up the steps as far as he could without being detected. He pulled out his phone again and reattached the telephoto lens. This time he was able to get much better pictures of the woman and her colleague, as they would occasionally turn enough for him to snap nearly three-quarter profile shots. He was also able to take several pictures of the man they were meeting.

From their interaction, Quinn sensed that the older guy held rank over the woman, and that she held rank over the man who had come with her. At one point, the woman turned to her companion and said something. In response, he handed the older man the suitcase.

Quinn was curious what it might contain, but unless they were going to open it, that would have to remain a mystery for the moment.

The trio spoke for a few more minutes, then the woman and her partner began to turn back the way they'd come.

Quinn dipped below the level of the stairs and looked over at Daeng.

"The older guy—you saw him?" Quinn said.

"I did," Daeng replied.

"See where he goes. Nate and I will keep on the other two."

Daeng nodded and moved down the stairs far enough that he could stand up without being seen. Then, as if he belonged on the premises, he headed back up again, his hands stuffed in his pockets.

When Quinn reached the bottom, he hurried along the path they'd taken into the courtyard. If he was right, the other two's business here was done and they were leaving. He needed to be back on the street when they appeared. He skipped the entrance to the hallway in favor of a door marked GARAGE. This led him down one level, where he quickly located the car ramp and reached the public sidewalk before the others reappeared.

His phone vibrated only seconds after he got there.

"The sedan's heading back to the drop-off point," Nate said.

"Figured. Looks like they've wrapped up here. Meet me same place as before."

Quinn headed down the sidewalk to be in position as soon as Nate arrived. Before he got there, however, he heard the door the man and woman had used earlier open behind him. He turned on his phone's front-facing camera and angled it so he could see behind him. As expected, the woman and man had exited the building.

The moment Nate pulled to the curb, Quinn jumped into the front passenger seat.

"Where's Daeng?" Nate asked.

"We'll pick him up later. Right now, let's see where these guys go."

DAENG DIDN'T EVEN receive a passing glance from the woman and man as he walked by them in the courtyard. A goateed Asian guy with hair down to his shoulders, he'd probably been pegged as a service-industry employee at one of the local hotels. The joys of racial profiling—an ugly practice he had taken advantage of on more than one occasion.

By the time he reached the door at the end of the walkway, the older man who'd met the two people had gone inside. Daeng wasn't worried, though. He had seen the guy turn to the right, but being overweight, the man wouldn't get far.

When Daeng stepped through the doorway, he found himself in a lounge area set up with seating and tables. It had a path curving through the lounge in a way that some architect must have thought was a flash of brilliance. The fat man was waddling down the thruway, so it took almost no effort at all for Daeng to close the distance between them to a mere ten feet.

Up close now, he could see the man wore an expensive

overcoat, and though Daeng couldn't see the man's suit from behind, he was willing to bet that it, too, was made from the finest of materials.

Because of the raised area in the courtyard, this section of the building was on the second floor. Ahead was a marble stairway leading down, and to its right, a set of elevators. The target skipped the former and headed straight for the lifts. Daeng thought this meant the guy had been intending to go up, but the man waited for and then entered a car heading down. Daeng and a few others shuffled on with him.

Before the doors closed, several buttons were pushed for the lower levels of a parking garage. That had to be it, Daeng decided. Taking the down elevator made sense to him now. Until the target reached out and pushed the button for level 1.

You lazy son of a bitch, Daeng thought. No wonder the guy was overweight.

A short ride down, the doors opened again and the target exited. Daeng tried to keep the disapproval off his face as he followed the man.

They were in a main lobby area, with dozens of people moving about and several more waiting in line at a coffee shop along the west wall. A podium was set up near the front door, and behind it stood a middle-aged man in a sharp black uniform, white shirt, purple tie, and black doorman hat.

As the target approached the podium, Daeng moved in as close as he dared.

"Mr. Boyer," the man behind the podium said. "Leaving us already?"

"I'm in a bit of a hurry," the target—Boyer—said, handing the man a ticket.

"I'll have your car brought up right way."

As the man picked up a phone, Boyer started to turn back to the lobby.

There was no time for Daeng to get out of his way, so he smiled and said, "Excuse me, is this where we arrange for a taxi?"

Boyer couldn't have looked less interested if he tried. "I wouldn't know," he said, barely even looking at Daeng.

Daeng watched him move near the doors to wait.

The man at the podium returned his phone to its cradle and said to Daeng, "How may I help you, sir?"

"Taxi?"

"Of course. I can signal one. If you'll head outside, it should be there in a moment."

"Thank you," Daeng said, handing the man a tip.

The promised taxi pulled to the curb a moment after Daeng stepped outside. As he got into the back, the driver said, "Where to?"

"Hold on a moment," Daeng said, pulling out his cell phone. "I need to check something."

"Hey, I can't just sit—"

Daeng dropped a twenty-dollar bill into the front seat. "Let's not be in too much of a hurry, shall we?"

The cabbie grabbed the bill. "This isn't part of the fare."

"Of course not."

The bill disappeared into the driver's pocket.

Daeng switched his phone to camera mode and looked out the window. Less than a minute passed before a dark blue Maserati Ghibli pulled to the curb in front of the taxi. A few seconds later, the door to the building opened and Boyer walked out.

Daeng shot a picture of the car and zoomed in on the license plate.

Expensive clothes. Expensive car. Whoever this Boyer was, he had access to cash—a lot of it.

Daeng texted the pictures to Orlando and Quinn, and then leaned forward and said to the cabbie, "A hundred-dollar tip if you do this right."

"Do what right?" the driver asked, more than a bit wary.

"Follow that car."

THOUGH ORLANDO HAD started to think the photo of Tessa would be the only thing of interest on Eli's computer, she wouldn't know for sure until she could finish a complete examination of the drive, a process being hindered by the pictures Quinn kept sending her.

The first set had been nearly useless—photos shot from a moving car, at angles far from desirable. The only one she could get enough data points on to feed through the facial recognition database was of the man sitting in the backseat. So far, an alarm hadn't gone off to tell her she had a match.

The next group was better. The woman and two men, neither of whom was the guy she was already checking out. The pictures of the woman and the younger man were also profile shots, but much clearer and showing more of their features. The pic of the older man was full face. With graying hair and more weight than he needed, he looked to be in his late fifties to early sixties. None of the three were familiar to her. Since she was almost done with Eli's computer, she decided to hold off on putting the photos through the recognition process until she finished. Fifteen minutes, tops.

Before she even got halfway to that point, her phone dinged again.

She cursed under her breath as she grabbed it.

She was expecting to see more photos from Quinn, but the two new pictures were from Daeng. These were different from the others, not pictures of people but a Maserati—one a wide shot of its back, and one a close-up of its license plate.

Curious, she ran the license number through the DC motor vehicles database. The car was not registered to an individual, but to a corporation called McCrillis International.

The name was vaguely familiar, which annoyed her.

Her memory had always been something she could count on, but lately it had begun to fail her on occasion.

"What's wrong?" Abraham asked.

She blinked and looked at him. She hadn't realized her frustration was noticeable. "Nothing," she said. "Sorry."

She returned her attention to the computer and searched for information about McCrillis International.

The first link that came up cleared the fog from her mind.

QUINN AND NATE followed the sedan through heavy traffic

east to Connecticut Avenue NW. There the others traveled only half a block north before pulling up in front of the Mayflower Renaissance Hotel. Bags were removed from the back and keys were given to a valet. Apparently the Renaissance was where they would stay.

Quinn had just told Nate to find a place to park when Orlando called.

"You get a hit on one of my pictures?" he asked.

"Not yet," she said. "But I did on Daeng's."

He had seen the pictures of the Maserati a few minutes earlier. "The license plate."

"Yeah. It's registered to, get this, McCrillis International."

"McCrillis?" he said, surprised.

McCrillis's public front was that of an international law firm that specialized in business partnerships and joint ventures. It did generate quite a bit of business in that area, but its lesser known private side was what brought in the bulk of the company's income. In effect, it was to the business world what the Office had been to the intelligence community, an agency that specialized in doing the things businesses themselves couldn't—industrial espionage, undercover smear campaigns, sabotage, and even the occasional target elimination. Since the skill sets needed for most of the company's projects were similar to those used in the secret world, some freelancers dabbled in both arenas, but the majority tended to keep to one sphere or the other.

And while it was true that intelligence agencies would often find it necessary to make incursions into the corporate world, it was nearly unheard of for industrial intelligence organizations to make a move in the other direction. When the latter did, they usually received more than a hand slap. So, having a company like McCrillis even tangentially connected to the death of a CIA analyst was highly unusual. And yet Quinn had witnessed a meeting that apparently connected McCrillis to the people who had been searching Eli's home less than twenty-four hours after the man's death.

"Do we know who the old guy is yet?" he asked.

"Just a second, I'm…" Her voice trailed off, and he could hear her working on her computer. After a moment she said softly, "Ah. There you are."

"There *who* is?"

"I'm on McCrillis's website. It has pictures and biographies of all their top executives. Our friend in the Maserati is one Ethan Boyer, Executive Vice President, Special Projects."

"Ethan Boyer," Quinn said, letting the name hang in the air for a moment. "Never heard of him."

"Me, neither," she said. "But how much you want to bet your other friends work for McCrillis, too?"

FINDING A CAB driver who was skilled at the art of following another car was a hit–or–miss proposition. Unfortunately for Daeng, his driver fell into the latter category.

While the cabbie was able to keep the Maserati in view, that was more due to the heavy evening traffic and some erratic driving than any talent on his part.

"Careful," Daeng said. "If he sees us, the hundred is off the table."

"I'm doing everything I can," the cabbie said angrily. "Do you want me to stop and just let you out here?"

Daeng was tempted to say yes, but a call from Quinn put it on hold.

"The guy in the Maserati's name is Boyer," Quinn said. "Give you the details later. Right now, go ahead and break off." Quinn told him where the SUV was parked. "We'll wait for you here."

As Daeng pushed his phone back into his pocket, he said, "Change of plans." He repeated the address Quinn had given him. "Quick as you can."

The cabbie looked at Daeng through his mirror, concerned. "What about the tip?"

ETHAN BOYER DID not take security lightly, especially his own. While he hadn't noticed the cab following him, the men who always monitored his position from a trail car had.

Whitmore, the driver of his shadow car, said, "They're turning off. What do you want us to do?"

"Has backup arrived yet?" Boyer asked.

"One minute out."

Crap. The idea of driving around without his security detail for sixty seconds was unappealing to say the least, but if it was the only way to find out who had been following him, he didn't see a choice.

"Go," he said.

"PULL OVER ANYWHERE in the next block," Daeng said.

As if he'd been waiting to hear those words, the cabbie immediately pulled to the curb and turned off the meter. "Forty-seven twenty," he announced.

Daeng paid the fare, with the extra hundred as promised.

Looking as if the weight of a thousand worlds had been lifted from his shoulders, the taxi driver said, "Next time, get into someone else's cab."

"You have a good evening, too," Daeng said as he climbed out.

He looked both ways and spotted what he was pretty sure was the Explorer on the other side of the street, down about a block. Traffic was bumper to bumper on that half of the road, but would be easy enough to weave through. All he had to do was wait until the cars on his side cleared out of the way.

There, he thought, after the dark Dodge Caravan. A large enough gap to pass through.

He stepped into the road about a foot beyond the vehicles parked at the curb. He looked toward where his friends were waiting, but his view was blocked by the traffic. He checked to make sure the opening on his side was still approaching, then took another step out.

A truck.

A compact.

And finally the van.

But instead of driving by, the Caravan pulled to a quick

stop, the front passenger window opened, and the man inside rested the suppressor-enhanced end of a gun on the frame. Not quite the family friendly image Dodge was going for.

"Stay where you are," the man ordered.

As much as Daeng would have liked to disobey him, he knew the guy would be able to get off a shot before Daeng could find cover. His only chance was to play it cool and hope for an opportunity to escape.

"We'd like you to take a ride with us," the man said.

"Thanks for the offer, but I'm not interested," Daeng replied.

The side door slid open, and a ropy man with intense eyes climbed out.

"It wasn't an offer," the guy in the front seat said.

Daeng didn't have to ask what this was all about. He knew it was that damn cabbie. The taxi had been spotted, and the man in the Maserati had apparently not taken kindly to the attention.

The ropy guy took a step toward Daeng and said, "Get in."

He grabbed Daeng by the arm and pulled him toward the van.

"Wait," the man up front said. "Search him."

His buddy pushed Daeng against the side of the vehicle and patted him down, pulling out Daeng's phone and his wad of cash. After stuffing the money into his own pocket, Ropy Guy showed the phone to the other guy.

"Get rid of it."

Ropy Guy tossed it on the ground, crushed it under his heel, and kicked the remains under a car parked nearby.

Now! Daeng thought.

He shoved past the man and darted toward the back of the Caravan, hoping the second guy would hinder his friend's view.

A single *thup*.

Daeng grabbed his left thigh as he stumbled forward and fell to the ground. He barely had time to register the burning pain of the gunshot before he was hauled to his feet and thrown into the van.

As they sped way, the man in front turned around, his gun peeking through the split between the seats. "So tell me, Mr. Nosy, what do we call you?"

CHAPTER
NINETEEN

"WHERE THE HELL is he?" Nate asked.

Quinn had his phone to his ear as he tried Daeng's number again, but like before, all he reached was voice mail. He called Orlando, putting her on speaker.

"I need to get a position on Daeng," he said.

"Something happen?"

"Not sure. Maybe nothing."

"Searching…" No matter where one of the team was in the world, Orlando could pinpoint that person via his phone to within a foot of his actual position. "Um…problem."

"What?" Quinn asked.

"I don't have a signal. Backtracking…okay, last ping was six minutes ago. Wait…"

When she failed to continue, Quinn said, "You still there?"

"According to his history," she said, sounding both surprised and confused, "his last position was a hundred and seventy-three feet east of you on the other side of the street."

Quinn and Nate whipped around and looked out the window. All Quinn saw were a few parked cars.

"We'll call you back," he said.

They jumped out of the SUV and sprinted between vehicles to the other side of the road. When they reached the ping point, Quinn scanned the ground and then dropped to his knees so he could look under the cars. With darkness falling, it was hard to see much of anything, but there was something just a few feet behind the rear tire of a Honda. A bump on the pavement.

By stretching his arm under the car as far as he could, he was able to get the tip of his fingers on the bump and work it toward him. Even before it cleared the bumper, he could feel that it was a phone, and once he had eyes on it, he knew it was Daeng's.

"Quinn," Nate said.

He was crouched next to a dark spot on the road. When he held up a finger, Quinn could see some kind of substance on it.

"It's not oil," Nate said.

"TELL ME YOU found him," Orlando said when Quinn called back.

"No," he said. "He was here, but something happened."

He told her about the smashed phone and the blood on the road.

"There are a few cameras on this street," he said. "Security, traffic."

"I'll look," she told him. "You want to stay on the line or…?"

"No. We're coming to get you."

"Okay."

As soon as she hung up, she closed Eli's computer and scooted it toward Abraham. "Put it away. We'll deal with it later."

"What happened?" he asked.

"Not now."

On her own laptop, she accessed the DC metro traffic monitoring system and identified the cameras nearest the Renaissance Hotel. Choosing the one with the widest view, she backtracked through the footage at double speed until she came to the point where a dark Dodge Caravan stopped next to Daeng.

The location of the incident was too far from the camera for her to see details clearly, so she noted the time and switched to one of the closer cameras. Unfortunately, since they were intended to monitor intersections, none were pointing directly at the spot where Daeng had been.

She looked at the map, noting the businesses and buildings in the area. There was the Renaissance, of course. It would undoubtedly have surveillance out front, but given the point where Daeng was taken, it was unlikely the hotel's cameras would be useful. There was, however, an office building close enough that its system may have picked up something.

After circumventing the firewalls into the building's security system, she discovered seven cameras covering the outside of the building—three in the back where deliveries were made, and four in front. The first of the front cameras was angled so that it caught only a thin slice of the Caravan. Daeng, though, was clearly visible, as was a man standing outside with him. The gunshot seemed to come from inside the van. She had to watch the clip frame by frame before she could identify the tip of a suppressor sticking out the front passenger window.

Her jaw tensed. She reversed the footage a bit and let the whole thing play out again at normal speed. Though she couldn't see exactly where Daeng had been hit, from the way he'd fallen and how he looked as he was pushed into the vehicle, she was pretty sure the bullet had struck him in the leg.

She checked the other three cameras but none provided a better view. She made her way back to the traffic camera and watched as the SUV began moving again. Once it reached its closest position to the camera, she froze the playback and enlarged the image so she could get a look at the license plate. The magnification distorted the picture but the number on the plate was readable. A quick run through the DC motor vehicles database returned the same result she'd received with the Maserati.

McCrillis International.

Next, she tried to trace the Caravan's path, jumping from traffic cam to traffic cam, but there were holes in the system and some cameras weren't working properly so it wasn't long before she lost the trail.

She didn't even check for any satellites that might have been overhead. The sky had been cloudy since they'd arrived and any overhead shots would be useless.

For the moment, she was out of options for tracking the Caravan, so she uploaded into the facial recognition system the images of the woman and the man who had met with Ethan Boyer.

She was setting the final parameters when Quinn called back.

"We're out front," he said.

Surprised, she looked at the clock on her computer and saw that forty minutes had passed since they'd last spoken.

"We'll be right there," she told him.

She input the final data, started the search process, and closed her computer.

"Are you sure you're all right?" Abraham asked as she stuffed her laptop into her bag.

"I'm fine."

"You seem—"

"I'm fine," she repeated and stood up. "Let's go."

MISTY BLAKE OPENED the townhouse door before Quinn had even finished knocking. Her smile was one of relief. Without a word, she stepped across the threshold and threw her arms around him. When she finally pulled back, she had water in her eyes.

"I'm so happy to see you," she said.

"Can we come in?" Quinn asked.

"Of course. Please." She stepped out of the way and gestured for them to enter.

When the door was closed again, she gave Nate and Orlando hugs, too, then stopped when she came to Abraham. "I don't believe we know each other." She held out her hand. "Misty Blake."

"Abraham Delger," he said as they shook. "A pleasure to

meet you."

"We appreciate you letting us use this place," Quinn said.

"It was just sitting here empty," she told him. "No big deal."

The townhouse was one that had been owned by Peter. He had controlled several hideaways throughout the DC area. After his death, the government had taken over all those listed as being owned by the Office, but a few had been completely in Peter's name. Per his will, Misty, his former assistant and right hand, had inherited them all.

Quinn knew he and his friends needed someplace anonymous and needed it fast, so he had called Misty while he and Nate were on the way to pick up the others. As he'd hoped, she had immediately offered him one of her places.

"I, um, put some food in the refrigerator," Misty said. "It's not a lot. I wasn't sure how long you'd be here. If you need more, just let me know."

"I doubt we'll be here very long at all, so I'm sure it's plenty," Quinn told her.

"There are clean sheets on the beds, towels in the bathrooms. Soap, shampoo—it's all there." She looked around as if searching for something else she needed to tell them.

"It's perfect. Thank you. You've done more than enough."

"Okay. Well, then, I, um, I guess I should…go."

"Thanks again," Orlando said.

Quinn knew Misty wanted to stay, but he wasn't about to bring anyone else into this until he knew exactly what it was they were dealing with. He put an arm on her shoulder and walked her to the door. "You have a spare key, correct?"

"Yes, of course."

"Then we'll slip ours through the mailbox when we leave." He paused before asking, "Do you have the other item?"

She stared at him for a second before her eyes widened. "Oh, right. Sorry." She dug into her purse and pulled out a small square object no bigger than a dime. As she handed it to Quinn, she said, "Spare bedroom closet, left side."

"Thank you."

"If you need anything else," she said, "seriously, let me know."

"We will."

Reluctantly, she opened the door. "It *is* good to see you."

"You, too, Misty."

The moment she was gone, Orlando set both hers and Eli's laptop on the dining table and showed the others the footage of Daeng's kidnapping.

"Boyer must have realized he was being tailed," Quinn said.

The computer dinged as a small window opened in the top corner.

"We've got a hit," Orlando said.

She clicked the alarm and the security footage was replaced by an information sheet. On it was a picture of the woman from the car, but not the picture Quinn had taken.

"This is interesting," Orlando said, reading the screen. "She's used at least eight different names, one for each time she's been arrested."

"On what charges?" Quinn asked.

"Breaking and entering. Reckless driving. Assault. Oh, and attempted murder."

"Any convictions?"

Orlando shook her head. "Charges dropped every time. Never even went before a judge. Her professional name is Gloria Clark." She read some more and then looked at Quinn. "She's a fixer."

"A fixer?" Fixers were the people you called to take care of a problem that required some creative thinking. "I've never heard of her."

"Me, neither, but she works directly for McCrillis, which makes her corp-intel, so we've likely never crossed paths."

Quinn turned to Abraham. "I don't get it. Why is corporate intelligence involved in this?"

"I honestly don't know. It doesn't make sense to me, either."

"What was the name of the guy who hired you to transport the girl again?"

"Gavin Carter."

"Who was *he* working for?"

"I've been under the impression that the CIA was at least partly involved. Could have been in conjunction with someone else, though. I just don't know."

"Did he do any corp-intel work?"

"I wish I could tell you, Johnny, but I have no idea."

"Do you at least know where he is now?"

"No. Last time I talked to him was right before I dropped off Tessa. I did halfheartedly try to track him down once, but no luck. Since I didn't really think he'd tell me anything, I didn't try again."

"I'll find him," Orlando said, turning back to her computer.

Quinn touched the nape of her neck. "Before you do that, I'd like you to locate Ethan Boyer. I mean exactly where he is right now. You can hunt down Carter after."

She looked at him the way she did when she knew what he had in mind. "It won't be easy."

"When is it ever?" He turned to Nate. "Need your help."

They went upstairs into the spare bedroom. There were two beds, made and ready, and a nightstand between them on which Misty had placed a pitcher of water and a couple of glasses.

Quinn slid the closet door open. A few blankets were on the shelf above the clothes rack, but otherwise the space was empty. Stepping inside, he knelt down at the left end and ran the tip of his forefinger along the baseboard. About seven inches from the corner, a section no wider than a Popsicle stick gave a little under his pressure. He pushed again, harder this time, and when he let go, a tongue of wood popped up. In the middle of the piece was a square depression.

Quinn inserted the square Misty had given him, and pushed the whole section back down. When it clicked into place, he could feel the ever-so-slight vibration of a motor below the floor of the closet. Behind them, in the right-hand corner, the wall that had looked as normal as the others slid out of sight, exposing a fully stocked equipment and weapons cupboard.

He looked at Nate. "Gear up."

CHAPTER
TWENTY

SIFTING THROUGH SAVED traffic-cam data, Orlando tracked Ethan Boyer's Maserati across the city to the McCrillis International headquarters. Twenty minutes later, he was back on the road, heading east into Maryland. She lost him five miles past the border, however, when he turned off the highway onto a road not monitored by traffic cameras.

A quick look at the map told her his route led through some of the more exclusive bedroom communities that surrounded DC. A search through property records told her all she needed to know.

"You find him?" Quinn asked when he came back downstairs.

She nodded. "I believe so. Last eyes I had on him, he was heading toward a gated community called The Hilltop, which happens to be where he owns a home."

"Text me the address. A layout of the place would be great, too."

"Already pulled. I'll send both to you."

He leaned down and kissed her. "Don't wait up."

"Be careful."

"I'm not worried about us," Quinn said. A moment later, he and Nate were gone.

Orlando sent him Boyer's address and the layout of the man's house, then considered what her next task should be. Finding Daeng was of utmost importance, but until Quinn came back with more information, there was really nothing she could do on that front.

Her time, she decided, would be best spent working on the Eli angle and trying to uncover the rest of the information he had planned to give Abraham. She delved back into his computer to finish her search but found nothing else.

"Do you think the photo was all he had for you?" she asked Abraham.

"I don't think he would have thought it necessary to meet in person if it was just a photo. There had to have been something more."

"What about Tampa? Was it random or did he want you there for a reason?"

Abraham looked surprised by her question. "I...I've been thinking it was random. It hadn't occurred to me that it might not be."

"Does it mean something?"

He thought for a moment, and then shrugged. "Nothing comes to mind."

She could see he was starting to feel defeated so she tried a different tact. "Why don't you tell me more about him? What was he like?"

"Like I said before, a bit of a loner. Cautious."

"Paranoid?" she asked.

"Perhaps a little, though I'm not sure I'd use that word myself." He paused before adding, "Clearly he was a collector. I knew he'd done a little bit of it, but didn't realize the extent."

"When was the last time you saw him in person?"

"Two summers ago," Abraham said. "Every few years he'd come to San Diego for Comic-Con and we'd get together for lunch one of the days."

"So...nerdy, kept to himself for the most part, borderline paranoid," Orlando summed up. "The perfect CIA analyst."

"Yeah, I guess."

"Okay, given those factors, even after he'd snuck out of DC, he would have still considered himself in potential danger, right?"

"Sure. That makes sense."

"Then he would have taken precautions, left a backup somewhere you could find it if something happened to him."

"But I searched the hotel room. If he left anything there, the others got it."

"You're looking at this wrong. I mean, yes, if you were just a normal guy, never worked in the business, you might hide the information in the room. But Eli wasn't a normal guy. He may not have been in the field, but he lived on the edge of our world."

"So...what? He dropped a copy in the mail to me? He knew I'd be there in a few hours so that seems unlikely, don't you think?"

"Exactly. *And* you're not a normal guy. You were an operative and he knew that. Now, think. What would he have done? What would he have done that *you* specifically would have been able to figure out?"

Abraham fell silent, his gaze resting unfocused on the tabletop. "I really don't know. He wouldn't have even been there long enough to do much by the time the ambulance came for him."

"That's true. There was a very finite window."

She grabbed her laptop and jerked it forward. Within seconds she was in the system for the Azure Waves Hotel. The security department monitored over a hundred cameras spread throughout the facility. From the amount of storage they had, she knew they wouldn't keep old footage for long. As she dove into the archive, she hoped she wasn't too late.

Her immediate impression was that the majority of old footage was dumped within twenty-four hours, but this tended to be true only for cameras in less traveled areas of the facility. The footage from those in and around the elevators, the lobby, the pool area, and the main entrances were held on to longer.

Since nothing remained from the seventh floor in the building where Eli had been staying, Orlando concentrated on the lobby, starting early evening. Running the playback at high speed, she scanned the comings and goings of the guests and employees, not spotting Eli until the timer on the image read 09:43:21 PM. She slowed the footage to double speed and observed as he checked into the hotel.

"He's nervous," Abraham said.

That was an understatement. Every fifteen seconds or so, Eli would shoot a look over his shoulder as if expecting someone to jump him.

When he received his key, he headed immediately to the elevators.

"He's carrying a bag," Orlando said. It was a small suitcase. "It wasn't in the room, right?"

"The room was empty."

As soon as Eli disappeared, she increased the speed again. She thought the next time they see him, he'd be on a gurney, but—

"Stop!" Abraham shouted.

Orlando paused the image.

"Go back," he told her. "He just walked through."

She scrolled back until Eli was clearly in frame. He had exited the elevators at 10:46:09 PM, walked straight across the lobby, and out the front door. She stopped the image and switched to a camera outside. Matching the time code, she found the point where he came out. He paused on the sidewalk for several moments, looking both ways. Three cabs were at the curb to the left. The driver of the first stuck his head out his window and said something to Eli. Eli shook his head and then turned right and walked off.

"So he was on foot," Abraham said.

"Or caught a cab somewhere else," she said.

She sped up the image. Eli returned twenty-four minutes later. Not really enough time to drive anywhere far away and get back, so she thought it unlikely he'd grabbed a taxi. She followed him through the lobby to the elevators. When he got on, a drunk-looking woman stumbled on with him, but not just any woman. The same one who had been in Eli's apartment and met with Boyer.

Gloria Clark.

Once more Orlando sped up the footage, this time slowing when the two men dressed as paramedics wheeled a gurney holding an unconscious Eli toward the front door. Right behind him was Clark.

"It's her," Abraham said, seeing it now, too.

Orlando nodded as she opened a new window on her browser and brought up a map of the area surrounding the Azure Waves Hotel. "All right. Eli could have gone, what? Maybe a mile and a half out and back, if he kept walking the whole time. But we've got to figure he would have stopped for a bit and—"

"Orlando, that was the woman," he said.

"I realize that. Not a big shock she was there, though, is it? Now, come on, I need you to concentrate." She created a circle with a mile radius around the hotel. "Wherever Eli went, I'm pretty sure it's in this circle. Think. What kind of place would he have gone to?"

"I don't know. Maybe he was getting something to eat."

"All right. Restaurants. We'll start there." She put in the parameters and the program highlighted all the known eating establishments in the area. There were dozens. "Does he have a favorite type of food?"

"When we met up, we sometimes went for Italian or Chinese or for steaks. Nothing in particular."

"If we're working off the premise that he did leave something behind, and it would be somewhere you could figure out, then I guess restaurants are out."

Abraham reluctantly nodded.

"What, then? Bars?" she asked, then remembered the stack of posters at his townhouse. "How about a movie theater? He liked movies."

"That could be it."

She searched for movie theaters, but the only two were right at the edge of the mile—unlikely candidates.

"Bookstores," she said, thinking back to his place again.

She tried that. There were seven hits. Five were used bookstores, one of which was only a couple blocks from the hotel. Another was part of one of the big chains.

"That's it," Abraham said, pointing at the last store on the list. "If he did leave something, that's where it would be."

She couldn't argue with him.

The seventh bookshop was a place called DeeDee's Comics, and was located somewhere between a five- and ten-minute walk from the hotel.

She brought up the store's website. "They're open to eleven. You want to give them a call?"

"Why not?"

The call connected after the fifth ring.

At first only loud rock music came out of the speaker on Abraham's phone—a classic Arctic Monkeys tune, if Orlando was correct—then a man said, "DeeDee's."

"Good evening," Abraham said. "I, um, have a bit of an unusual question to ask."

"You wouldn't be the first. What is it?"

"I'm wondering if a friend of mine left something there for me."

"This isn't a mailbox store," the guy said, sounding like he was about to hang up.

"I realize that," Abraham said quickly. "He would have come in three nights ago just before you closed."

"I wasn't on three nights ago."

"Well, is there someone there who was?"

An exasperated "Hold on."

The Arctic Monkeys filled the absence until a woman came on and said in a much friendlier voice than her colleague's, "This is Vanessa. Can I help you?"

"Yes, my name is…Abraham Delger. I think a friend of mine may have left something there for me the other night."

In an unexpectedly cautious tone, she said, "It's possible. Who was your friend?"

"Eli Becker," he said. "Oh, or he may have been going by Charles Young."

"May have been going by?" the woman asked.

"His name is Eli. It's…well, it's a long story. *Did* he leave something for me?"

If it weren't for the fact they could still hear music, Orlando would have wondered if they'd been disconnected. Finally Vanessa asked, "What was the girl's favorite game?"

Orlando could see that Abraham was shocked by the question.

"Hey, you still there?" the woman asked.

"Checkers," he blurted out. "She loved checkers."

"Then yeah. I do have something for you. When do you want to pick it up?"

CHAPTER
TWENTY ONE

IF THERE WAS one thing you didn't do, it was mess with the people important to Quinn.

Those who had tried to harm his mother and sister had found that out, as had those who'd caused Nate to lose half of his leg, and the ones responsible for nearly killing Orlando. Unfortunately, not everyone seemed to have been clued in to that particular nugget of information, so it fell back on Quinn to hammer home the lesson again.

The section of the Maryland countryside he and Nate were driving through was a haven for those who made their living trying to suck the US government dry—lawyers and businessmen and lobbyists and those who were a bit of all three. Five-bedroom, six-bedroom, seven-bedroom homes on an acre or more of land. Some with columns, some with guesthouses, and almost all with more cars than could fit into oversized garages.

Ethan Boyer's home was in a gated community called The Hilltop, on a street named River View Lane. The Hilltop's security staff appeared to be competent, with two vehicles constantly roaming the development and pairs of guards stationed at the three separate entrances. Competent, yes, but little problem for Quinn and Nate.

The two cleaners entered over the wall into the backyard of a darkened house whose owners were either not home or early sleepers. Sticking as much as possible to the shadows, they moved silently through the community to River View

Lane. Behind some bushes across the road from Boyer's property, they found a spot that would serve as the perfect observation point.

Nate pulled the pack off his back and removed the two sets of night vision goggles they'd procured from Peter's stash. In addition to allowing them to see their surroundings as if during daytime, the goggles were equipped with two magnification settings, turning them into adequate if a bit underpowered binoculars.

Each man donned his pair and scanned the area. Boyer's home was a Federal-style clapboard house, three stories high with a four-car garage off to the side. Though they couldn't see it from their position, they knew from the layout Orlando had obtained that a two-story annex stretched behind the house, with a room on the second floor designated on the plans as OFFICE.

"See anything?" Quinn whispered.

"Nothing," Nate replied.

While The Hilltop did have its own security force, Quinn was positive someone in Boyer's line of work would employ his own people to ensure his safety.

Motioning toward a copse of trees fifty yards to the left, he said, "Let's reposition."

Quietly, they moved straight back from the bushes, away from the road, before skirting the front of a neighboring home and entering the small grove. Staying low, they shuffled forward again until they were only a few feet from where the trees ended. Once more, they scanned Boyer's property.

"Got one," Nate said.

"Show me."

Nate touched the side of his goggles, pushing the button that would put a digital tag on the sentry he'd seen. A second later, a yellow dot appeared in Quinn's view, showing him where the man was. By the time they were through with their visual search, they had tagged three total.

"Probably two more on the other side," Quinn said. "Maybe three."

"D-guns?" Nate asked.

Quinn nodded. "They're all in range."

In addition to the goggles, they had procured two SIG SAUER P226 pistols with matching sound suppressors, four flash-bang stun grenades, and a pair of high-tech dart guns—D-guns—complete with scope and set of twelve tranquilizer-filled darts. Since they were operating in a highly populated civilian area, the less noise they made, the better.

Nate removed them from his pack, attached the clip that contained an extra three darts beyond the one already chambered, and handed one of the weapons to Quinn.

"Left to right, one, two, and three," Quinn said. "You take one, I'll take two, and whoever gets there first gets three."

Nate grinned. "We both know who that'll be."

Quinn placed his dart gun's barrel against a tree to steady it, and then aimed through the scope at target number two.

"Set," Nate said.

"Set," Quinn echoed. "Ready. Now."

Together they pulled their triggers, each man keeping an eye on their target to make sure their shot hit home. Quinn's man staggered backward, his hand grasping at the dart, but before he could pull it out, he collapsed on the ground.

Quinn immediately moved his scope to target number three, but as he was lining up his shot, he heard the *pfft* of Nate's gun again, and a second later number three was on the ground.

"Told you," Nate said.

"Keep up the cocky attitude and you'll have firsthand knowledge of what these darts do to you."

After Nate reshouldered his backpack, they sprinted across the street and dropped into a shallow ditch that lined the other side of the road. They made a quick study of the grounds but saw no one, so they headed toward the side of the house.

Partway there, they came across the first of the sleeping sentries. Together, they moved him to the other side of a leafless hedge so he wouldn't be noticed by any community patrols driving by. The other two they didn't need to worry about. They'd been farther in on the property and were lost in the darkness.

When the cleaners reached the house, Quinn pointed at Nate and then at the rear corner. With a nod, Nate headed there while Quinn moved to the front of the house. Very carefully, he leaned around the edge and searched the yard. Once he was sure the area was clear, he headed back to Nate's position.

His former apprentice held up two fingers, and then pointed at an angle through the wall at two different spots to show Quinn where the guards were located. After silently deciding who was responsible for whom, they dropped all the way to the ground and eased around the corner.

"Set," Nate whispered.

"Ready. Now."

At the exact second Quinn pulled the trigger, his target moved. Not a problem if the dart traveled as fast as a bullet, but at its subsonic speed, it sailed harmlessly behind the man's back. It did not, however, do so in complete silence.

As the sentry whirled around to see what had made the sound, Quinn pulled the trigger again. This time the man did not get out of the way.

Five down.

Nate took the lead as they followed the property line to a group of hibernating shrubs that delineated the back end. There, they got their first good look at the rear of the house.

Just like the plans showed, a two-story wing stuck straight out along the southern edge of the house. The only window on the property emitting any light was the one corresponding to the second-floor office.

Quinn carefully swept his goggles from one side of the property to the other. The only heat signatures he was picking up were those of the unconscious guards. There was still one side of the house they hadn't checked yet, though—the south. They crept along the bushes until the wing was no longer blocking their view.

A sixth sentry was about midway along the side.

"I got this," Nate said.

Quinn didn't argue. Nate's marksmanship had won him the opportunity, so Quinn stayed by the bushes and watched. Nate retraced their path until he was out of the man's potential sightline before cutting across the lawn toward the back of the wing section.

That's when Quinn saw the guard move. Nothing fast, not a reaction to having heard Nate, but the man did start walking toward the back of the house. That would have been something Nate could easily handle, but then the guy plucked something off his belt. When he held it up to his mouth, Quinn realized it was a radio, and knew their stealth arrival was on the verge of being exposed.

Since it was impossible for Nate to get into position for a shot in time, Quinn didn't even bother clicking on his mic. Instead he rushed forward and closed the distance between him and the sentry.

The man still had his walkie-talkie at his mouth when he spotted Quinn. The radio dropped as he went for the gun on his belt.

Quinn pulled the trigger of his D-gun, sending a dart zipping through the air. The man tried to duck but the tip caught his shoulder, only an inch from his neck. His hand flew up and yanked it free.

Quinn shot again, hitting the sentry in the chest this time.

The man staggered to his left, bumping into the side of the house as he tried to rip out the second dart. Though he was able to extract it, he was too late. Enough of the tranquilizer had already entered his system, causing him to crumble to the ground before he could even drop the dart.

Nate rushed around the wing and reached the man at almost the same time Quinn arrived.

"What happened?" Nate whispered.

Quinn picked up the man's radio and showed it to his partner. He was about to put it back on the ground when it crackled to life.

"Mr. Richards, what's going on out there? Sounded like

something just hit the house." When there was no immediate answer, the voice said, "Mr. Richards, come in, please. I want to know what's going on out there."

Boyer, Quinn thought.

Having no choice, he snatched up the radio and said in a hushed voice, "Sorry, sir. One of the men slipped." It was as good an excuse as any. Several patches of snow had turned to ice, some very close to the house.

"Jesus," Boyer said. "Tell your people to watch their fucking step! I'm trying to work here."

"Yes, sir. Sorry, sir."

Quinn waited for Boyer to say more, but apparently the man was done. The cleaner turned the volume way down, put the walkie-talkie into his pocket, and motioned for Nate to follow.

As they passed beneath the lit office window, they could hear snippets of Boyer's voice.

"...sure of that?...tell if the congressman...Wednesday. No, no. Wednesday...doesn't matter. What does is if that asshole....Exactly..."

Upon reaching the door into the wing section, Quinn retrieved a device identical to the one Orlando had used at Eli's townhouse, and used it to deactivate the alarm in a way that would not alert Boyer to their actions. He then stepped out of the way and let Nate pick the lock.

Just inside was a well-lit mudroom that made use of the goggles no longer necessary. Quinn noted only a single jacket on the hooks, all but confirming Boyer was alone.

After trading their dart guns for the SIGs, they proceeded into the hallway that ran the length of the wing. At the end, where the annex met the house, was a set of stairs.

Quinn went first as they headed up, quick and quiet, and emerged into an open area with a couch, a few chairs, and a television. Beyond was a shorter hallway running against the south side of the building. Two doors on the north side, with a third straight back at the very end of the hall, light leaking from under it.

They stopped at the other two doors only long enough to

make sure no one was inside before walking to the end.

"...care. We can't do it that way and you know it," Boyer was saying. Though his voice wasn't raised, his words were delivered in a way that said: Don't mess with me. "Tell them to get it done, and then get the goddamn information to the client. I don't want to hear about this again. Am I understood?....Good."

When Quinn was sure the call was over, he gave Nate a quick nod and pushed the door open.

Boyer turned to them as quickly as his girth would allow. "Who authorized you to come in here?"

In their dark clothing, they looked somewhat similar to the sentries outside but not exactly the same. A realization that took Boyer a moment to reach.

When he did, he moved toward the large desk in the center of the room. But Nate got to him long before Boyer could reach it and jerked him back.

"Get your hands off me!" Boyer yelled as he tried to twist free.

"This will go much easier if you cooperate, Mr. Boyer," Quinn said.

Nate manhandled the McCrillis executive into one of the puffy leather chairs in front of the desk.

"Sit," he said.

"Go to hell," Boyer replied.

"I said sit," Nate told him as he kicked him in the back of the knees, forcing Boyer to flop into the chair.

"Who the fuck do you think you are?"

"People you shouldn't have screwed with," Quinn said.

"Oh, really?" he said. "I'm the one who shouldn't be screwed with. That's a life-changing mistake. My men will be here in a moment so I suggest you—"

"I assume you mean the same men who stopped us from coming up here," Quinn cut him off. "Yeah, none of them are going to be doing anything for a little while. Or do you mean the men who will be arriving because of the alarm we should have tripped getting in? Sorry, not happening, either."

Quinn had to give the man credit. Instead of looking frightened, Boyer's anger seemed to increase. "You have no idea what I am capable of doing. I will ruin you."

"No," Quinn said. "You will not."

With a nod from Quinn, Nate whipped the barrel of his gun into the side of Boyer's head.

Boyer yelled in pain. "You'll fucking pay for that!"

Quinn smirked. "I doubt that."

Boyer forced a laugh.

Quinn took a step forward. "Where is the man you abducted earlier this evening?"

"I don't know what you're talking about."

Quinn signaled Nate, who hit Boyer again.

"Fuck!"

Quinn leaned in again. "Your people grabbed him, put him in a car. Where is he?"

Boyer tried to spit at Quinn, but only succeeded in dribbling saliva down his chin.

"Where is the man you took?"

"You can go f—"

Nate's pistol slammed into the man's head a third time.

"Where is the man you took?" Quinn repeated.

Boyer spit out some blood before looking at Quinn again. "If you know who I am, then you know I would never cower to little fucks like you."

Quinn placed his suppressed SIG against Boyer's right knee and pulled the trigger.

A loud, agonizing scream filled the room. If there hadn't been so much space between the homes at The Hilltop, one of the neighbors might have heard Boyer, but with the way the community was laid out—not a chance.

Quinn moved the gun to the other knee. "Where is the man you took?"

Boyer writhed in his chair. "Goddammit! Oh, shit! Oh, shit! Oh, shit!"

"Answer my question or I pull the trigger again."

"Wait! Wait!" The man fell back against his chair, his jaw tensing in pain.

After a moment, Quinn shifted the position of the suppressor half an inch to remind Boyer he was still there. The man's eyelids popped open.

"Where is he?"

"I…I don't know."

Quinn pulled the trigger.

Another scream, but shorter than before because Boyer blacked out.

Quinn let ten seconds pass, then said to Nate, "Wake him."

Nate slapped Boyer's cheeks until the man sucked in a deep breath and looked around as if unsure where he was. Then the pain hit him again and he began to groan. "Oh, God!"

"Where is the man you took?"

"I don't know!"

Quinn moved the gun to Boyer's shoulder.

"No, please! I'm serious! I don't!"

"Then what happened to him?"

"He's…with one of…my people."

"Who?"

A hesitation. "Gloria…Clark."

"The same woman you met in the courtyard near the Ritz-Carlton this afternoon?"

Even with all the pain, Boyer looked surprised. "Yes…the same."

"What is she going to do with him?"

"She's supposed to find out why…he was following…me, and who he's…working for."

"I can answer that last part for you right now. Me."

The man looked like he'd already figured that out.

"You must have some idea where she took him," Quinn said.

The guarded look in Boyer's eyes told Quinn he was right.

"Tell me," the cleaner said, poking the man's wound again.

Boyer moaned, "I don't know."

This time Quinn grounded the muzzle deep into the wound. Boyer's scream was so intense, it was almost soundless.

"One of…one of our local facilities."

"Which one?"

Boyer shook his head. "I prefer not to know that…information."

Quinn could see Boyer was telling the truth, so they'd have to use what he'd given them and figure out the rest on their own. But that didn't mean Boyer didn't have more information to give.

"What was in the suitcase Gloria Clark gave you?"

"Suitcase? Oh…clothes, mainly…some travel stuff."

"Whose?"

"A guy named…Becker. We're checking it…for a data chip."

"And did you find one?"

"The lab's looking now."

"So what's supposed to be on this chip?"

"Information…about…about a girl."

"What girl?" Quinn asked.

"A girl who's supposed to be dead."

"And is she?"

Boyer's response was lost in another tidal wave of pain. "Please," he finally said. "Call…an ambulance…"

The man's voice was growing weaker, and Quinn knew they didn't have much more time to get anything out of him. "What did you tell the woman to do with my friend after she's done?"

The man looked away, acting as if he hadn't heard the question.

"What did you tell her to do?" When Boyer still didn't answer, Quinn grabbed his chin. "Look at me."

The man kept his eyes averted, so Quinn squeezed his jaw.

"Look at me."

Reluctantly, Boyer did.

"Did you tell her to eliminate him?"

Boyer didn't need to speak to provide Quinn an answer.

The cleaner stood up and raised his gun.

"No," Boyer pleaded.

"I told you already—you screwed with the wrong people," Quinn said, and then shot Boyer through the forehead.

They siphoned gas out of the cars in the garage and doused every room in the house. Before the now deceased McCrillis International executive vice president received a thorough soaking, Nate emptied the emergency container of dissolving chemicals from his kit into the wounds on Boyer's head and knees. It wouldn't completely hide the damage from the coroner, but it was fast acting enough to confuse things, leaving a mystery about what had happened here.

After dragging the unconscious security guards far enough away from the building to be out of harm's way, Quinn started the fire.

Unlike the blaze in Copenhagen, this was one act of arson for which he felt no regrets.

CHAPTER
TWENTY TWO

VIRGINIA

MCCRILLIS INTERNATIONAL HAD three permanent black ops sites within fifty miles of the capital, each well equipped for Gloria's purposes. The one closest, near College Station, Maryland, was being used by another team, so she had been assigned the facility in an industrial park in Springfield, Virginia.

The interrogation room was below ground in a soundproof space with one-foot-thick concrete walls, a chair bolted to the floor, and cameras that could be turned on or off, depending on what the situation dictated.

The prisoner, an Asian man with a goatee and shoulder-length black hair, had been brought in by a McCrillis transport unit twenty minutes after Gloria and her team arrived. The man was immediately taken to the interrogation room and strapped to the chair.

Gloria had then spent the next fifteen minutes watching him on the monitor, hoping to pick up something she could use, but the whole time he just sat there, staring straight ahead, his expression blank. Even the bullet he'd taken didn't seem to be fazing him. The wound had been treated before he was brought to the facility—nothing fancy, just a clean-and-bandage job. Given what was about to happen, any further treatment would have been a waste of resources.

"Going in," she said to King.

"You want me to record?" he asked.

She thought for a moment and then nodded. "Until I say otherwise."

She pushed the cart holding her bag of tricks toward the door.

THIS WASN'T THE first time Daeng had been shot. It wasn't even the first time he'd been shot in the leg. And as wounds went, this one hardly rated mention. It was a through and through, the bullet cutting a tunnel in his thigh muscle before exiting his leg. No bone hit, and, based on the fact his body hadn't drained of blood, no artery, either.

As for the pain, the mental training he'd received during the brief time he'd been a monk back in Thailand helped him let much of what he was feeling flow out of him. What pain remained, he was able to mask, cringing with each burning wave on the inside, while outwardly showing nothing at all.

After being shoved into the van, he had been taken to the lowest level of a parking garage, where, about ten minutes later, a dirty white cargo van screeched down the ramp and pulled into the adjacent spot. One of the men he'd been squeezed between climbed out and then wagged his gun at Daeng and said, "Let's go."

As Daeng gingerly scooted across the seat, the side door of the cargo van opened. From his angle, he could see four people inside—two up front and two in the cargo area.

"I don't need to tell you what to do, right?" the man with the gun asked.

Daeng answered by hobbling over to the van and sitting in the opening. From there, he could see a fifth guy in back.

"All the way in," someone behind him said.

If only these assholes had shot him in the arm instead. He could have made quick work of the guy with the pistol and then run like hell. He could still accomplish the first part in his current condition, but escaping on foot was not going to happen, so he swung his legs inside and scooted out of the doorway.

"Ari, you're up," the guy closest to Daeng said as he closed the door.

The guy in the back picked up what looked like a hard plastic toolbox and moved over to Daeng. From the box, he removed a pair of heavy-duty shears that he used to cut away the portion of the pant leg covering Daeng's wounds. He then cleaned everything out and bandaged Daeng.

"That should hold him," the man announced.

With that, the van left the garage.

Though there were no windows in back that allowed Daeng to see where they were going, he knew by the time the vehicle stopped that they were well out of Washington.

The guy in the front passenger seat hopped out, and a few seconds later, Daeng could hear the squeaky sound of a metallic roll-up door being chained open. When it stopped, the driver pulled the van several feet forward and turned off the engine.

It wasn't much of a stretch to guess they were now inside a building. This was confirmed a few moments later when the side door opened. No one asked Daeng to get out this time. Instead, two of the men grabbed him by the arms, hoisted him out of the vehicle, and guided him to a stairwell in the corner of the room. At the bottom they entered a dimly lit hallway that looked to Daeng to be concrete all the way around.

The room they took him into was three doors down and no more than twelve feet square. It had a single chair in the center of the room, facing away from the door. As he was pushed onto it, he discovered it was bolted to the floor. The men handcuffed his wrists and ankles to the chair and then left.

He had seen the cameras when he was brought in, so he knew someone was watching him. The watcher no doubt expected to see a man in pain and fear. Instead, he kept his expression blank and pictured himself lounging on a hammock in Chiang Mai, the scent of pepper and basil in the air, and a Thai pop song somewhere in the distance.

Finally, he heard the door behind him open.

Footsteps. The *click, click, click* of a woman's shoes. And the rolling of wheels.

Not far into the room, the moving wheels stopped but the *clicks* continued.

Out of the corner of his eye, Daeng saw her come around his left side. He kept staring ahead, so it wasn't until she was standing right in front of him that he got his first good look at her.

The woman from the courtyard. Of course.

She studied his face and then looked him up and down. "Well, you are an interesting specimen," she said. "I understand you haven't told anyone your name yet. Perhaps you don't speak English." She slowed her speech, pronouncing each word carefully. "Do you understand me?"

Using the southern California accent he'd perfected while living in L.A. as a teenager, he said, "I understand you better when you speak normally."

"So you do talk. Then how about giving me your name?"

"You're the host. You should go first," he said.

"All right, then. I'm Gloria. And you are?"

"Not in the habit of giving my name to someone who holds me hostage. You can appreciate that, can't you, Gloria?"

The smile she gave him was closed lip and humorless. "And you can appreciate that cooperation is the much easier path."

"For you, perhaps."

"Why were you following the Maserati?" she asked.

Daeng knew he had one job—buy time. And to do so sometimes meant dangling a carrot. "Why did *you* meet with the man who was in the Maserati and give him a suitcase? Was it full of items you took from Mr. Becker's townhome? Or were you with him in Florida, too?"

She stared at him, fake smile gone. "Who the fuck are you?"

"Careful. Your lack of control is showing."

She stepped forward and punched him in the cheek.

He stretched his mouth and said, "That was more for you than for me, I believe."

Predictably, that brought on a second hit. "Who are you?"

Blood trickled out of Daeng's mouth, but he kept his expression relaxed. "You choose what you want to call me. I'm flexible."

Breathing heavily, she raised her fist as if she were going to strike a third time, but seemed to get ahold of herself at the last moment and lowered her arm.

As soon as her breathing steadied, she walked back to whatever it was she had wheeled into the room. Daeng didn't try to see what she was doing. He'd know soon enough.

He heard a latch opening, followed by a squeak of movement. There was a moment or two of things knocking together, then relative quiet. When she walked back into view, she was holding a syringe.

"You're not going to enjoy this," she said. "Not only will this make you tell me everything I want to know, it's going to make you feel like shit, too."

He smiled and said, "I appreciate the warning."

MARYLAND

QUINN COULD SEE the glow of the fire in the rearview mirror as he and Nate drove away from The Hilltop. He gave it another couple miles to make sure they hadn't been spotted, and then called Orlando.

"Did you find Boyer?" she asked.

"Yes," he said.

"And you two are all right?"

"Of course."

"Then give me a second." The speaker went silent as she put him on hold.

"I guess we're not priority anymore," Nate said.

Quinn grunted.

After nearly a minute, Orlando returned. "Sorry."

"Everything all right there?" Quinn asked.

"Yeah, just had to talk to someone. Did Boyer know where Daeng is?"

"Not exactly, but he pointed us in the right direction."

He gave her a quick rundown of his discussion with Boyer. "I'm hoping that you can track down where these McCrillis facilities are located, then Nate and I will do drive-bys and see if the tracker on the woman's car is still working." The trackers, unfortunately, only had an effective range of four miles. After that, the signal became spotty before dropping off to nothing.

"I should have enough time to do that."

That wasn't quite the answer he expected. "You have other plans?"

"I do, actually."

As she spoke, Quinn heard what sounded like an announcement over an intercom system in the background. "Where are you?"

"Reagan Airport."

He exchanged a look with Nate. "Okay. Why?"

"I think we found where Eli left the information he had for Abraham."

"That's great news. Where?"

"Tampa," she said.

"You're kidding me."

"I wish I were." She told him about Eli's stroll in the hour before he was abducted, and of the conversation she had with a woman at a place called DeeDee's Comics. "I called around and was able to get us on a charter heading there in a half hour."

"You might not be the only one looking for it down there," Quinn said. "I can send Nate with you."

He wasn't exactly keen on the idea of Orlando and Abraham going down there alone. If she had been at full strength, then, sure, he wouldn't have worried so much, but her injuries still limited her abilities and she was still tiring easily. And Abraham? Well, he was in relatively good shape for a man of sixty-seven, but he was still sixty-seven.

"You'd never get him here on time," she said. "But don't worry. I can handle it."

"I'd feel better if you had some backup. I don't need you trying to be a hero."

"Not a role I'm interested in, either. I've already pulled up a few names of people who are available, all right? If I think anything's wrong, I'll call someone in. That work for you, Dad?"

"Yeah, that works for me."

"Now if you want me to find these McCrillis locations for you before I leave, I gotta get off the phone."

"Right. I love you."

"I love you, too."

He disconnected the call.

"For the record," Nate said, "she doesn't call you Daddy when you're alone, does she? Because that would be—"

"Shut it."

"I mean, I guess everyone is into their own thing. I just never pictured the two of you doing the—"

"I will kill you if you do not shut up now. I don't care how long we've known each other. I don't care if you *are* dating my sister. I will kill you and dump you in the deepest part of the ocean. Understood?"

"I'm, uh, not sure if I should answer. You made it pretty clear I should say nothing, but then you asked a question. Conflicting signals."

Quinn glared at him.

Nate held up a hand in surrender before using it to pull an imaginary zipper across his mouth.

Five minutes later, Quinn's phone pinged several times with incoming texts. A different address was in each of the first three messages, and in the last, a note from Orlando:

Heading onto plane now.
Takeoff sched. 15 mins.
Should be back online not
long after that if you need me.

The closest McCrillis facility was only ten miles away, right there in Maryland.

VIRGINIA

THE CAPTIVE'S NAME was Daeng, information he sounded almost eager to give up when Gloria started asking him questions again, this time post-injection. He was apparently from Thailand, though he spoke English like he'd been in the States his whole life. When asked about this, he told her about his teen years living in Los Angeles and going to Hollywood High.

With the subject sufficiently primed, she turned to the questions that really mattered.

"Who do you work for?" she asked.

"Work for?" he said, his head bobbing loosely on his neck, a half smile on his face. "Who do any of us work for?"

"Answer my question."

"I work for myself."

"Doing what?"

He tried to shrug, but his shoulder moved independently of each other, creating more of a wavelike motion. "Many, many things. Whatever needs to be done." He looked at her. "Do you need something done?"

"I do. I need you to tell me who was paying you to follow the Maserati."

"Maserati. Beautiful car, but too showy for me."

"*Who* was paying you?"

He blinked. "As far as I know, no one was paying me for that."

"Then why were you following it?"

"To see where it went."

"Why?"

His eyes narrowed in confusion. "I told you why. To see where it went."

"But you stopped following before it got to where it was

going."

"No longer necessary."

Gloria could feel her frustration level rising. "Mr. Daeng, who—"

"Just Daeng."

"Fine. *Daeng*, who told you to follow the Maserati?"

He seemed to struggle with himself for a moment before he said, "Quinn."

The name meant nothing to her, but at least it was a name.

"Why did he want you to follow it?"

"To find out where it went."

She grabbed his face and tilted it up. "I want to know *why*."

A grin still on his lips, he said, "Already told you.

She shoved his head back and knocked it against the chair. But even this didn't seem to faze him. While the dose she'd given him had indeed made him more compliant, it was clear this wasn't the first time the man had been drugged, and he was able to exert some directional control over his responses.

"This Quinn. Who is he?"

"He's my friend."

"Okay, he's your friend, so tell me about him."

Daeng's head lolled to the side. "He likes to swim."

"Why would he ask you to follow the man in the Maserati?"

"Because he was busy following you."

The woman stared at him. "What did you say?"

His eyes closed. When they fluttered open again, his smile was gone and the color was draining from his face. "I think…I'm going…"

Whatever the man ate last raced out his mouth and onto the floor beside his chair. Gloria leaped back but still ended up with a few droplets on her shoes.

Daeng's head rolled forward, his chin collapsing against his chest. She grabbed his hair and tilted his head back. His eyes were closed and his facial muscles slack.

She slapped him and shouted, "Wake up!" But all she received was a groan. A second slap didn't even garner that much.

He was out.

Her experience with other guests told her he would be useless for at least twenty minutes, perhaps more.

She stormed out of the room. Unfortunately for King, he was the only one downstairs with her. Nolan and Andres were patrolling the business park above. "Get a bucket and some towels and clean up that mess," she ordered. She then grabbed the walkie-talkie off the observation-room counter and pressed the button. "Nolan, do you read?"

"This is Nolan," Nolan answered.

"There's something I need you to check."

CHAPTER
TWENTY THREE

QUINN AND NATE drove within three miles of both the McCrillis facility southeast of DC and the one just outside College Station, Maryland. Neither location emitted a signal from the tracker on the woman's car.

"They could have found it," Nate said as they drove away from the second location. "Or maybe they changed cars."

Both possibilities had been playing through Quinn's mind, but with no other clear option at the moment, they headed toward the third location, some fifty miles south of the capital in the city of Springfield, Virginia. They talked for a while, speculating on exactly what Orlando and Abraham might find in Florida, but it wasn't long before their conversation was replaced by a quiet tension.

A year ago, neither Quinn nor Nate had known Daeng, and yet now he was one of their closest friends and an integral part of their team. Quinn knew it was possible Daeng was already dead, but he kept the thought shoved in a corner, not willing to give it any credence until he saw a body. If that did happen, Boyer wouldn't be the only casualty at McCrillis International.

About seven miles out from Springfield, Nate sat up in his seat. He'd been holding Quinn's phone and was now staring at the screen.

"I've got something," he said, and then frowned. "Well, I had something."

As they drove on, he kept his gaze glued to the cell.

After another mile, he said, "There it is again."

The signal grew stronger as Quinn entered the town and made his way to the last address Orlando had given him. It turned out to be located in a business park consisting of long buildings subdivided into separate workspaces.

Instead of driving into the park, Quinn cruised the road that ran alongside it and parked a few blocks down, in front of a church.

"The car's there, at least," Nate said, handing Quinn his phone.

Quinn looked at the display and nodded, then brought up a wider map of the area. There were main entrances off the road to the south and to the west. The east side butted up against a housing tract, while a wall bordered the northern end, separating the park from a similar but smaller one.

"Here," Quinn said, pointing at the wall between the business zones. "We can get over in the east corner."

Nate nodded. "Perfect."

They grabbed their gear and headed down the street.

The smaller business park appeared to be deserted as they hurried between the buildings to the back corner. There they looked at Quinn's phone again. The car was pinging from a point on the other side of the north wall, about ten yards from where Quinn and Nate were standing.

"Give me a boost," Quinn whispered. "Just high enough to take a look."

Nate laced his fingers together and Quinn stepped into the cradle.

"Here we go," Nate said as he pushed up.

As soon as Quinn could see the other side, he tapped the wall and Nate stopped lifting.

There were five rows of buildings, the McCrillis facility in the one straight in front of him but at the other end. Along the wall starting right below him were lines denoting parking spaces. At this time of night, only five were filled. Three were identical vehicles. Company cars, no doubt. Another was a pickup truck parked way down near the west end. The last was the sedan Gloria Clark and her men had been using.

He scanned the area for any signs of life, and was about to tell Nate to push him over when he heard a pair of low voices. Though the words were lost to him, he was pretty sure they were coming from somewhere between the building in front of him and the next one to the west. After a few seconds, the voices were replaced by the sound of someone walking on asphalt. The sounds of the steps started out almost as low as the conversation had been, but they steadily increased in volume as the walker headed in Quinn's direction.

Quinn signaled Nate to lower him until only his eyes and the top of his head were above the wall, but the background he was up against was dark enough that he was confident he wouldn't be noticed.

Several moments later the walker appeared from between the buildings. Quinn had just enough light to confirm the guy was one of the men who'd been in the car with Gloria Clark, and though Quinn couldn't see a gun, he was sure the guy had one. He continued to watch as the man paused long enough at the end of the building to check both directions before walking over to the sedan.

When the guy reached the car, he didn't get in, nor did he open the trunk to retrieve anything. What he did do was considerably more curious. He first stood a few feet behind the trunk and scanned the vehicle. Then he knelt down and began running a hand behind the bumper.

Son of a bitch, Quinn thought. He was checking for a bug.

Quinn motioned for Nate to lower him. When he was back on the ground, they moved along the wall until they were at the spot directly opposite the sedan. Quinn could hear the guy moving along it.

Quinn set his backpack on the ground and mouthed to Nate, "Up."

Nate pushed Quinn high enough so that Quinn could look all the way over the edge. The man was nearing the front fender, right below him. If the guy kept to form, he would move around the front end and be only inches from the tracker.

Quinn didn't care so much if the bug was discovered. The real problem was the alarm that would be raised when the man found it.

With extreme care, Quinn climbed onto the top of the wall, stretching out prone as he monitored the man's progress. Slowly, the guy felt along the inside bottom of the car, up the wheel well, along the top, and down the other side. When he moved toward the front corner, Quinn sat up and tucked his knees against his chest.

The man rose a few inches as he came around the corner, which was exactly what Quinn had been waiting for. He shoved himself off the wall and slammed his shoes into the side of the man's head. The guy rocked backward and landed in a heap on the ground. Before the man hit the asphalt, Quinn dropped beside him, ready to follow up his initial blow. But the man was unconscious.

Worried that whoever the guy had been talking to might be near, Quinn whipped around and scanned down the alley between the buildings. All was clear, so he used the hood of the sedan to give him enough height to lean back over the top of the wall.

He took both packs from Nate and then helped his partner up and over.

They relieved the unconscious man of his radio and weapon, then zip-tied his hands and ankles and used the guy's own shirt to gag him.

"There's at least one more walking around somewhere," Quinn whispered.

After pulling out their night vision goggles, they donned their packs and moved over to the alleyway between the last two buildings. Quinn carefully scanned the building to either side, in case someone was leaning in a doorway, but no one was there. He was about to suggest they move a couple alleys over to be farther from the McCrillis facility and less likely to be spotted, when a man walked across the opening at the far end, heading toward the east wall, and then disappeared again. The distance had been too far for them to recognize any facial features, but the gun in his hand had been plain as day.

They went to the alley between buildings two and three, and then down to the other end. Once there, Quinn slipped the lens portion of his phone far enough past the corner for them to see the other side. There was no sign of the other man.

Was he heading down the far side of the last building? If so, he might discover his tied-up buddy. Quinn motioned for Nate to head back the other way for a look.

As soon as Nate was gone, Quinn used his phone to check around the side again.

"What the hell?"

The alarmed voice had come from less than ten feet away. Quinn dropped the phone and whipped off his goggles as he rushed around the corner. He miscalculated the man's position by half a foot, so instead of hitting him center mass, he rammed the man shoulder to shoulder.

The man's weapon flew out of his hand and the two men slammed onto the asphalt. The sentry tried to shove Quinn off but Quinn was having none of it. He recognized the guy now as the same one who'd been with the woman when she met Boyer.

Quinn whacked his palm into the side of the man's face and stunned him enough for Quinn to get an arm around the guy's neck, cutting off blood flow to the brain until the sentry blacked out.

Quinn heard someone running up behind him. He jumped to his feet, ready to fight, but it only was Nate.

"Subtle," Nate whispered. "I almost couldn't hear you fighting from way down at the other end."

Ignoring the commentary, Quinn said, "Help me secure him."

After they had the guy trussed up like his partner, they moved him under a hedge that lined the parking area.

"That's got to be it," Nate said. "If there was anyone else, they would have come by now."

"Outside, anyway," Quinn said.

They hurried over to the second-to-last building and peered into the alleyway. The McCrillis unit was two down from where they were. A camera was located above the main entrance, and identical ones were above the entrances to the units on the left and right, which probably meant McCrillis owned them, too.

Quinn had a signal jammer in his pack but decided not to pull it out. The woman had been traveling with three men, two of whom they'd already danced with. It was possible the facility came with its own personnel, but if that were the case, the guards would have been on outside watch since they would be more familiar with the area. So it was likely only the woman and her other man were inside, in which case they might not be actively monitoring the camera feeds, but if the signal was jammed, that might very well trigger an alarm that would draw their attention.

He studied the front of the unit. There were two doors, one a large, roll-up garage type and the other a standard-sized security door. Next to the standard-sized door was a security pad that didn't appear to have any keys for inputting a code.

"Wait here," he told Nate.

He ran back to the man they'd left by the hedge and gave him a thorough search. In the front pocket of his jacket was an employee badge identifying him as Kelvin Andres of McCrillis International. There were some letters and numbers and other symbols that meant something to someone, but what was most important to Quinn was the microchip sure to be embedded inside.

He returned to Nate and explained his plan.

Keeping their faces angled away from the cameras, they walked up to the security door. On the outer wall just above the security pad was a plaque that read:

NEYER-HOLT ENGINEERING
By Appointment Only

On the security pad itself was a logo. But it wasn't really a logo. It was a symbol that matched the one on Andres's ID card.

Quinn tapped the card against the symbol and the door clicked open.

GLORIA LOOKED OVER King's shoulder at the monitor. The prisoner was finally starting to show signs of life again.

"Restart the cameras," she said.

"Yes, ma'am."

She headed back to the interrogation room.

As she opened the door, Daeng lifted his head but kept his focus on the back wall.

"Hello again," she said. "Where were we?"

THE INTERIOR OF the Neyer-Holt Engineering unit consisted of a large open space with what looked like a small, walled-off office in the front corner, and another self-contained space in the back with a sign on the door that read: SUPPLIES.

Along the walls were shelves and workbenches filled with lathes and drills and presses and testing equipment—all the items needed to sell the engineering front to the casual observer.

But this was no engineering firm.

Quinn waved his gun once at the supply-room door. Nate moved over and put his ear against it. When he pulled away, he shook his head.

Quinn ran the alarm detector around the door but it was clean, so he turned the knob and slowly pushed it open.

Instead of the supply room, they found a stairwell.

This, he was sure, was not a standard option the business park had offered tenants. The concrete steps led down approximately twenty feet, creating a nice soundproof barrier between the subterranean facility and those above ground.

Quinn went first, and as he neared the bottom he heard the distinct rumble of voices. A doorless opening led into a corridor about twice as wide as a household hallway. He paused at the threshold.

The noise was now intermittent, a single voice coming from the left.

208

A woman's voice.

He edged into the corridor and shot a quick look in both directions. There were several doors in both directions. The only one open was to the left, where the noise was coming from.

Keeping next to the wall, he and Nate made their way down to the room, stopping right outside it.

"…in your best interest. Now answer the question. Yes or no?" Definitely a woman's voice, though it had an amplified quality, telling Quinn it was coming from a speaker.

"Sure…yes. Is that what you want?" It was Daeng. A bit weak, though surprisingly strong.

"Then why did he follow me?" the woman asked.

"To find out where you were going."

This was followed by the sound of a loud slap.

"Give me a better answer than that," the woman said.

"Ask me a better question."

Quinn pulled out his cell phone, crouched down, and used the camera to peek inside the room. The space was longer than it was wide, maybe twelve feet by six. A built-in desk stretched along the length of one wall, and on it were several monitors and computers. At the moment, only the center monitor was on. Unfortunately, he couldn't see what it was displaying. It just looked like motion and light.

Seated in front of the screen was the third man Quinn had seen in the sedan. No one else was around.

Quinn looked over his shoulder at Nate and whispered, "Dart."

Nate retrieved his dart gun from his pack and handed it over. Quinn checked his phone's screen again, noting the man's exact location and distance from the door. Standing, he raised the gun, and then inched out until the muzzle was pointed at this target.

At the last second, the man seemed to sense something, but as he turned to look, the dart was already flying through the air. It hit him in the upper right portion of his chest.

"Son of a bitch!" he yelled as he pushed himself out of

his chair and reached for the dart.

Before he could get it out, Quinn shot again, hitting him in the thigh.

The guy started to say something else, but his words came out in a slur as he began to sway. Quinn got there just in time to catch him before he fell. Quinn laid the man on the concrete and retrieved the darts.

"It's Daeng, all right," Nate said, looking at the computer monitor.

The image was of an almost barren room, the only pieces of furniture a wheeled cart and a chair in the center. On the chair was Daeng. His pant leg had been cut off along the thigh where he was shot, but that was about the extent of his exterior damage. It was clear, though, from the odd bobbing of his head that he'd been drugged.

Standing in front of him was Gloria Clark.

"*Why* are your people interested in the girl?" she asked.

"Already answered."

"Is she alive?"

"Come on," Quinn said.

Back in the hallway, he raced to the closest door and listened. All quiet inside.

He moved to the next. Same.

Door number three. Same.

He switched to the other side. That's when he heard her.

"What about Eli Becker? Do you work together?" she asked.

Daeng said, "Becker...poor, poor Becker..."

"Down here," Quinn whispered to Nate.

GLORIA WAS NOT satisfied in the least. She had no doubt Daeng knew more than he was sharing, but even with the drug he was able to hang on to his secrets.

"*Why* are your people interested in the girl?" she asked yet again.

"Already answered."

The response he'd given—"Because we want to know"—was little more than babble.

210

"Is she alive?"

"No clue. Is she?"

At least he was consistent in answering that question. Which meant he and whoever this Quinn was weren't any better off than she and her team. But who exactly were they? And why would they be interested in the girl? That's what didn't make sense.

She had been working under the belief there were only two interested parties—one, the group who had used the .xuki virus to expunge all information about Operation Overtake from CIA computers, and the other, McCrillis's client.

When a CIA contact leaked to McCrillis what the virus had really done, Boyer, with the client's approval, reactivated the long dormant job and put Gloria in charge of the investigation team. In the first months after the .xuki attack, as Gloria sifted through the history of the job, she began to think the client was simply paranoid, her concern about this girl—who was dead, by all accounts—bordering on the maniacal. But the more Gloria dug, the more things didn't quite add up, and then, just a few days ago, Eli Becker had shown up on her radar, forcing her to seriously reconsider her opinion.

And now there were Daeng and his boss Quinn, pushing the thought of client paranoia further and further from Gloria's mind.

The problem was, the way the prisoner had been answering questions led her to believe his group had not been responsible for the virus. That would make him and his boss a third interested party.

"Do you know where she is?" she asked.

He grunted what might have been a laugh.

"She's alive, isn't she?"

"Did you…hear me say that? I didn't."

She decided to come at it from a different direction. "What about Eli Becker? Do you work together?"

Daeng said, "Becker…poor, poor Becker. Were you the one…who killed him?"

She narrowed her eyes. "Did you work together?"

QUINN GRABBED THE door handle. "Ready?"

Nate nodded.

"One. Two." On three, he threw the door open and rushed inside, his gun pointed at the woman. "One step backward," he ordered. "Then freeze."

"Who the hell are you?" she demanded.

Daeng peeked over his shoulder and smiled. "Quinn. Been waiting."

"Sorry we couldn't get here sooner." Quinn glared at the woman. "Take that step back *now*."

She remained where she was a moment longer, her jaw set, but then did as he ordered.

"Check him," Quinn said to Nate.

Nate moved over to Daeng and began undoing the restraints. "You all right?"

"Been better…been worse," Daeng said.

"We'll get you out of here and fixed up."

Daeng swayed a few inches to the side before righting himself. "That works for me."

Quinn studied the woman. "Hands."

"Go to hell."

"Let me see them."

Hesitantly, she brought them forward. Her right was empty, but in her left she held a syringe.

"Drop it," he said.

"Or what? You'll shoot me?"

"Yes."

BY THE MATTER-OF-FACT way he said it, Gloria knew he would have no problem putting a bullet in her, so she let the syringe fall to the floor.

"What now?" she asked.

"Now you and I talk," he said.

"Do I get to ask questions, or…?"

"One, and you just used it."

This Quinn guy was a pro for sure, but why had she

never heard of him?

She shoved the thought away. That was something she could worry about later. Right now she needed to concentrate on getting out of this alive.

Keeping her gaze aimed at the man, she checked the door behind him. No shadows moving around out in the hall, so did that mean it was just Quinn and his partner?

"My people were concerned when we realized your friend was following us. Naturally, we'd want to find out who he was and why he was interested. You'd have done the same."

Quinn said nothing.

"I suggest we all back off and be on our way. How does that sound?" she said.

"Like another question," he said. "But I'll answer it with this—do you really think your bosses back at McCrillis will be happy you let us walk away?"

She'd guessed he already knew the name of her employer since he'd found the facility, but it still bothered her, especially since she didn't know anything about his organization.

"I heard some of the questions you were asking my friend," Quinn went on. "I would actually be interested in your response to a few of them. Why are your employers interested in the girl?"

She laughed. "Very good. But I'm sorry, I'm not at liberty to discuss confidential matters."

Off to her side, Quinn's partner helped Daeng out of the chair.

"Get him out of here," Quinn said. "I'll be right behind you."

The two men left the room at a slow shuffle and turned toward the stairs.

As their footsteps faded, Quinn said, "You're the one who killed Eli, aren't you?"

"Becker's dead?" she asked.

He smirked. "You're not as good an actress as you

think."

"Really, I had no idea he was—"

Without warning, she juked to the right then dove left, ramming her forearm into his hands and sending them flying upward just as he pulled the trigger.

"And you're not nearly as badass as you think!" she yelled as she landed a left jab to his gut and raced out the door.

Knowing she wouldn't be able to make it all the way to the stairs before he could gun her down, she ran toward the observation room. King had most likely been taken out, but hopefully his weapon was still there.

She was a step away from the room when she heard Quinn burst into the corridor. He took another shot as she turned through the doorway. His bullet grazed her waist before she could get all the way inside.

Ignoring the burning pain, she grabbed the door and shoved it closed, and then jammed a chair under the knob.

GIVEN THAT THE woman seemed to be his friend's principal interrogator, Quinn couldn't help but ask, "You're the one who killed Eli, aren't you?"

All innocent and shocked, she said, "Becker's dead?"

"You're not as good an actress as you think."

He should have seen it, should have known it was coming. But he had let his emotions get the better of him and found himself momentarily focused on what she'd done instead of what she might do.

"Really, I had no idea he was—"

By the time he got off a shot, her arm was already shoving the gun away. She yelled something as she slugged him but he didn't hear it. He followed her into the hallway just as she was turning into the room where the computers were. He shot again. He thought his bullet might have nicked her but it certainly didn't stop her.

He reached the door seconds after she'd closed it. He yanked the handle and it turned but the door wouldn't budge.

He took a step back. He'd seen no other exit from that

room when he checked it earlier, so at some point she would have to come out. But wasting even one second waiting for her while Daeng was in need of help was not an option.

He turned and headed for the stairs.

CHAPTER
TWENTY FOUR

TAMPA, FLORIDA

THE CHARTER LANDED right after eleven p.m., and the Audi
A6 Orlando had arranged for during the flight was waiting for
them at the private terminal.

As soon as she climbed behind the wheel, she called
Quinn.

"You there yet?" he asked.

"Just arrived," she told him. "Did you find Daeng?"

"We did."

"And?" she asked, concerned.

"He's a little drugged up and has two holes in his leg that
are getting stitched right now. Probably won't be running
anytime soon, but otherwise he's all right."

"Thank God. And you and Nate?"

"We're fine."

"No one got hurt?"

"Not on our side." He gave her the highlights of what
had happened, ending with their trip to a discreet DC-area
doctor Misty had arranged for them. "How are you feeling?"

"I'm fine."

"Did you get any sleep on the flight?"

"Some, yeah." Twenty minutes, but she wasn't going to
elaborate.

"Get more tonight."

"You my doctor now?"

"If I need to be."

She and Abraham then headed into the city, arriving at DeeDee's Comics twenty minutes before midnight. While the sign in the window said CLOSED, lights were still on in the back of the store. As they walked up to the glass front doors, they could hear music blaring from inside. Orlando rapped on the glass.

"I don't think anyone can hear you," Abraham said after a few minutes.

Orlando waited until a lull between songs and then knocked again.

The head of a woman with long dark hair popped up from behind a high counter near the back. When Orlando waved, the woman disappeared. After a few seconds, the volume of the music dropped to a more conversation-friendly level, and the woman reappeared, moving between the stacks. As she drew near they could see tattoos covering one arm and peeking out under the collar of her shirt.

"We're closed," she said when she reached the door.

"Are you Vanessa?" Orlando asked.

"Yeah."

"I talked to you earlier this evening," Abraham said.

She studied him for a moment. "So you're the guy, huh?"

"I am the guy, yes."

"Hold on."

Vanessa grabbed the lanyard hanging around her neck. She picked out one of the keys attached to it, unlocked the door, and let them in.

"We appreciate you staying late for us," Abraham said.

"For the couple hundred bucks your friend gave me, I figure I should do a little something to earn it." She looked at Orlando. "And who are you?"

"I'm Orlando. Abraham's friend."

As they shook, Vanessa said, "Please tell me you don't live in Florida with a name like that."

"No, I don't."

"Good, 'cause I don't even want to think about the crap some people might give you."

"You have what my friend left for me?" Abraham said.

"This way." Vanessa led them through the store to an office in the back. "I have to be honest. I've been a little annoyed with myself for agreeing to hold on to this. I mean, your friend swore there was nothing illegal about it, but two hundred bucks to hold on to an envelope with just a piece of paper and a memory card inside for a few days? Seemed over the top, you know what I mean?"

"You looked in the envelope?" Abraham asked.

"I made him show me," she said. "He wouldn't show me what was on the card, but at least I could see there weren't any drugs or something like that. Police find that crap, they shut this place down."

"So why *did* you take it?" Orlando asked.

Vanessa shrugged. "He seemed sincere, you know? And a little bit desperate. I'm a sucker for desperate." She opened a large door on a cabinet behind the desk, revealing a safe. "Didn't know where else to keep it."

As she input the combination, Orlando asked, "Did our friend say anything else when he was here?"

"Just gave me a description of him," she said, nodding at Abraham. "Pretty accurate, too. Then he told me if you called to ask you the question about the girl."

She finished with the last number and opened the door. The space inside was crammed with papers, files, a cash box, and a few other items. She moved some of the files and pulled out a 9x12-inch manila envelope from behind them.

After shutting the safe again, she held out the envelope. "Here you go."

Abraham's name was scrawled on the front in thick, black pen.

Looking wistful, he said, "Eli's handwriting."

He turned the envelope so he could open it, but Orlando put her hand over his. "I'm sure Vanessa would like to go home. We can look somewhere else."

"Of course," Abraham said. He smiled at Vanessa. "Thank you so much for holding on to this for me."

"Like I said, it was really nothing."

"No," he said. "It was much more than that."

Orlando pulled five twenties out of her bag and put them on the desk.

"Your friend already paid me enough," Vanessa said.

"Take it," Orlando said. "Consider it part of your fee. All we ask is that if anyone else comes around asking about this, act like you don't know what they're talking about. I don't think anyone will, but just in case."

Vanessa considered her for a moment before picking up the money and stuffing it in her pocket. "I can do that."

ORLANDO MADE ABRAHAM wait until after they checked into the Embassy Suites Hotel to open the envelope.

The moment they stepped into Orlando's room, Abraham slit open the top and pulled out the piece of paper and memory card. Printed on the sheet was an address for a location right there in Tampa. Below this was a short, handwritten note:

> This first. Your answers start here.
> Eli

"Well, that's annoyingly cryptic," Orlando said. She pulled out her laptop. "Give me the card."

As soon as he handed it over, she stuck it into a slot on the side of her computer. But before she clicked on the icon, she decided to check the address first, so she opened Google Maps, selected satellite view, and plugged in the information.

"Oh," she said, surprised.

"Well?" Abraham asked.

She turned the computer so he could see the screen.

A red arrow was pinned in the middle of a large green area that could easily have been mistaken for a park if not for the identifier typed across it.

GARDEN OF MEMORIES CEMETERY

"You don't think…" he said. "I mean, she couldn't be…"

"We don't know anything," Orlando said in a calm voice. "And until we do, there's no reason to speculate."

She could see him struggling to accept her words and not think the worst. He didn't quite get there, but at least his growing panic seemed to subside a bit.

Clicking on the memory card icon brought up a password screen. She tried one of her decryption programs but the screen was proving difficult to crack. Given time, she knew she'd break through, but she thought there might be a quicker way.

"Hand me that," she said, pointing at the paper with the address.

As soon as Abraham gave it to her, she reread Eli's note.

"'This first,'" she read aloud. She turned to Abraham. "Do you think he's saying we have to go here before we open the card?"

"Possibly? I don't know."

"We're going to want to check this place out anyway. Might as well do it now."

"But it's after midnight. It's going to be closed," he said.

"When has that ever stopped us?"

WHILE THE GARDEN of Memories Cemetery was indeed closed, it had no fence around it. All they had to do was walk in without drawing the attention of the small security staff.

The street address on Eli's note had a number at the end. When Orlando first saw it, she had taken it for an apartment or unit number. It was, in fact, the location identifier for a specific grave.

Using an online map of the cemetery as a guide, they weaved their way around headstones, careful to avoid walking on anyone's grave. They had to hide only once when a patrol vehicle came down one of the roads, but its headlights had given them plenty of warning and they were safely tucked out of sight as the car drove by.

The grave they had come for was located near the eastern end, far from the main road.

Orlando checked the map again before pointing two rows ahead and down to the left. "Should be over there." She paused, then added, "Maybe I should go first. Check it out."

"No," Abraham said. "We both go."

They moved to the appropriate row and passed grave after grave until they reached the one matching the number on Eli's note.

The name was not Tessa's, but it was still surprising. Carved into the marker was:

GAVIN CARTER

"What?" Abraham said, astonished.

"Look at the date," Orlando said.

Carter's date of death was listed as two days after Abraham had handed Tessa over to the pickup team.

Abraham stared at the marker, his lips moving but no words coming out.

Orlando rubbed a hand across his back. "You told us you never heard from him again," she said. "I guess we know why now."

Not sure he had heard her, she decided to step back and give him a moment.

"I don't understand," he finally said. "What does this mean? Does his death have something to do with Tessa?"

"I don't know."

Using the night vision function on her phone, she snapped several photos of the grave and a close-up of the headstone.

"Seen enough?" she asked.

He looked at her, shell-shocked, and whispered, "Yeah."

She put her arm around his back and turned him from the grave. "Come on, then. We'll grab some coffee."

THEY FOUND AN open diner a few blocks from their hotel and took a back booth far from the handful of other customers. Abraham was going to sit across from her, but Orlando patted the bench beside her.

"Here," she said.

As he scooted in, Orlando told the waiter they'd have only coffee for now. Once their server was gone, she pulled out her laptop and inserted the memory card again. When the password box came up, she tried inputting *Gavin Carter* first, but after she hit ENTER, the box emptied and remained on the screen. She then tried Carter's date of birth, but that didn't work, either. Nor did his date of death. She decided to throw it all in there—name followed by date of birth followed by date of death.

This time when she hit ENTER, the box disappeared. For a moment nothing happened, and then a window opened, listing the files on the card. Eleven total. One she recognized immediately. It had the same file name as the .xuki file she'd found on Eli's laptop, only instead of ending with the virus extension, it ended with .tiff, indicating an image file. She clicked on it and a few seconds later, she and Abraham were looking at the same photo of the older Tessa.

"Here you go," their waiter said as he walked up. "Two coffees." He set their cups on the table. "Anything else?"

"I think we're good for now," Orlando told him. "Thank you."

"Give me a holler if you change your mind," he said, then left.

Orlando turned back to the computer, minimized the photo of Tessa, and scanned the rest of the files. Several documents and a movie were labeled: FOR_ABRAHAM. She clicked on the latter. When it open, it showed a still image of Eli looking straight at the camera.

Before hitting PLAY, she dug a set of earbuds out of her backpack. "I only have the one," she said as she plugged them in. "So we'll have to share."

She gave one bud to Abraham, donned the other, and

clicked on the PLAY arrow.

"Abraham, hello. This is Eli…which, I guess, you can probably see. I've made this video in case we don't have enough time to go over everything in person. As you know by now, I'm going to disappear for a while, and you should do the same. At some point, they will find out about you, like they found out about the others. I can't deny that I'm annoyed with you for dragging me into this." Eli sighed. "But I realize you couldn't have known. If you did, you would have given up the hunt a long time ago.

"Here's a confession. The last few times you called me, I really didn't do much checking at all, just enough to make me feel like I was doing something. This whole business seemed a waste of my time. When you called last week, I did what I always did—put out a few anonymous feelers, did a minor data check, and, well, that was actually it. I found nothing new so I didn't lie about that.

"The day after I told you there was no news, I got a message. Only it wasn't from one of my sources. It was from an e-mail address as anonymous as the one I was using. I tried tracing it using some resources at work, but it just led to a dead end.

"The message itself contained a name, an address, and a link to a Flickr account that contained only one photo. You've seen the picture by now. It's your girl, Tessa. She looks a lot older than the four-year-old you transported, so I guess she did live.

"The name and address, you've also already figured out. If you haven't, I'm talking about Gavin Carter. A dead Gavin Carter. And in case you doubt it's him in the grave, don't. I confirmed it. He wasn't killed in the field, per se. Car accident. Hit and run. Autopsy photos, the whole works. It's him.

"I'm sure you took special note of the date of his death. Suspicious, to say the least. That and the picture are what provoked me to see if I could find anything else out. Yeah, I guess you could call it guilt for having blown you off these last few times.

"I started first by taking a deeper look into the members of Overtake that I had names for. Guess what? Three are confirmed dead. And two—Akira Hayashi, the head op in Osaka, and Desirae Rosette, the one in charge of the pickup team in Amsterdam—have been missing since the operation. You told me your name was kept out of the official mission report. I have a feeling that's the only reason you're not dead now, too.

"You understand what went on here, right? A complete cover-up. I'd be willing to bet everyone associated with the job has been eliminated. I'll get to who did it in a minute, but spoiler alert—I don't really know.

"Okay, so I decided to try again at prying something loose from the Overtake files in the CIA system, but it turns out the files are gone. You've been out of the loop, so I'm not sure if you heard about the dot-xuki virus. I'll include a report about it with this video in case you want to read up, but the short story is, someone infiltrated the CIA data storage system and erased several drives. Included in this were all the files associated with Operation Overtake. Well, not quite all of them.

"See, it would have been easy to assume the Overtake stuff had just been caught in the larger viral attack, but it felt screwy to me. There's this girl I know who's part of the computer network team here. A friend, I guess…I don't know, whatever. Anyway, I got her talking about the attack, and after a while she tells me a couple files had been salvaged, only instead of their original designation, they'd been turned into dot-xuki files. She said the thought was, these were files the virus was trying to steal. After hunting around, I was able to find where one of them was being kept and downloaded a copy. It was an image file of the same damn photo of Tessa I'd received in the e-mail.

"At first I thought if the dot-xuki virus was meant to get rid of all the Overtake files, then whoever was behind it must also have been responsible for the deaths of the Overtake team members. But the large amount of time between the events bothered me. I mean, the team members had all died or vanished seven years ago, and it's only been a couple months since the dot-xuki attack. It got me wondering—if the girl was alive, which seemed so from the photo, then what if the cyberattack was carried out by someone who was trying to protect her? While the earlier deaths were conducted by someone trying to *find* her?"

He ran a hand through his hair and looked at his watch. "Shit, I need to wrap this up, so whatever I have will be on the disk. See this?"

He picked up a piece of paper off his desk and held it up to the camera. It was heavily creased but they could still make out the message written on it.

Mr. Becker. Please call.

Below this was a phone number.

"I found this about twenty minutes ago. Someone had pushed it through my mail slot. I tried looking up the number but there was no listing for it. If you're wondering if I called it, of course I did. There was a part of me that didn't want to, but how could I not?

"A woman answered. Don't ask me how old she sounded, because I don't know. She had a slight accent, European of some kind, I think, but she spoke perfect English. The moment she picked up, she said something like 'You should have never looked into her history. You were not supposed to do that. Why couldn't you have been satisfied? Why did you continue to look?' Before I could say I had no idea what she was talking about, she went on. 'If you stay in your house, they will find you. I can distract them for a few hours at most, but that is it. Be gone by then.' I asked her who she meant, but she'd already hung up. I called back probably a dozen times, but the line would just ring and ring and ring.

"Abraham, she told me I should have never looked into 'her history.' She's got to be talking about Tessa. I mean, who else would it be? And the people she's warning me about?

What if they're the ones who killed Carter and the rest of Overtake?

"I can't ignore her warning so I'm leaving here right now." Eli reached forward. "See you in Florida, buddy."

The video stopped.

Orlando and Abraham stared at the screen, speechless. After several seconds, she backtracked the footage to the best frame of the piece of paper Eli had held up. She captured a clean image of the number.

"We should call it," he said.

She closed the computer. "Yes, but not here."

They left cash on the table and returned to the Audi. Not wanting to chance someone overhearing them while they were parked in the lot, Orlando started the engine and headed out. At the first stoplight she opened her computer and handed it to Abraham. The image of the phone number was still on the screen.

"Go for it," she said.

He pulled out his cell and dialed.

Five rings.

Six.

Seven.

Eight.

"Abraham," Orlando said softly.

Nine rings.

"Abraham."

He finally looked over as the tenth ring began.

"They're not going to answer."

"Just a moment longer," he said.

The twelfth ring cut out halfway through. Abraham leaned forward as if his wait had paid off, but the voice that came through the speaker was merely a recording. "Please try your call again later."

His shoulders sagged as he dropped the phone into his lap. Orlando gently took the cell from him and disconnected the call.

After they were back in her room at the hotel, she said, "Why don't you go and get some sleep? We can start fresh in the morning."

"I'm not tired," he said, though clearly he was.

She considered her next words very carefully, but even though she knew what his response would be, she had to say them. "Abraham, perhaps it's time to drop this. The picture tells us that Tessa's probably alive, so you know that much. But looking into this is what got Eli killed. It could happen to you, too. Maybe you should let it go and disappear like he suggested."

His jaw tensed. "Don't you get it? The people who killed Eli and took your friend Daeng are hunting for Tessa. What do you think they're going to do to her when they find her? I guarantee you it won't be good. So tell me, if you were in my shoes, would you just disappear?"

"No," she said after a moment. "No, I would never do that."

"So why on Earth would you think I would?"

CHAPTER
TWENTY FIVE

VIRGINIA

NEARLY FIFTY MINUTES passed before Gloria finally heard someone in the hall outside the observation room.

"King? Ms. Clark?" Nolan's voice. "Are you down here?"

Gloria pulled the chair out from under the handle and opened the door.

Nolan and Andres were in the corridor. They had turned at the sound of the door and aimed their guns at the opening. Once they saw it was Gloria, they lowered their weapons.

"Thank God," Nolan said. "Are you all right?"

"Where's King?" Andres asked.

Ignoring the questions, she marched over to them and asked, "Where the fuck were you two?"

"You found them," a third voice said. "Good."

Gloria looked past her men toward the stairway. Standing near the entrance was Scott Foster, head of the McCrillis emergency response team. They had undoubtedly come in response to the call she'd made from the observation room.

She turned back to her men. "Answer my question!"

Nolan swallowed hard. "They knocked us out and tied us up."

"They knocked you out and tied you up? Are you

serious?"

Neither Nolan nor Andres said anything.

From the stairwell entrance, Foster said, "What's the word on the prisoner?"

"Gone," she told him.

Foster frowned.

"Hey, I'm not pleased about it, either," she said. "But there wasn't a hell of a lot I could do when the people who were supposed to be watching my back weren't doing their job."

In a hesitant voice, Andres asked, "Is King all right?"

She glared at him for a second before nodding back at the observation room. "He's in there."

When Andres caught sight of the other man's body, he asked, "Is he dead?"

"Out cold."

"So they got him, too," Nolan said.

"True, except he wasn't supposed to be guarding the place."

She pushed past them and headed for the stairwell.

When she neared Foster, he said, "Mr. Davis said for you to call in as soon as we found you."

"Davis isn't my boss," she said.

"He is now."

"What do you mean?"

"Mr. Davis will tell you."

Cursing to herself, she pulled out her phone and headed up the stairs. A moment before she hit the top step, the line was answered by one of the night operators.

"McCrillis."

"It's Gloria Clark. I believe Mr. Davis is expecting my call."

Hold music, low and unobtrusive.

It had barely played two measures when—

"Clark?"

"Mr. Davis, you wanted to talk to me?"

"What the hell happened over there?" he asked. Perry

Davis was McCrillis's vice president of general operations, a man who was reportedly a competent organizer. Gloria had no firsthand knowledge of this. Her work had never strayed into his arena before.

She grimaced. It wasn't his place to ask that kind of question. "We had an incident, sir."

"What kind of incident?"

Another pause. "An incursion."

"Any casualties?"

"None, sir."

"Any idea why they were there?"

"Sir, I should really be speaking to—"

"Please answer my question, Ms. Clark."

"Yes, sir. They came to get the man we were questioning."

"And did they?"

"Unfortunately."

Davis said nothing for a moment. "I don't know what the hell's going on. I've barely had time to take a breath, let alone go through Boyer's files."

"Sir, where is Mr. Boyer? I'm sure he's expecting me to update—"

"He's dead."

She had been walking across the ground-floor room toward the exit, but his words stopped her in her tracks. "Dead? How?"

"He was in his house when it burned down."

"Jesus. Was it an accident?"

"Unlikely. His security team was found unconscious in the backyard. They'd apparently been drugged."

Drugged? She'd been unable to revive King while they waited for the response team, which had led her to believe he was drugged.

Quinn, she thought. If he'd played a role in her boss's death, it would certainly explain how he'd found out where she was.

"Ms. Clark, are you there?"

She blinked. "Uh, sorry, sir. I'm here."

"I need to know exactly what you're working on."

"It's a KV job, sir." KV was McCrillis's highest secrecy designation, meaning phone conversations about it were strongly discouraged.

"Of course it is, goddammit. Fine. Get your ass in here as quickly as you can and give me a full report. I'll be in my office."

WASHINGTON, DC

GLORIA STOOD ON the other side of Davis's desk as she filled him in on her assignment. The offer to sit had not been extended, nor would she have accepted it if it had. Though one of Foster's men had patched her up before she left Virginia, she'd refused any pain medication, so it felt like she had a hot poker constantly pressed against her side and sitting made it worse.

"So the job is to find out if the girl is alive or not?" Davis interrupted, apparently having a hard time comprehending the mission.

"Part one, yes," she said, working hard to maintain her patience.

"And what is part two?"

Her training made her not want to answer the question, but with Boyer out of the picture she had no choice. "If she's still alive, eliminate her."

"A child."

"Yes, sir."

She would have understood if he looked disgusted, but instead he appeared merely annoyed as he said, "And do we know why?"

"That's not part of the job, sir," she told him, though she actually did know the answer.

"Unbelievable. Who approved this?"

"The client has worked with McCrillis for many years, sir, and I do believe a premium is being paid for this project."

"As well it should be." He reached for his phone. "Please

231

step into my waiting area. I'll call you back in when I'm ready."

"Yes, sir," she said, and headed for the exit.

As she entered the waiting area, she heard Davis say, "Don? This is Perry. We have a situation here that I need a little…"

After the door closed behind her, she could hear him no longer, but she had no doubt who he was talking to.

Donald McCrillis. President and CEO of McCrillis International.

The corner of her mouth ticked up.

Exactly seven minutes after she stepped out of Davis's office, the door opened.

"Please come back in," Davis said, his tone contrite.

As she entered, she felt her phone buzz in her pocket. She pulled it out and looked at the text on the screen.

Davis. Keep it natural.

There was no sender's name, only a number she was sure belonged to a burner phone. It didn't matter. She knew it was from Don McCrillis.

In a few hours, when the sun came up, instead of being down one vice president, McCrillis International would be down two.

"Ms. Clark, please have a seat."

She smiled and lowered herself into the chair.

CHAPTER
TWENTY SIX

TAMPA, FLORIDA

ORLANDO'S ALARM WENT off at 6:30 a.m., barely four hours after she'd fallen asleep.

Forcing herself up, she shuffled into the shower, shocking her body first with cold water and then gradually adding some heat. By the time she was toweling off, she felt like she probably wouldn't spontaneously fall asleep in the next fifteen minutes. Anything beyond that, all bets were off.

Coffee. She needed coffee. Now.

Forgoing even the small amount of makeup she usually wore, she ran her fingers through her hair, pulled on some clothes, and headed downstairs to the coffee shop in the lobby. She knew there would be a line—there were always lines at hotel coffee shops, no matter the time of day—but what she didn't expect to see was Abraham sitting at one of the small tables out front, sipping from a cup and eating a muffin.

Orlando purchased her coffee, waited for it to be prepared, and then joined her former mentor.

"You did get some sleep, didn't you?" she asked.

"More than enough," he replied. "The older you get, the less you need."

"Then I need to get older fast."

A small grin, but no snide comment. That wasn't like

him.

She stirred her coffee and gave it a taste. A little too hot still, but she was willing to risk a scorched mouth for the brew's revitalizing effects.

"I...I tried again," he said.

"Tried what?"

He touched the phone sitting next to his half-eaten muffin. "The number. I tried again."

"And?"

"Same as before," he said, disappointed.

"Whoever it belonged to probably tossed their phone."

He nodded in reluctant agreement. "It's just...whoever Eli called was trying to help him. So that has to mean they know something about Tessa, doesn't it? I thought...I mean..." He took a breath and picked up his coffee. "I don't know where we go from here."

"I might," she said.

He looked at her, hope creeping into his eyes. "Did you find something?"

She held up a hand. "Can I finish my coffee first?"

DESPITE ABRAHAM'S PERSISTENT questioning, she refused to go into further detail until they were back in her room.

Once she woke up her laptop, she brought up the files Eli put on the memory card for the members of Operation Overtake. "According to Eli, three are dead," she said. "I double-checked and he was right. These other two, though, were only listed as missing. Akira Hayashi and Desirae Rosette. I checked to see if either of them had taken any jobs after Overtake but found none. Granted, I didn't have a ton of time so it wasn't a thorough search, but it was enough of a sample to form my opinion. Before I went to sleep, I set up a few search bots. First, to see if any unidentified bodies had been recovered in the months following the job that matched either of them, and second, to hunt down any personal information such as friends and family who they might get in contact with."

"What did they find?"

"Have no idea." She moved the cursor across the screen. "Shall we take a look?"

She accessed the server where the bots had dumped their information into presorted files. She checked Hayashi first. During the time frame she had specified, three male bodies had been recovered in Japan with the correct height and general size. The one discovered nearly three months after the operation was the most intriguing.

It had been found in the wreckage of a building fire. Though the body had been severely burnt, the medical examiner found that the man had been shot in the back of the head and not recently. The doctor was able to extract some cells that hadn't been wrecked by the fire, and discovered damage usually associated with extreme cold. To Orlando this meant only one possibility—the victim had been killed, put on ice, and, after a desired amount of time had passed, placed in a building that was then set ablaze.

"I've seen this method before," Orlando said. "And if you ask me, that's Hayashi."

It took Abraham a bit longer to finish reading the file. When he did, he said, "I think you're right."

Orlando moved on to the files that might be the woman. There were four bodies—three in Canada and one in France.

"Why did you include Canada?" Abraham asked.

"That's where Desirae is from."

"I thought she was French."

"French-Canadian. She's from Quebec."

"Oh," he said, surprised.

Orlando went through the reports one by one, but while they found some similarities in each to Desirae Rosette, none was a perfect match.

"Could be they never found her body," Abraham said.

She nodded. "Could be."

She opened the file where information pertaining to Desirae's personal life had been gathered. There were only a few names—a half dozen acquaintances in the business, and the name of a civilian woman the bots had dug out of a deep

NSA file. The name was Nadine Chastain, and the search indicated an 85% chance of the woman being Desirae's mother. She lived in the town of Lac-Saint-Charles, north of Quebec City.

Orlando first checked to see how long Chastain had lived in Lac-Saint-Charles—nearly forty years at the same house—and then found the name of a local newspaper. She searched through the obituaries for the years right after Operation Overtake.

Five and a half months after the job was over, there was a small, two-paragraph obituary for a woman identified as Nadine's daughter. An accident overseas. No memorial service scheduled. Most interesting of all was the daughter's name. Desirae.

After letting Abraham read what she'd found, Orlando said, "So, how do you feel about a trip to Canada?"

PENNSYLVANIA

QUINN STAYED AS far to the side of the two-lane road as he could get without stepping off the asphalt. The temperature the day before had topped out at forty-five degrees, and it was supposed to reach the same level again today, allowing the softening ground and melting snow to form a dark muck that seemed hell bent on tugging his shoes off his feet.

The morning traffic was heavy, most of it going north toward the two factories outside Welton, Pennsylvania, the small town where Quinn, Nate, and Daeng had spent the night. The convenience store that the motel clerk had directed Quinn to was just up ahead. Quinn could have driven, but being on foot gave him a better chance to look around and make sure no one was keeping tabs on them.

After his and Nate's encounters in Maryland and Virginia the night before, he was sure they would be on McCrillis's most wanted list, but Quinn thought it unlikely someone from there would come as far as Pennsylvania to look for them. Still, prudence was always the best course.

At the store, he purchased orange juice, fruit labeled

FRESH FROM FLORIDA, and some bagels, then made his way back.

Nate looked up from the computer when Quinn entered the room. "Any problems?"

Quinn shook his head. "We're clean."

Nate pointed at the laptop. "Story here about Boyer. 'Hilltop House Fire. One Dead.' Doesn't call him by name, 'pending notification of next of kin,' but says he was trying to get out when he was consumed by smoke. No mention of the guards. Think they're going the natural-causes route."

Quinn tossed one of the bottles of orange juices to Daeng, who was sitting up on one of the beds.

"Much appreciated," Daeng said.

"Picked up some fruit and bagels, too." Quinn set the bag on the other bed. "But I'm not serving anyone."

"Cream cheese?" Nate asked.

"Sorry."

"How are we supposed to eat a bagel without cream cheese?"

"Do you really want me to answer that?"

Orlando called as Quinn was helping himself to a tangerine.

"Good morning," he said.

"Good morning back," she replied. "How's the patient?"

Quinn glanced at Daeng. "You know him—always the same. What about Eli's stuff? Anything of interest there?"

"Lots, actually." She told him what they'd found, then said, "We're going to check out the potential mother. Should be there in the afternoon."

"You want company?"

"We could always use company."

"I'll see what I can work out."

CHAPTER
TWENTY SEVEN

WASHINGTON, DC

THERE WAS NO missing the somber mood when Gloria returned to McCrillis headquarters at 9:15 a.m. First the news of Ethan Boyer dying in a house fire, and then the discovery of Perry Davis in his office, collapsed over his desk, dead from an apparent heart attack.

Gloria felt a tinge of guilt about the secretary who'd found him, but that was the way it had to happen to sell the scene.

She exchanged a word or two here and there with people she knew, but avoided any lengthy conversations as she made her way to see Toby Martinez, assistant deputy head of research and her main contact in the department. He was on the phone when she walked into his office, but he waved her in and motioned for her to take a seat.

"Yeah, right...okay. Got it. Give me at least an hour. Two would be better....Thanks." He was smiling as he talked, but as soon as he hung up, it seemed as if the weight of the world had just fallen on his shoulders. "You heard the news, right?"

"I heard."

"Man, two people in one night. What are the odds? And both VPs, too." He looked at her with a start. "Crap. Boyer was your boss. I'm really sorry."

"Me, too. He was a good guy."

"Fire. What a way to go."

Though she had not seen the true reports yet, she was positive fire was not the way her boss had gone. She said nothing.

Martinez shook his head and leaned back. "So you're here about the stuff in the suitcase?"

"Yeah."

He clicked around his computer for a moment, and then turned the screen so she could read the report he'd brought up.

"Sorry," he said. "They were all clean. Nothing hidden."

That was disappointing.

Becker had been keeping information somewhere, she was sure of it.

"Well, thanks for taking a look. E-mail me a copy when you get a chance."

She started to get up.

"Hold on," he said. "You don't want to know about the phone number?"

"Phone number?" she asked, lowering herself again.

He stared at her as if she might be crazy. "You put in a request to look into any calls Becker made or received before he fled."

"Right," she said, remembering. It had been a routine request, and not high priority after Becker was in her custody.

Martinez hit a few more keys and a new report came up listing six phone numbers.

"This is his call log for the twenty-four-hour period you asked about," he said. "Not a big talker, apparently. Most recent first, with outgoing in green and incoming in red."

Becker had placed four calls and received two.

He pointed at the top number, an outgoing call that occurred at 12:41 p.m. the afternoon he left town. "This number is for his office. We used a contact to check the records and apparently he'd called in sick."

"Interesting," she said.

"It is." He pointed at the second number on the list,

another outgoing that occurred at 12:03 p.m. the same day. "With the exception of this one, all the calls were from the previous day. The two incoming calls were from his doctor and the Red Cross blood donation line—and before you ask, the number's confirmed. One of the outgoing was also his doctor, and the other to a Chinese place around dinnertime. Again, that number has been confirmed. This is the interesting one." He pointed once more at the second from the top. "It's a dummy. No number exists, and yet he was on the line for two minutes." He looked at her. "Talks to someone at a nonexistent number, thirty minutes later he calls in sick, and then he leaves town? My opinion, whoever he talked to on this call"—he tapped the number again—"warned him to get out of town."

Exactly the way she saw it.

Finally, a real break. Whoever warned Becker had to know about the girl. It was likely the person knew more than the late analyst. "I need to know where that call came from," she said.

"Without a number, it would be extremely difficult."

"But not impossible."

He hemmed and hawed for a moment before he smiled. "Nothing's ever impossible. My boys are already working on it. In fact, they've gotten a partial trace already."

Martinez loved to make a problem seem insurmountable before giving a solution. She'd learned long ago it was easier to play into this than fight it. "That's fantastic," she said. "Please extend my thanks to your team. So, what have they learned?"

"Well, there were a lot of bounces and reroutes, but they've narrowed down the location to this." He opened a map on his screen.

"What am I looking at?" she asked.

"Here. This'll help."

He widened the map, and water appeared at one edge of the land, and then at another and another until she finally recognized the area.

"That's Hawaii."

"Specifically a four-hundred-square-mile area of Oahu," he clarified.

"I think your guys must have made a mistake. This is a perfect bounce location. It must go somewhere else."

"I thought the same thing, but it's not a bounce. They've checked it a dozen times. This is where the signal ended."

"Hawaii."

"Oahu."

She was having trouble buying it, but in the years she'd worked for McCrillis, Martinez had never let her down.

"Four hundred square miles? Any chance of narrowing that down?" she asked.

"Possible, but it's going to take a bit of time."

"Send me everything you have so far and keep me updated via e-mail." She stood up and held out her hand. "I'm counting on you guys, Toby. This could be big for the both of us, so the sooner you can pinpoint a location, the better."

The gleam in Martinez's eyes as they shook hands told her that her request had just moved to the top of his to-do list.

"As soon as we know, you'll know," he said.

"Excellent," she said. "There is one other thing I need you to look into for me. But I'd appreciate it if you kept it on the down low. Kind of a personal matter."

"It shouldn't be a problem," he said.

"I need to find out everything you can about an operative who goes by the name of Quinn."

CHAPTER
TWENTY EIGHT

QUEBEC, CANADA

QUINN, NATE AND Daeng's closer proximity to Quebec City meant that their flight, though later than Orlando and Abraham's, still arrived first. By the time Orlando and Abraham walked out of the airport, a three-row SUV had been rented and the route to Lac-Saint-Charles worked out.

Nate was behind the wheel with Quinn up front, leaving the two bucket seats in the middle row for the late arrivals. Daeng, crutches bound, had claimed ownership of the bench seat in the back, where he could stretch out his wounded leg.

"Comfy?" Orlando asked him as she buckled into her seat.

"I could use a pillow," Daeng said.

"I bet you could."

As soon as Abraham was strapped in, Nate took off.

"How do you want to play this?" Quinn asked Orlando.

"I don't think Nadine Chastain will just roll over because we walk in there and start asking questions," she said. "If we can swing it, I'd rather try a self-guided tour first. See if we can find something that proves Desirae is her daughter. Even better, something that points in Desirae's direction. If we can avoid talking to Nadine at all, that would probably be best."

Lac-Saint-Charles wasn't officially a town on its own anymore, but a district within Quebec City. Even then, it had a remote country feel. It was located at the southern end of the lake for which it took its name, in a heavily forested area. The homes were quaint and colorful, most without fences, just snow-covered lawns and leafless trees, reminding Quinn very much of his hometown of Warroad, Minnesota.

"Left ahead," he said, consulting his phone's GPS.

They turned onto the road where Nadine lived. Like elsewhere, the houses here were on similarly sized lots, only these all seemed to back up to the woods. Nadine Chastain's home was a half mile in on the north side, a mustard yellow two-story cottage with dual dormer windows in a black-shingled roof and a single-car garage to the side. The driveway was cleared of snow but had no cars parked on it.

They kept driving to the dead end of the street and were happy to find an area where they could not only turn around but park behind a snowbank, out of view of the homes.

"Did anyone see signs of someone home?" Quinn asked.

A chorus of nos.

He looked at Orlando. "You're up."

Orlando called the cell phone number she'd found for Nadine. After a few seconds, she leaned forward and said, "*Bonjour. Êtes vous Madame Loge?....Je suis vraiment désolé. J'ai fait le mauvais numéro....Je m'excuse de vous avoir dérangée.*"

As soon as she hung up, she opened an app that would track the location of the woman's phone. "She's definitely not home."

"How far away?"

"Ten point three miles, and doesn't seem to be going anywhere."

"Okay," Quinn said. "Daeng, think you can drive?"

"I'll manage."

"Hopefully you won't have to go anywhere, but I want you behind the wheel just in case." Quinn turned to Abraham. "You're staying with him."

"I am not," Abraham said.

"You are, and it's not open for discussion."

"But—"

"No."

The retired op leaned back and sulked.

Orlando pulled out a leather bag from her pack and removed several sets of comm gear. "I only have four. I'm sorry, Abraham, you'll have to go without."

"Of course I will," he said. "Maybe I should have just stayed in Florida."

Nate looked like he was going to throw in a quip, but a withering glance from Quinn nipped that in the bud.

As soon as they had the receivers in their ears and the mics attached to their collars, Quinn said, "Let's go."

It wasn't quite as cold outside as it had been when they'd stepped out of the airport, but that wasn't saying much. Anything below sixty-five degrees was unacceptable in Quinn's book.

He checked Google Maps' satellite image of the area and then pointed at the trees to his left. "We go back about one hundred and fifty feet, then head right until we're behind her house. Should be able to stay in the woods all the way."

Nate took point, with Orlando in the middle and Quinn a few steps behind her. In most places the snow wasn't more than a foot deep, but there were a few drifts where they sank in to above their knees, soaking their pants. When they finally arrived behind Nadine's house, they crouched and surveyed the scene. There was a shed in the yard and a wooden swing set near the back. As for the house, it had a single door along the rear, accessed up a short set of brick steps, and five windows, three on the first floor and two more dormers up top. Overall, the place seemed quiet.

Quinn scanned the neighboring houses and noted that the curtains were drawn on the house to the right, while the view from the place on the left was blocked by the shed and the back of the garage.

"Any change in her position?" Quinn whispered.

Orlando looked at her phone. "Same relative area as before."

"Okay. Up the left side and over to the garage."

Staying low, they hustled across the yard.

When they reached the garage, Orlando said, "Did either of you get a good look at the swing set?"

Nate nodded. "Couldn't be more than a few years old."

"Grandkids from another child?" Quinn asked.

"The obit said Desirae was it."

They moved up to the door at the back of the house, where Orlando used the detector to check for an alarm.

Her eyebrow rose when she viewed the results. "Same system we've got at my place."

"Are you sure?" Quinn asked.

She nodded.

A Garber Sentry 231 was way more firepower than a person like Nadine Chastain, or most any civilian, needed. It was marketed only to high-end clients who wanted a more secure environment than what conventional systems offered. Most interesting was that the Sentry 231 had been around only about eighteen months. So who had helped Nadine make that choice?

The system took Orlando three times as long to disarm as the system at Eli's place. Once she did, she picked the lock and they stepped inside. The only light came from the early afternoon sun streaming through the windows. That and the silence was more than enough to confirm no one else was there.

"Fifteen minutes and we're out," Quinn said.

They checked their watches and split up—Nate hitting the basement, Quinn taking the ground floor, and Orlando upstairs. Though Quinn had the largest area to search, he was able to quickly clear the entryways, guest bathroom, and dining room, leaving him with the kitchen and the living room.

It was amazing how many people hid secrets in kitchens, sometimes in plain sight in an old-fashioned address book, sometimes wrapped in plastic then frozen in a block of ice in the freezer, and sometimes taped to the bottom of a drawer. Quinn rapidly worked his way around the room, checking for all these possibilities and more, but if Nadine was hiding secrets about her daughter, she did it somewhere else.

He moved into the living room and did a quick scan. An old green cloth couch, a matching recliner, a coffee table, an entertainment stand with TV, a stand-up piano against the wall, a bookcase stuffed with glass figurines and other knickknacks, and a fireplace. He sensed something was missing, but it took him a moment before he realized what it was.

Photographs.

Usually a house someone had lived in for a long time was brimming with photos. But there were no framed pictures on the piano or in the bookcase or on the walls. Maybe Nadine was one who preferred her photographs in albums or kept them on her phone.

He searched the room, tipping back the couch and the chair, looking under the coffee table, and feeling for secret compartments in the entertainment center. Two figurines were sitting on a crocheted doily on the piano. He moved them to the side, glancing at them only long enough to get the sense they were some kind of Native American totems, and then pulled the doily off and opened the lid.

Strings and hammers and the usual things that were inside a piano. He moved his fingers under the lip that ran across the top, and stopped halfway across. A key was taped against the panel, out of sight.

Leaving it where it was, he activated his mic. "Either of you come across anything that needs unlocking? I have a key here."

"Haven't seen anything yet," Orlando said.

After a few seconds of silence, Quinn said, "Nate?"

More silence.

"Nate, can you hear me?"

Nothing.

"Coming down," Orlando said.

Quinn grabbed the iron poker from the hearth and hurried to the basement door, reaching it a few seconds before Orlando arrived. Stepping carefully, he went down first, surveying the room as it came into view.

It was an old, unfinished space full of ancient, overstuffed shelves and the smell of earth. Lighting was poor, a few naked incandescent bulbs in fixtures screwed to ceiling beams.

"Nate!" Quinn yelled as soon as he reached the bottom.

The sound of movement deeper in the room, then Nate stepped out from behind one of the units in the back. "What?"

"Why didn't you answer me?" Quinn asked.

"I just did."

"I mean a minute ago on the radio."

"You never called me on the radio."

Quinn frowned. "Check your battery."

Nate turned on his mic and said, "Test, test. Can you read me?"

Quinn did, so he turned his own mic back on and said, "How about me?"

"Loud and clear."

Quinn turned back to the stairway. Orlando was waiting halfway down.

"Go upstairs and shut the door," he said. Once she did this, he clicked his mic back on. "Orlando, do you read me?"

No answer.

He looked over at Nate. "You got that, right?"

"Yeah."

"You try."

"Orlando?" Nate said. "You there?"

Not a crackle.

Quinn went up a few steps. "Come back down," he yelled.

Orlando opened the door and started down. "Did you try me?"

Quinn nodded.

"Didn't hear a thing," she said. She pulled out her phone and looked at the screen. "No signal."

Quinn looked up at the ceiling. "There's got to be some sort of shielding. The question is why?"

"That, I might be able to answer," Nate said.

He led them through the basement to the aisle between the last set of shelves and the stone wall at the back. The nearest light was partially blocked by the shelves so the area was dim at best. Nate pulled out a flashlight and flicked it on.

"What are we looking at?" Quinn asked.

"Here," Nate said, shining his light on the wall where a stone seemed to be missing.

"Check this out." Nate reached down and picked something up off the ground. "High quality work."

As he ran the light across it, Quinn saw it was the face of the missing stone. But by the way Nate was handling it, it appeared too lightweight.

"The problem was the grout," Nate explained. "At first I thought it was a hairline crack running through it, but it was too even. I'd just figured out how to get it open when you came down."

"So what's behind it?" Orlando asked.

Nate aimed the light into the recess where the fake stone had been, and Quinn and Orlando crowded in behind him to look. A keyhole.

"I should be able to pick it pretty quickly," Nate said.

"I don't think that will be necessary," Quinn said.

He made a quick trip up to the piano to fetch the key and then returned to the others.

"I guess that'll work, too," Nate said.

Quinn slipped the key into the lock and turned it as far as it would go. He felt around, found a handhold, and pulled.

The door swung out within an inch of the shelves. This created a temporary wall that blocked the view of the doorway from elsewhere in the room. Behind the fake wall was another door. No lock on this one, so Quinn turned the knob and pushed.

The space beyond was pitch-black. Quinn grabbed his own flashlight and pointed it into the darkness. He'd been thinking this was some kind of secret storage room, going back half a dozen feet or so. What he found instead was a set of stairs leading down into another room. He played the beam along the wall next to the doorway until he found a switch. As soon as he clicked it up, warm light filled the stairway and the room below.

"What is this?" Nate said as they moved down the steps and into the room. "A bomb shelter?"

"More like a safe house," Quinn said.

There was a living area and a kitchen and two other doors that led off to other rooms. Quinn took a quick look inside each—a bedroom and a bathroom.

"This must extend under half the backyard," Orlando said. "If she's not Desirae's mother, then she's in the business herself."

"Let's spread out and look around," Quinn told them.

While Orlando disappeared into the bedroom, Quinn and Nate tackled the main living area. On a credenza near the kitchen, Quinn spotted a couple figurines that were a perfect match for the pair up on the piano. He realized he'd made a mistake earlier as to what they were. Not Native American. Polynesian—maybe Tahitian or Fujian or Hawaiian.

"Quinn, come here," Orlando called.

He entered the bedroom and found her on the other side of a queen-size bed, wearing her look-what-I-found smile. She beckoned him over, and then leaned down and pulled on what appeared to be a long drawer under the bed. But it was no drawer. It was a single-person trundle bed, the mattress covered by sheets with cartoon princesses.

A young girl's bed.

Orlando ran her finger over the edge of the bed frame, leaving a trail in the dust. "Don't think anyone's been down here for a while."

They looked at each other, clearly thinking the same thing, but neither wanting to openly speculate about who had slept in the trundle bed.

"Let's keep looking," Quinn said. "See if there's anything else around."

While the room had no closet, it did have a wardrobe cabinet and matching dresser.

"There's some shirts and pants here," Orlando said, looking in the top drawer of the dresser. She pulled out one pair of pants and unfolded it. "Women's. I'd say for someone around five foot seven or so." She returned them to where she'd found them and opened another drawer. "Old pair of tennis shoes, a couple of belts." She closed that and opened the bottom drawer. "Okay, here we go."

She held up a nightgown. A girl's, with the picture of a dog on the front. Orlando put it back and hunted through the rest of the drawer.

"Looks like a variety of sizes," she said. "The older stuff is smaller. Everyone's different, but I'd say the newest stuff is for a girl somewhere around nine or ten."

Nate stuck his head into the room. "Found something you're going to want to see," he said, and then disappeared as quickly as he'd appeared.

Quinn and Orlando returned to the main room. Nate was standing next to a waist-high cabinet right outside the kitchen area. The top was open, making it look like one of those console record players from the 1950s, but as Quinn drew near, he saw no turntable inside. Instead, there were connectors attached to long wires curled neatly next to a tablet computer inset in the shelf.

"Let me see," Orlando said, nudging Nate to the side.

She examined the setup for a moment, and then crouched and felt along the sides of the cabinet. After a few seconds, there was a quiet click and the front panel swung open.

Quinn and Nate both leaned down to look over her shoulder.

Three electronic devices took up the lower half of the space, with some wires running between them and the top shelf where the tablet and connectors were.

"Give me a flashlight," she said.

Quinn handed his over. She moved the beam through the interior, and then leaned into the cabinet as far as she could to get a closer look.

"So, what is it?" Quinn asked when she pulled herself out.

"Just a second and I'll show you."

After giving him the flashlight, she stood up, looked into the top half again, and pushed the button that brought the tablet to life. A password screen appeared, asking for four numbers. Instead of punching in any, she retrieved her phone and plugged it into one of the connectors. She then used it to hack into the tablet.

The home screen offered several app icons. She touched one that looked like the handset for an old home phone. Two things happened simultaneously: the screen went black with the exception of the words STAND BY in bold white letters across the middle, and the equipment in the lower half of the cabinet began to hum.

The message on the screen then changed from STAND BY to INITIATING to CALL in a matter of a few seconds.

Orlando turned to Quinn and Nate and held up her phone. "Suddenly I seem to have a signal."

"A booster," Nate said.

"Oh, it's a lot more than that," she said.

She placed a call.

Three rings, then a wary Daeng said, "Yes?"

"You guys bored yet?" she asked.

"Orlando?"

To Quinn and Nate, she said, "Not only a booster, but a number and location scrambler. My guess is that it routed the signal all over the place before Daeng's—

"Did she find you?" Daeng asked, cutting her off.

Quinn's brow furrowed. "Who?"

"A woman drove up a few minutes ago and went inside. I assume she's Nadine Chastain. I've been trying to call you, but none of you have been answering your phones."

Quinn shot a look at the safe-room entrance but no one was there. "We'll call you back."

CHAPTER
TWENTY NINE

NADINE CHASTAIN BARELY thought about the cold as she left the elementary school where she volunteered in the library and helped students with their homework after classes ended. The temperature was part of living in Quebec.

The weak winter sun had nearly set as she pulled out of the parking lot. She made one stop on the way home, picking up a few groceries at the market so she could prepare her favorite split pea soup.

As she pulled into her driveway, she clicked the remote that deactivated her alarm and received the double beep that told her it was already off. This was not the first time she'd come home to find she'd forgotten to arm it so it didn't concern her. It wasn't as if crime was high in the neighborhood.

Groceries in hand, she hurried to the front door and let herself in.

She smiled and sighed as the warmth of her house wrapped her in its arms. She loved her little home and her little town. She couldn't imagine living anywhere else, especially a big city. It was too easy to get lost, something that had happened to her four or five times when she'd been in Washington, DC, a few days ago, running the errand for her daughter.

She left her coat and boots in the mudroom and carried the food into the kitchen. Very neatly, she set the ingredients for the soup on the counter in the order she would need them.

That done, she went to get the slow cooker from the sideboard in the dining room. As she was returning to the kitchen, something in the corner of her eye caught her attention. She paused and looked into the living room. It took a moment before her eyes settled on the tiki figurines on her piano. Or, rather, the space where the tikis and the doily should have been.

She looked behind her, positive someone would be standing there, but she was alone. She rushed into the kitchen, set the cooker on the sink, and grabbed the largest carving knife she had.

In her head, she could hear her daughter yelling, "Where's the gun I gave you?!"

Right where it had been since the last time Desirae visited, locked in a metal box at the bottom of Nadine's closet. She was scared to death that if she ever had to use it, she'd end up shooting herself, or, worse, one of her neighbors.

She moved out of the kitchen and over to the piano. The tikis and the doily were sitting on the piano bench. She hadn't put them there. She hadn't touched them since dusting last week. Why would someone—

Oh, no.

She lifted the top of the piano and felt under the lip for the key. It was gone.

Every few weeks, per Desirae's instructions, she changed where she kept it. It had already been in the piano for two weeks. Another few days and it would've been time to move it again.

She tiptoed across the room until she could see that the door to the basement was cracked open.

Get out! Desirae's voice yelled at her.

Nadine tried to swallow but her mouth had gone dry. Yes, she had leave immediately, but there was something she could do that would give her an edge. She returned to the kitchen, quietly opened her junk drawer, and rooted around until she found the old basement key. Taking careful steps, she walked back to the basement entrance, turned the knob so the latch retracted, and eased the door back into place.

Her heart was beating so rapidly she could hear the blood racing past her ears as she inserted the key into the hole below the knob. In her mind, she imagined someone rushing up the stairs and ripping the door out of her hands, but the door remained closed as the bolt slipped into place.

Get out!

She wasn't about to ignore her daughter's voice a second time.

AS DUSK SETTLED on the area, it became less likely the SUV would be seen, so Daeng moved it into a position where he had a clean view of the woman's house. He imagined in the summer the neighborhood was pretty active, with everyone getting as much outdoor time as they wanted. At least that's what he would do. Now, though, the only people he saw were all moving from car to house or house to car.

Five minutes after he repositioned, a late-model Volvo pulled into the driveway of the woman's house. He tried calling Quinn first, then Nate, and finally Orlando, but no one was answering.

As he made the calls, he watched the driver—a woman with shoulder-length gray hair—get out of her car and walk inside the house.

"Maybe they heard her," Abraham said, "and that's why they aren't answering."

Daeng grunted noncommittally as he tried Quinn again.

No response.

"Should we go in?" Abraham asked.

"We stay here," Daeng said.

Several minutes later, as he was contemplating moving closer to the house, his phone rang. He snatched it up, thinking it would be Quinn, but the number on his screen was not familiar to him, and the locator below it read: CARSON CITY, NEVADA.

He let it ring one more time before deciding to answer. "Yes?"

It turned out to be Orlando. She started explaining

something about scramblers and routed signals, but there was no time for that right now.

He said, "Did she find you?"

"Who?" Quinn asked.

Daeng told them about the woman and how he'd been trying to reach them.

Quinn said, "We'll call you back."

It couldn't have been more than thirty seconds after the call ended when the front door of the house opened and the woman rushed out.

Daeng tried calling Quinn again but had the same luck as before. He was about to cycle through the other two when the woman jumped into her car and started backing out of the driveway.

He tossed his phone at Abraham and said, "Keep trying them until you get through."

As soon as the Volvo headed down the street, Daeng put the SUV into Drive and followed.

QUINN WAS THE first up the safe-room stairs and into the basement, with Orlando and Nate only steps behind him. There they paused and listened, but it didn't sound like anyone was in the basement with them, nor did Quinn hear any creaks from the floorboards above. He did, however, hear the faint scrape of metal on metal and a click.

A lock.

The realization hit all three of them at once. They raced through the basement toward the stairs, but before they could even reach them, they heard someone running through the house and then what sounded like the front door opening and slamming shut.

Taking the steps two at a time, Quinn hustled to the top and grabbed the knob. But as he feared, the door was locked.

"Son of a bitch," he said.

He tested the door and found it was a little loose in the frame, so he grabbed the railing and repeatedly kicked the door just below the lock until it broke free.

Standing just inside the stairway, Quinn called in French, "Madame Chastain, are you there?" He was all but positive she wasn't, but caution was dictated. "We just want to talk. We're not here to hurt you."

The only response was Nate muttering, "Which is why we busted down your door."

Quinn glared at him before stepping through the doorway. "Madame Chastain?"

While Orlando followed him into the living room, Nate paused near the door and pulled out his phone.

"Hello?" he said. "No, we're okay. She didn't—" He paused, listening. "All right. Good....Call you right back." He lowered the phone. "That was Abraham. Apparently the woman jumped in her car and drove off. They're trailing her and want to know what we want them to do."

Quinn looked at Orlando. "Your call."

"Given what we've found, I think it would be a good idea to try to talk to her, don't you?" Orlando said.

THIS WAS OFFICIALLY the most frightened Nadine had been in her life.

Desirae had warned her that someday someone might try to use Nadine to reach her, but as the years passed, the possibility had become more unreal, like it was only a story her daughter had made up.

Until she realized someone had been in or was still in her house.

A horn honked. She blinked and saw she'd started drifting across the centerline. She jerked the wheel and brought the Volvo back to her side.

Get it together, she told herself.

A normal person would have driven directly to the police station. But as straitlaced and boring as she might appear, her life was far from normal.

"Yes, Officer. Someone deactivated my professional-grade alarm and found the secret apartment under my backyard. No, no, there aren't any building permits. My dead daughter had it built. And no, that gun you found upstairs is not registered. She got that for me, too."

Besides the awkward questions she'd have to answer, Desirae herself had said that while the local authorities could probably be trusted, the same could not be said of others who might gain access to their reports. That was something that needed to be avoided at all costs.

Nadine's most obvious option was her sister's house. It was only fifteen minutes away, but she figured if the intruders knew about her, they'd know about her sister, too. So where the hell should she go?

God, she wished there was a way to easily reach Desirae. Her daughter would know what to do. But that was not going to happen so Nadine would have to find a solution on her own.

As she reached the south end of the lake, an answer occurred to her.

Beatrice's place.

Of course.

It was back in the other direction on Lac Delage, but Nadine's friend was in Arizona for the winter and the place would be empty. And Nadine was one of the few who knew where Beatrice kept the spare key.

She circled around to the other side of Lac-Saint-Charles and headed northwest toward Lac Delage, feeling for the first time since this started that things would be okay.

FOLLOWING DAENG'S DIRECTIONS, Quinn drove to Lac Delage in the Lexus sedan he'd anonymously borrowed from one of Nadine's neighbors.

"There they are," Orlando said, pointing ahead.

Barely visible in an overgrown turnout at the side of the road was their rented SUV. Quinn killed his headlights as he pulled in behind it, and then he, Orlando, and Nate relocated into the other vehicle.

"There's a driveway on the other side of the road, fifty yards down," Daeng said. "That's where she is."

"Anyone with her?"

Abraham shook his head. "No other cars, and the only person I saw inside was her."

"*You* saw?" Orlando said.

"Someone had to check, and Daeng's in no condition to sneak around, so who else was it going to be?"

Orlando looked over at Daeng, skeptical.

But Daeng shrugged and said, "When he's right, he's right."

"Was she calling anyone?" Quinn asked.

"Not when I was watching," Abraham said. "She was just pacing back and forth in the big room at the back of the house."

Quinn had a pretty good idea why she hadn't called the authorities, but he thought she would have reached out to her daughter. The people Desirae might send in response were what worried Quinn.

"Entrances?" he asked.

"Main out front. Three sets of sliding glass doors on a high deck out back. Also an attached garage so there's probably a way in through there."

Quinn quickly told Abraham and Daeng what they'd found in Nadine's basement.

After he described the trundle bed and the girls' clothes, Abraham said, "Do you think—"

"There's no way to know anything right now," Orlando jumped in. "That's why we need to talk to Desirae's mother."

Abraham reached for the door. "Let's go."

"Abraham," Quinn said. "We don't know how she's going to react when she sees us, but I promise we'll bring you in as soon as the situation is settled. Deal?"

"So I stay," he growled. "Again."

"I'm sorry."

Abraham shrugged in annoyance. "I obviously have no say so whatever you want."

Quinn, Orlando, and Nate headed back out into the cold night.

As a gust of wind blew down the road, Nate said, "Times like this make me long for Isla de Cervantes. I mean, other than the electric shocks and the whippings."

"You'll excuse me if my memory of the place isn't quite as fond," Orlando said.

Quinn glanced at her. She looked even more worn out than she had when they'd met her at the airport.

"You want to sit this one out?" he asked. "Nate and I can handle it."

She sneered. "Right. Who do you think Desirae's mom is going to want to talk to? You guys or me? I'm fine. Really."

The driveway led down to a large, two-story chalet. Most of the windows were dark, the only illumination coming from the rear of the house like Abraham had said. The garage off to the right was of the two-car variety, with a wide automatic door along the front and a regular-sized one on the side near the back. They headed toward this last one.

After Orlando checked for an alarm—there was none—Quinn did the honors of picking the lock. No cars were inside, only a workbench and some storage boxes, and, as hoped, a door into the house. Quinn put his ear against it, but the only thing he could hear was the low drone of the home's heating system.

The lock was an easy pick. On the other side was a laundry room with an open doorway at the other end. He crossed through the space and peered into the other room, which turned out to be a kitchen.

Just as he stepped across the threshold, his phone vibrated twice in quick succession, letting him know he'd received a text. Whatever it was, it would have to wait.

There were two exits to the kitchen, one to the right leading to the back portion of the house where Abraham had seen the woman, and one to the left into a dining room. He signaled to Orlando and Nate what he wanted to do. Orlando nodded and headed to the door on the right, while he and Nate entered the dining room and made their way to the corridor at the far side.

They moved into the hallway, which bisected the house front to back, and inched as close as they could to the back room without entering it. The woman was pacing in front of a large leather couch, lost in thought.

Quinn looked over at Orlando, who was peeking around the kitchen doorway, and gave her the go signal.

Keeping her movement slow and smooth, she stepped into the room and said in a soft voice, "Madame Chastain?"

The woman whirled around in panic. "*Non! S'il vous plaît! Laissez-moi tranquille!*" She backed toward the exit where Quinn and Nate were.

Nate moved to block the doorway, but Quinn grabbed him and shook his head. She was already frightened enough. He didn't want to make it worse by letting her discover they were there yet.

"We're not going to harm you," Orlando said in French. "We just want to talk."

"I don't have anything to say to you," the woman said. "Go. Get out!"

"We need to talk to your daughter," Orlando said.

"She's...she's dead," the woman said, trying to sound defiant. "Long time ago."

"You're trying to protect her. I get that. I would, too, if she was my daughter. But we don't want to hurt her. We just need to talk to her."

The woman was only a few steps from Quinn and Nate. "I said she's dead!"

"She's not dead, Madame Chastain. She goes by the name Desirae Rosette, or at least she did." There must have been confirmation on the woman's face because Orlando said, "She has the girl, doesn't she? She has Tessa."

Nadine nearly tripped over her own feet as she turned to run out of the room.

Quinn swore under his breath as he was forced to step out in front of her and grab her.

She screamed.

"Take it easy," Quinn said. "I'm not going to hurt you."

She pounded her fists against his chest as she tried to squirm out of his arms.

"Let me go," she said. "Let me go."

"As soon as you calm down, I will. I promise. Nothing's going to happen to you. My friend was right. We're only here to talk."

"You're lying," she said, the defiance back, real this time. "She said you might come someday. That you would try to get me to talk about her. Well, you won't get anything from me!"

While Quinn had been corralling Nadine, Orlando had hurried over. "Why don't we sit down? If you don't want to talk, then don't talk."

"Right," Nadine said. "I'm sure that's how it's going to work. Then you...what? Start cutting me up?"

"No one's going to cut you up," Quinn said.

In a fit of rage and terror, she began twisting even faster as she screamed for him to release her.

Quinn sensed someone move in behind him.

"Let her go, Johnny," Abraham said.

Quinn held on to the woman for a moment longer before releasing his grip. The woman looked back and forth as she searched for some way out, her chest heaving with each breath.

"I told you to wait in the car," Quinn said to Abraham.

"If I may," Abraham said, gently trying to push Quinn to the side.

The sound of crutches moved through the dining room and then Daeng appeared beside Nate. Quinn gave him a what-the-hell look as he kept himself between the woman and the exit behind him.

"Sorry," Daeng said. "It's not like I could stop him. I *did* text you."

"Please," Abraham said, his hand still on Quinn's arm.

Reluctantly, Quinn moved to the side.

"May I call you Nadine?" Abraham said to the woman as he stepped around Quinn.

"You may not," she shot back.

"All right. Madame Chastain, then. My name is Abraham Delger, and my friends here are Orlando, Quinn, Nate, and

Daeng. I assure you we mean you no harm at all. Nor do we mean any harm to your daughter, or...the girl." Abraham's reassuring tone seemed to have a calming effect on the woman. "Would it be okay if we sat down?"

Nadine hesitated before nodding.

Quinn motioned for Nate and Daeng to hold back to not overwhelm her, and then he moved over to the seating area with the others. He and Nadine took chairs on opposite ends of the coffee table, and Orlando and Abraham shared the couch.

"You're concerned, of course," Abraham said, leaning forward, his forearms resting on his thighs. "You think we want to hurt Desirae."

"My daughter's dead," she said, sounding now like she was reading from a book.

"I worked with her, you know," he told her. "On my last job before I retired. I'm starting to think it might have been your daughter's last, too. Maybe one she's still working."

"I don't know what you're talking about."

"You would have never allowed her to build secure living quarters under your house if you didn't have some idea," he gently countered.

Nadine made no comment.

"The truth is, Madame Chastain, it's not your daughter that we are most concerned about. It's Tessa."

She stared at him for a moment, and then in a near whisper said, "I've never heard that name."

"I'm the one who delivered Tessa to your daughter," he said. "I'm the one who brought the girl halfway around the world. I don't want to harm Tessa. I would never do that." He glanced back at Orlando and Quinn. "None of us would."

While he spoke, the woman's expression changed from one of disbelief to dawning realization.

"What is it?" Orlando asked her

Nadine's gaze remained on Orlando's old teacher. "Abe," she said softly. "You're Abe."

The room went quiet.

Nadine finally blinked and seemed to get control of

herself. "Or maybe you're just using that name to try to trick me."

"Not a trick."

"Then prove it."

"So you do know about the girl," Orlando said. "Do you know where she is?"

Nadine shot her a quick look. "I never said that. I never said anything about a girl." She turned back to Abraham. "Prove it."

"I could show you my driver's license," Abraham said. "But you'll just think it's fake."

"That's not what I mean."

"Tessa?" he asked.

She said nothing.

Abraham frowned. "I was only with her a few days when she was four years old. I can tell you she liked noodles then but wasn't crazy about rice. I can tell you she used to have three freckles that formed an arc right here." He touched his collarbone where it met his neck and traced the pattern. "I can tell you she liked her hair in a single ponytail, not two."

"What else?" she asked, as if looking for something specific.

"Well, checkers, of course," he said. "I taught her to play. I even gave Desirae the set we used."

Almost in a daze, Nadine said, "She still has it."

It was as if time froze. No one moved. No one breathed. No one said anything.

Orlando finally broke the spell. "Tessa's with Desirae, isn't she?"

Nadine glanced at her and then away, her lip trembling.

"It's okay," Abraham said. "I told you. We're not here to harm them."

"Terri," Nadine said. "Her name's Terri now."

"How did she end up with your daughter?"

"I don't know. Really. One day Desirae showed up with her. Within a few days there were these people in my basement building the apartment."

"How long did they live there?" Quinn asked.

"A couple of years. Until Desirae thought it was safe enough to leave."

"Where did they go?" Orlando asked.

Nadine said nothing.

"Tell me about Terri," Abraham said.

A hint of a smile graced Nadine's face. "What can I say? She's my granddaughter. She's the best girl on earth."

"Does she still ask about her mother?"

"Her mother?" she asked, confused.

"Before Desirae," Abraham said.

"I don't know anything about her…first mother. If she talks about her, it's not with me."

"She is healthy, though, right?"

The smile was back. "She broke an arm once when she was out—" She stopped herself. "Look, I've already said way more than I should."

"Could you at least tell us if you have a way of getting ahold of Desirae?" Quinn asked.

"What does that have to do with anything?"

"We need to warn her," Abraham said. "Someone's looking for her and…Terri. Someone whose intentions are not good."

"Who?"

"If we told you a name, would it even matter?" Quinn asked.

"Try me."

"McCrillis International."

The woman thought about it and then shook her head. "Never heard of it."

"We need to warn your daughter. Is there a way to contact her?" Quinn said.

"Sorry. There isn't," she said, a tad too quick.

"Your daughter and your granddaughter are in *serious* trouble. We can help them."

She crossed her arms, her face tense. "Or maybe you're trying to trick me."

"No one is trying to trick you," Abraham said. He rubbed

his eyes and sighed. "Don't your understand? I should have gone with Tessa last time. I should have made sure she was safe."

Orlando put a hand on his shoulder. "Abraham, she was safe. We know that now. Desirae took care her. She's okay. Maybe it's time to give it up."

"Give it up?" he said, pushing her hand off. "You know what? All of you can just leave. Thank you for your help, but you can go on to your next job now. I have to help Tessa. I will not make the same mistake I did before."

Quinn had been keeping an eye on Nadine throughout the exchange, and could see she was affected by his response.

"Madame Chastain," he said. They all looked at him. "Could you tell us about the tikis?"

Her face dropped. "How did you—"

"Which island are they on?"

CHAPTER
THIRTY

ABOVE THE PACIFIC OCEAN

GLORIA RECEIVED THE information in Los Angeles right before boarding the second leg of her flight to Hawaii. She took her seat and patiently waited for the announcement allowing the use of electronic devices. When it came, she fired up her laptop and opened the waiting file.

Her researchers had been able to locate four operatives who had used Quinn as either a first name or surname. One was a woman so she was out, as were two others who were long retired. The last was a man who called himself Jonathan Quinn, with a presumed age range in the late thirties to early forties, right in the ballpark of the Quinn she'd encountered. There were some conflicting reports that mentioned him being at least a decade younger, but those were in the minority. The only picture was a police sketch from a few years earlier. It was not the best drawing, but she was certain this was her guy.

He was a cleaner who worked exclusively in the intelligence world. So why had he crossed over into corporate?

The lack of other information about him despite the fact he displayed the skill level of someone with years in the business at least shed light on how he'd been able to outmaneuver her men and infiltrate the Virginia facility.

She knew Mr. McCrillis would want this information. She had no doubt that Quinn was responsible for not only freeing his friend Daeng but also killing Boyer.

But Gloria wasn't above a little revenge of her own. When she finally finished her business with the girl, she would go after Quinn and make him pay for getting in her way. If she could use his termination as a means to advance her career at McCrillis, that was just a bonus.

Everyone would be happy in the end.

Well, except for Quinn.

AFTER QUINN TOLD Nadine about Eli Becker and their encounters with the people from McCrillis International, she finally agreed to tell them what she knew.

Yes, Desirae was on one of the Hawaiian islands. Oahu. But where on the island, Nadine did not know.

"How do you contact her?" Quinn asked.

"I don't."

"No phone number? No e-mail?"

She shook her head. "We agreed that Terri needed to be her priority. And it would be safer if I didn't have a number someone could…torture out of me, I guess. She checks in with me every few months."

"You must have some way to get ahold of her in an emergency."

Nadine went quiet for a moment before saying, "There is one."

The method involved an in-person visit to a gift shop on Oahu, and the name of a woman who worked there and could get a message to Desirae.

As Daeng drove them to the airport, Quinn said, "I want you to stay here and keep an eye on Madame Chastain. I don't think anyone will show up, but just in case."

"In other words, you don't want my crutches in your way," Daeng said with a knowing smile.

"Fifty-five percent what I said, forty-five you."

Daeng laughed. "It will be my pleasure."

They were too late to catch a flight to anywhere useful, but since they'd have to connect through one of the major hubs anyway, it made more sense to rent a sedan and drive the seven and a half hours to Toronto so they could catch one of the first flights the next day to the West Coast. By the time they deplaned in Honolulu and rented a car, it was a quarter to three in the afternoon.

The gift shop was located in the Windward Mall in Kaneohe on the other side of Oahu from the capital. After they parked, Orlando pulled comm gear out of her bag and handed a set to Quinn and Nate.

"What about me?" Abraham asked.

Reluctantly she gave him one, too. "But you stay with Nate, understand?"

"Yeah, I know. Stay in the car. It's becoming my mantra."

"Tell me about it," Nate said.

As Quinn put his receiver in his ear, he said, "Letter?"

Orlando pulled the sealed, white envelope out of her bag. The last thing they'd had Nadine do before they left Quebec was write Desirae a note and print the name of the contact on the envelope. Since none of them looked like they could be Desirae's mother, it was the best plan they could come up with at the time.

"All right," Quinn said. "Let's give it a whirl."

The mall was doing all-right business for a weekday afternoon. The mix seemed to be almost fifty-fifty local and tourist. Two things kept the place from looking like it could be anywhere in the United States. The first was the abundance of men wearing Hawaiian shirts, so many that Quinn felt like he stuck out. The second was the number of stores with Aloha in the title. Among these was the Aloha Kaneohe gift shop.

The store was brightly lit, with tables and displays of pretty much any type of souvenir a visitor might want. Quinn and Orlando entered separately. While Quinn browsed through the displays, Orlando headed to the checkout counter. On her way, she paused in front of a glass cabinet with locked doors.

"Well, looky here," she said over the radio.

"What is it?" Quinn asked.

"A couple of very familiar-looking tikis."

Orlando grabbed a hoodie off one of the shelves and a hat off another before entering the checkout line. By the time she reached the cashier, Quinn had moved over to the postcard rack not too far away.

"Aloha," the cashier said. "Did you find everything you were looking for?"

"All set," Orlando replied. "Thank you."

The woman rang her up and Orlando paid with cash. As the bag containing her purchases was handed to her, Orlando said, "Oh my gosh, I almost forgot why I came in here in the first place. Does..."—she looked at the envelope—"Sandra Wiley still work here?"

"Ms. Wiley? Sure, she's the manager."

"Is she here right now?"

"Should be. Would you like me to check?"

"That would be wonderful."

The cashier picked up a phone from the counter behind her. After she finished her call, she said, "You can wait by that door over there. She'll be right out."

As Orlando headed over, Quinn repositioned himself again to stay close and pulled out his phone. The moment the door opened and a thirtysomething woman stepped out, he activated the app on his screen.

"Hi, were you the one looking for me?" the woman asked.

Immediately a large circle appeared on Quinn's display. It was filled with red dots, each representing a cell phone in range that it had just pinged. There was only one blue dot, Orlando's phone. Right next to it, corresponding to where the woman was standing, was a red dot. Quinn tapped the dot and all the others disappeared as the app began tracking the woman's phone.

"Are you Sandra Wiley?"

"That's right."

"So nice to meet you," Orlando said, holding out her hand. "We have a friend in common."

"We do?" the woman said, shaking Orlando's hand. "Who?"

"Nadine Chastain."

The woman looked at first confused, then surprised.

"I was in Montreal for a conference last weekend," Orlando said as if she hadn't noticed the woman's reaction. "Nadine came down to meet me for lunch. So great seeing her again. When I told her I had meetings in Oahu this week, she insisted I stop by here and say hello. Oh!" Orlando reached into her pocket and pulled out the envelope. "She also wanted me to give you this."

"What is it?" the woman asked, not taking it.

Orlando shrugged. "Just a note, I think." She laughed uncomfortably. "I didn't watch her write it."

Wiley hesitated a moment longer before her full smile returned. "Of course," she said, taking the envelope. "Thank you."

"No problem. So…um…nice shop. Have you been here long?"

"A while. I'm sorry. I do apologize, but I need to get back to work. I hope you understand."

"Of course. Have a great day."

"You, too."

The woman disappeared back the way she'd come.

The moment the door was closed, Orlando whispered, "I don't think her good-bye was sincere."

Quinn huffed but added nothing as he watched the screen.

The red dot representing Sandra Wiley's cell phone had moved twenty feet beyond the door and stopped. Her office? That seemed logical. The dot flashed yellow, indicating the woman had sent a text. No way to know what it said or who it was sent to, but given the timing, Quinn had little doubt it had gone to Desirae.

As the dot moved again, he said, "She's on the go."

Instead of heading back into the shop, though, Wiley

went in the opposite direction and made a sharp left turn.

"Service corridor heading north," he said. He hurried out of the store to where Orlando had repositioned.

So that he didn't have to focus on the phone, he handed it to her and began walking quickly through the mall, parallel to the path the woman was taking. Keeping his eyes on the shops, he searched for an unmarked entrance to the employees-only area.

Before he found one, Orlando said, "She's descending."

He spotted the nearest escalator and took it down to the ground floor.

"Which way?" he whispered, as he reached the central area where the three wings of the mall met.

"North…no, no, changing to northwest."

Quinn looked toward the wing that jetted off to the right, just in time to see Wiley pass through another doorway to a service corridor.

"Nate," Quinn said. "Wherever she's going, it should be off the northwest wing somewhere."

"Got it," Nate said.

Quinn angled over to the access door Wiley had used and found it unlocked. As soon as he passed inside, he could see her in the distance. When she looked back at him, he kept his pace normal and acted as if he were another mall employee on some random errand. Given that she didn't race away, he figured his ruse had worked.

About three quarters of the way to the end of the wing, she exited through a doorway on the right.

"Think she just went outside," he said. "The northeast-facing wall."

"Pulling into that area right now," Nate replied.

As Quinn neared the door, he said, "Update."

"She's stationary," Orlando replied. "Hasn't moved for the last fifteen seconds."

Quinn could think of only one reason for that. "She's in a car. Nate, did you get that? She's—"

"I see her," Nate said. "A green MINI Cooper."

"On the move again," Orlando said.

"That's because she's pulling out," Nate told them. "Am I go with follow?"

"Yes," Quinn said. "Go!"

THROUGH HER BINOCULARS, Gloria surveyed the narrow strip of land Martinez's techs had narrowed the search area down to.

The mountain valley sat on the windward side of Oahu, northwest of the town of Kaneohe. According to official records, a total of eleven homes were scattered along it, each sitting on multiple-acre lots. Research in DC had run the names of all the owners and known residents, but only a few traffic tickets and one police response to a domestic dispute were kicked back.

By all appearances, just a quiet, if spread out, neighborhood.

She walked back to the sedan where her team was waiting.

"I've double-checked the maps," King said. "The road peters out about a half mile above the valley so there's only one way in or out."

"Good," she said. "We start at the bottom and work our way up. Everyone in."

NATE AND ABRAHAM followed the MINI Cooper east on Haiku Road and then north on Kahekili Highway, never letting the vehicle get more than four cars ahead.

"Relax," Nate said, sensing Abraham's tension.

"I am relaxed," Abraham snapped.

"Really?"

"I mean…it's just, well, we're so close."

Nate couldn't begrudge him his anticipation. The man had been obsessing about this for seven years.

A few minutes later, the MINI turned onto Kamehameha Highway, but only stayed there for about a minute before turning onto a side road into what seemed a more residential neighborhood.

Nate gave the MINI a little more distance before he took the turn. When he did, he found himself at the top of a slope. The MINI had reached the bottom and was pulling off into what appeared to be a park. Nate angled across the street onto the shoulder and killed the engine.

"Call Quinn," he said to Abraham. "Tell him where we are. But *stay* in the car."

He jumped out before Abraham could respond, and headed down the small hill. Unlike Quinn, he was dressed for the islands, having put on shorts and a T-shirt before they landed. To finish the look, he pulled out a set of earbuds, plugged them into his phone, and started nodding his head to music that wasn't playing.

When he reached the bottom, he saw that Wiley had pulled into a small parking lot next to the park. A few other cars were there, too—all, including the MINI, empty.

The park itself was not large. There was a basketball court near the parking area, and to the side a grassy area big enough for a decent game of international football. Near the center, close to the road, was a tan cinderblock building that had to be restrooms, and not too far away a sign that read: LAENANI BEACH PARK.

Nate entered the restrooms, going in only far enough so that he was masked by the shadows. There were three people in the park, a woman playing with a dog down at the far end of the grassy area, and two teenage boys shooting hoops. Sandra Wiley was nowhere in sight.

He looked past the parking area, wondering if she had gone into one of the nearby homes. As he swept his gaze back across the park, he noticed the top of someone's head just beyond the edge of the park across from him.

The beach. It was below the level of the park a good four and a half feet. Needing a better view, he walked around the court to a picnic table near the ocean side and leaned against it.

The person on the beach was indeed Wiley, so he took off his shoes, hopped over the short wall onto the sand, and walked into the water. It was warm and inviting, just the way he liked it.

After a few seconds, he turned and started walking parallel to the land, expecting to see the woman still standing where she'd been, but instead she was heading back to the parking area access way.

What the hell? She was leaving, but without meeting anyone?

Maybe she'd been killing time until she was supposed to meet Desirae somewhere else. Which would mean he needed to get back to his car in a hurry. But wouldn't she have left her shop later? He stepped out of the water intending to return to the car, but his gut was telling him he was missing something, that Wiley didn't come here on a whim.

He looked toward the spot where she had been leaning against the wall, and noticed a crack between the blocks running halfway up from the bottom. Nothing special; there were other cracks. But this was the only one that had a spot of white peeking from it.

He looked toward the parking lot. The woman had almost reached her MINI. If he sprinted, he might be able to get back to Abraham before she drove past, but not without her seeing him and likely wondering what he was doing.

He moved back into the water, trusting his instincts, and started walking again. Behind him he could hear the MINI's engine spring to life, followed soon by the roar of it driving away.

The crack was now only a dozen feet ahead and across the beach. He swung his gaze left and right, taking in the beauty of his surroundings. His pace didn't falter as he passed the crack. No one would have been able to tell he had the slightest interest in it.

His gamble had paid off. The woman was now unimportant.

Jammed in the crack was a white envelope.

CHAPTER
THIRTY ONE

ORLANDO FLIPPED THE page and stared at the words without actually reading them.

As soon as she and Quinn caught up to Nate and Abraham, she had taken over observation duty and was now sitting at the picnic table, reading a trade paperback copy of *Wool* by Hugh Howey that Abraham had been carrying around.

Since she'd moved into position, only two other people had ventured onto the beach, neither coming close to the crack containing the envelope.

"It's starting to get dark," she whispered without moving her lips. After the sun set, pretending to read would no longer be a viable ruse.

"You've got at least ten minutes," Quinn said.

"Maybe we've already been made."

"Let's hope not."

She let the appropriate amount of time pass and turned the page again.

"Car," Nate said. He and Abraham had moved into the parking lot of the Episcopal church at the top of the rise. "Turning onto Laenani Drive now."

"I see it," Quinn said. "And old Jeep CJ7. Dark blue. Black hardtop. Pulling into the parking lot. Hold on...okay, got the license." He read off the number.

"Running it now," Nate said.

Quinn took up commentary again. "Door's opening. I

have…a woman exiting. She's the right age but her hair's black and long. Don't have a good angle on her face so can't say for sure. Heads up, Orlando. She's headed your way."

Orlando made no move to acknowledge the steps echoing off the asphalt behind her. She was just someone enjoying a good story. As the person from the Jeep moved past the table and onto the beach, Orlando turned the page again. The clacking echoes were now replaced by shifting sand along the wall.

Orlando softly clucked her tongue once, letting the others know the woman was heading toward the crack.

"Got an owner on the car. Karla Bishop. Age thirty-seven." Nate read off an address. "Checking the map…okay, got it. It's in the hills northwest another ten miles or so. Satellite image doesn't really show much. Looks pretty overgrown."

"Move to position number two," Quinn told him.

"Copy."

"Orlando, what's going on there?"

"She's almost there," she said as low as she could.

The woman slowed as she approached the crack, and then leaned against the wall and looked out at the ocean. So normal and natural. A real pro. Orlando's position prevented her from seeing the crack itself, but when the woman leaned to the side, she knew it was to tease out the envelope.

Orlando clicked her tongue three times.

"Copy," Quinn said. "Tagging the vehicle."

While Orlando continued pretending to read, she kept the woman in sight, ready to warn Quinn the moment she neared the parking area, but the woman seemed content to remain at the wall. Again, a pro move, selling the sense that nothing was up.

"Clear," Quinn said. "We're all set."

"Ready on our end, too," Nate said. He and Abraham would now be waiting closer to the main highway to follow the Jeep.

When the woman finally began moving again, Orlando clucked once, staying focused on the book.

Footsteps coming up the ramp, growing closer and closer and—

"Getting a little dark to read, don't you think?"

Orlando looked up. The woman was standing five feet away, and though the color of her hair had changed, Orlando knew from the picture Nadine had shown them that the woman was indeed Desirae Rosette.

"Not too bad yet," Orlando said. "I can probably get in another twenty minutes." She turned back to the book but could feel the woman's gaze on her.

"What is it?" Desirae asked.

"I'm sorry?"

"The book. What is it?"

Orlando held it up so Desirae could see the cover.

"What's it about? Sheep?" Desirae said.

"No," Orlando said with a smile. "It's actually science fiction. Kind of."

"What do you mean, kind of?"

Orlando could tell Desirae was testing her, but as a proponent of being prepared, she'd asked Abraham to give her a quick rundown of the plot.

"There are these people living in a silo with no apparent way out. Thousands of them. Not sure why. Haven't gotten there yet."

"Good?"

"Yeah. Really good."

"Well, have a nice evening," Desirae said, and then headed into the parking lot.

"THAT SOUNDED LIKE fun," Quinn said as Orlando climbed into the car and tossed the book into the backseat.

"She didn't bash my head in so I'll take that as a win," she said.

Quinn hit the gas and headed for the highway.

On the console between them was his phone, open to the app tracking the Jeep. Orlando picked it up and looked at the screen.

"Heading northwest," she said. "Fits with the address Nate found. Who was the Jeep registered to again?"

"Karla…Bishop, I believe."

Orlando leaned between the seats and retrieved her laptop. Within moments she had a mobile connection and her browser open. Unfortunately, she wasn't able to turn up anything more about Karla Bishop. The address on the Jeep's registration had a different name as property owner—Susan Drake. A search of that name also came up blank.

AS GLORIA HAD done at the four houses they'd visited so far, she approached the door of house number five with only King as company while Nolan and Andres waited by the sedan, ready to spring into action if things went bad.

Her knock was greeted by an elderly Asian man. "Yes?" he said.

"I'm sorry to bother you. I'm Detective Baker and this is Detective Kendrick. We're with the county crime investigation unit."

The man looked surprised. "How can I help you?"

She asked him a few innocuous questions, hinted at an investigation of someone else in the valley, and in the end decided he and his wife—the only other person who lived at the house—were unlikely to have been the ones Eli had talked to.

With a thank you and good-bye, she and her team moved on to house number six. Like several of the other places, there was a gate across the driveway. On one side was a mailbox with the name Drake printed on it, while on the other an intercom at driver level. When Gloria pushed the button, she received no response.

She peered past the gate and down the long drive. She could make out a portion of the house off to the right, tucked beneath several trees and surrounded by brush. The rest of the property seemed overgrown, too, as if the owner had given title back to the jungle. What she didn't see were any cars.

She pushed the button again but again no one answered.

"Mark this one," she said. "We'll come back."

She backed out of the driveway and headed down the road to house number seven.

THE GOLDEN TONES in the sky had begun to give way to black as the Jeep turned onto the mountain valley where the property owned by Susan Drake was located. Since there was no other way out of the area, Quinn had Nate and Abraham wait for him and Orlando at the base of the valley. By the time they met up, the Jeep had stopped moving at the exact coordinates they'd expected.

After consolidating into one car, they headed into the valley. The Bishop/Drake residence was the sixth property up the road. There was a gate across the driveway and an intercom to the side. While he couldn't see any, Quinn was sure a camera was there, too.

He started to roll down his window to access the intercom.

"She knows me," Abraham said. "Let me try."

It was a sound idea. Quinn pulled forward enough so that Abraham could lean out his window and press the button.

For a long moment, it seemed as if no one would answer, and then the same voice Quinn had heard speaking to Orlando on the beach blared out of the speaker. "This is private property. Leave now or I will call the police."

"Desirae," Abraham said. "We just want to—"

"Get off my property!"

"It's Abraham Delger. I know you haven't forgotten the last time you saw me. When I brought her to you."

Silence.

"Please," he said. "Please let us in."

A few more seconds passed before they heard the sound of an electric motor and saw the gate swing open. Quinn drove forward before Desirae could change her mind.

"Nice job," Nate said to Abraham.

"I don't think the job's done yet," Quinn said as the front lanai came into view, revealing Desirae Rosette standing at the top of the steps cradling a Tavor assault rifle.

CHAPTER
THIRTY TWO

"DO NOT GET out of the car," Desirae said. "I don't care why you're here. I don't know what lies you told my mother. I don't want to hear any of it. I only let you come this far so you could see how serious I am. You are *not* welcome. Just your presence here has already ruined our lives. If you come back tomorrow, we will be gone. Now turn around and don't come back." She emphasized the last of her words by leveling the barrel of her rifle at them.

Orlando said, "All we need is a few minutes of—"

"Leave. Now." Desirae braced the rifle against her shoulder.

"Anyone have a suggestion?" Quinn whispered.

"Maybe we *should* go," Nate said. "Let her cool down a little and come back in a few hours. One of us could keep an eye on the place, make sure she doesn't leave."

Quinn knew as unsatisfactory as Nate's suggestion might be, it was probably the best solution for now. But as he reached to put the car in reverse, he heard one of the back doors open.

"What are you doing?" Nate said.

"Do not step another foot outside!" Desirae shouted. "Get back in your vehicle."

"Go ahead and shoot me, then," Abraham said, climbing all the way out of the car. "I'm not going to leave. Not until you've heard us out."

"I said get in the car, Abraham! Right now!"

He moved around the back of the sedan and started walking toward the house, his hands raised.

"I swear to God, I will kill you where you stand."

"Then go ahead," he said.

Quinn opened his door.

"You get back in!" Desirae said, shifting her aim to him.

"There are people looking for you," he said.

"I *know* there are people looking for me. They've been looking for me for years."

"They're getting close," Abraham told her.

"Because of you," she said, pointing her gun back at him.

"All I wanted to know was if Tessa was alive. I realize I should have left it alone, but I can't take it back now." He paused. "These are the worst kind of people. They killed a good man, a friend who was helping me."

Surprise flashed across Desirae's face. "What friend?"

"His name was Eli. Eli Be—"

"Becker?" she said. "They killed Eli? Oh, God. I told him to run."

Another car door opened. "You're the one who warned him," Orlando said as she climbed out.

Nate, apparently feeling left out, opened his door and joined them.

Still holding her gun on them, Desirae repeated, "I told him to run."

"He did run," Quinn said. "He went to Florida."

"I was supposed to meet him there," Abraham said. "But they found him before I arrived. We followed his trail but we didn't get to him in time. They knew he'd found some information about Tessa. They tried to torture it out of him. We don't know how much they got before he died."

"Oh, my God. Abraham, why couldn't you stop? Why did you have to keep looking?"

"This isn't Abraham's fault," Quinn said. "These people aren't looking for you because he wouldn't stop. They took another friend of ours, but we were able to get him out before they could kill him. When they were interrogating him, they never asked him about Abraham. They don't even know about Abraham."

"The dot-xuki computer virus at the CIA," Orlando said. "I'd be willing to bet that's what started it. At least this latest round."

The front door of the house creaked open, and a scared young voice said, "Mom, what's going on?"

Desirae looked over her shoulder and said, "Get back inside."

"Who are these people?"

"Terri, I told you, wait in your room."

From Quinn's vantage point, he could see the girl standing in the doorway. Abraham, however, had to take a few steps to the side to see around Desirae.

"Tessa?" he said.

"Inside!" Desirae yelled at the girl.

But the girl had frozen in the doorway at the sound of Abraham's voice.

Abraham took a step forward. "Tessa, I-I don't know if you remember me, but I knew you when you were very young. My name is Abraham. I—"

"Abraham?" the girl said, her eyes widening. "Abe?"

Abraham's own eyes were swimming in water as he continued forward. "Yes. I'm Abe." The girl stepped onto the lanai.

"Terri, please," Desirae pleaded. "It's not safe out here."

But the girl walked on as if she couldn't hear Desirae.

"Abe?" she said again. "You...you took me on a plane."

"A few. A couple trains, too."

"I don't remember trains." She hesitated. "You promised you'd come back."

"I wanted to for a long time, but I'm here now." He was almost to the lanai now. "Do you still play checkers?"

A surprised half smile. "Every day," she said. "Just like you taught me."

Desirae's shoulders sagged as she lowered her gun. "For God's sake, come inside before I kill all of you."

HOUSES EIGHT AND nine were both occupied by large families Gloria quickly dismissed as possibilities.

House ten, like house six earlier, appeared to be unoccupied. There was not, however, a locked gate across the entrance, so they drove all the way up to the house and had a look around.

Not just unoccupied. Empty. Whoever had lived there was gone.

The caller, perhaps? Or was this only the location the caller had used?

They let themselves in through the back door and found enough dust in the place to know that no one had been inside for weeks.

She mentally crossed number ten off the list and ordered her men back to the Suburban. They had one more house in the valley to check.

Two, she corrected herself. They still had to go back to number six.

"DON'T GET TOO comfortable," Desirae said as they walked into the living room. "And don't expect me to get you anything to drink."

Orlando and Nate sat on the couch while Abraham took one of the chairs. Quinn didn't feel much like sitting and remained on his feet. Apparently, Desirae was feeling the same.

"I can't tell you how good it is to see you," Abraham said to Tessa as the girl took a seat on a nearby footstool.

Still unsure about how she should react to him, she paused before saying, "Thanks."

"I never knew what happened to you after...after we separated."

She took a quick glance at Desirae. "I've been okay. Mom takes care of me."

"How long have you been here?" Orlando asked Desirae.

"None of your business," Desirae said. "Tell me about Eli."

"Do you think maybe…" Quinn let the sentence hang as he glanced quickly at Tessa then back at Desirae.

Desirae considered his suggestion for a few seconds. "Sweetheart, why don't you go to your room for a few minutes?"

"I want to stay," Tessa said.

"I know, and I'm sorry. But I promise, I will tell you everything after."

Tessa looked disappointed as she stood up. "Everything?"

"Yes, everything."

As soon as Tessa disappeared into the back of the house, Desirae said, "I don't hide anything from her. That way, she doesn't question me if we have to do something…unusual."

"Like living in a secret underground apartment below your mother's house?" Orlando asked.

Desirae didn't seem fazed by the question. "Something like that." Her face hardened. "Now tell me about Eli."

Abraham carried the load of the story, taking it back to when he had first approached Eli for help not long after leaving Tessa with Desirae. Quinn and Orlando added points here and there in regards to the most recent events.

"I was angry at myself for leaving her when I thought she needed me most, I guess," Abraham said. "Apparently, I shouldn't have worried."

"No, you shouldn't have," Desirae said.

"Your turn," Quinn said. "What happened after Amsterdam?"

"I never agreed to take turns," Desirae said.

"Abraham needs to know," Quinn countered. "You owe him that much. He *did* bring Tessa to you."

Looking annoyed, Desirae finally sighed and said, "She wasn't supposed to stay with me. I was head of the pickup team, that's all. We were to take her to Mexico City and await further instructions from Carter. Those instructions never came."

"Someone killed him," Quinn said.

"Yes, but we didn't know that yet. At that point, there

were two of us with Terri…with Tessa. The guy with me went out to try to make contact, but he never came back. It was obvious something was up. Since Carter's group usually did sub work for the CIA, I used a contact I had there to see if she could find anything out. That's when I learned about Carter, and the fact that nearly everyone else associated with Operation Overtake had been killed. Not exactly a good feeling knowing you're probably the last link in the chain." She looked at Abraham. "For a while, I assumed you were dead, too."

"What about the person you were supposed to be taking Tessa to?" Orlando asked.

"Carter was the only one who knew who that was. Kept it in his head. Took it with him when he died."

"So you decided to keep her?" Quinn asked.

"I was *asked* to help," she said. "You have to understand, this was a mess. While the Agency wasn't directly involved, and would have liked to wash their hands of the whole thing, they knew there was a slim but real possibility that if Operation Overtake was exposed, it could be linked back to them. The abandonment of a little girl? Or God forbid, her death? Think of the careers that would have ruined." She paused. "The offer was a well-paid early retirement, and access to additional funds for whatever other extras I might need. The trade-off was that once I accepted the job, Tessa would be my responsibility alone. If something happened to her, all the blame would fall on me."

"And you said yes to this," Quinn said.

"I wasn't a bad agent, but I wasn't jumping at the chance to get shot at every day, either," she said. "It was an out."

Abraham scoffed. "It was more than an out, wasn't it? How long were you with her when they made you the offer?"

Desirae said nothing for several seconds. "By then, a few weeks."

Abraham nodded. "If I had been watching her that long, I would have said yes, too. Hell, I probably would have said yes if you'd asked me in Amsterdam."

Desirae said nothing, but by the look on her face, Quinn knew Abraham had hit close to home.

"So you moved her into your mom's basement?" Quinn asked.

A reluctant nod. "The Agency arranged the construction."

"And then?"

"When I felt enough time had passed, we moved here."

"So until now there haven't been any problems?"

"I wouldn't say that," she said hesitantly. "Though I wasn't to have any direct contact with anyone at the Agency anymore, my friend there did set me up with access to their system so I could watch my back. She contacted me a few times after that, telling me someone seemed to be trying to find out if Tessa had really died in Osaka or not. I kept tabs on things to make sure no one was getting close. The searches seemed to be coming from two different sources. One I tracked back to Eli Becker right there in the CIA. At first I thought he was a mole working for those who had killed the rest of the Overtake team, but after a while I figured out he was working for you." She looked at Abraham. "That's when I realized you were still alive.

"The real problem, though, was this other group. It took me a few years, but I was able to ID them as McCrillis International. Familiar with them?"

"You might say that," Quinn replied. "They're the ones who killed Eli."

"I guessed as much. In the first few years, they would probe several times a week for info about Tessa. After that, it dropped off some, occasionally there were months with nothing. This last time was over six months, and I thought maybe they'd finally given up." She hung her head for a moment, then looked at Abraham. "It's my fault they're on me again, not yours. I'm sorry I said it was."

"What do you mean?" he asked.

"I thought I was being so smart. See, the one thing McCrillis hadn't been able to get their hands on yet was a full copy of the Agency's file on Overtake. About a year ago they got close. Scared the crap out of me when I found out. I'd been told the report had been sanitized to reflect that Tessa had been killed along with Jennifer Kagawa, her…mother, but I hadn't seen the files myself and couldn't be sure there wasn't something in them that would lead back to us. So I knew I had to do something.

"The dot-xuki virus was yours," Orlando said, leaning forward.

Desirae shook her head. "I can't take credit for creating it—that was done by a tech I still trusted—but I did execute it. Good thing, too. It wiped out the files at the Agency and delivered a copy to me. The stupid son of a bitch who had asked me to take care of Tessa had created a special subfolder detailing the decision and had subsequently been adding updates of her status. If McCrillis had found that, we'd both be dead right now."

"What about the recent picture of Tessa?" Quinn said.

"The one Eli was sent? That came from me." Once more Desirae looked at Abraham. "I thought maybe it would be enough to satisfy you. See that she was alive and well. I should have never sent it. Within twenty-four hours, not only had Eli somehow been able to dig up more information, but I was also receiving notifications that McCrillis's activities seemed to have kicked into high gear and I realized they were on his trail. I couldn't have that. Eli had the picture of Tessa. McCrillis would know she was definitely alive if they got ahold of it." She took a breath. "I called, told him that someone was after him and he had to leave town. Then I set up some quick and dirty false trails I hoped would keep McCrillis busy for a while. Apparently, it wasn't enough."

"Who took the picture?" Orlando asked.

"I don't know. I used one that was in the file, so someone from the Agency, I assumed."

"I have news for you, then. Your virus left a few things behind. Eli had a second copy of the picture on his computer, only he'd found it in the CIA system and it had a dot-xuki extension."

"What? Oh, my God. How many files were left?"

"I don't know. The message Eli left made it sound like only a few. The good news is they've been isolated, so it's doubtful McCrillis has gotten to them."

Desirae didn't look convinced, and Quinn was willing to bet she would attempt a second purge in the future.

"Have you ever been able to figure out why these McCrillis people would want to kill Tessa in the first place?" Abraham asked.

Desirae stared at him for several seconds, as if caught off guard. "I live with this every day. I guess I forgot that information was kept from us during the operation. It's her father. He's Frank Rostov."

Silence.

"*The* Frank Rostov?" Orlando asked. "Rostov Dynamics Frank Rostov?"

"Yes."

Frank Rostov had turned his father's small San Francisco electronics company into one of the largest tech firms in the world, rivaling Apple and Google and Microsoft. Aside from making much of the equipment and software that served as the backbone of the Internet, his company had also become one of the largest tech-related defense contractors in the country, easily making him worth more than thirty billion dollars.

"Didn't he get sick or something?" Nate asked.

Desirae nodded. "A severe stroke. Hung on for a little while before he finally passed away."

"That was what? Five or six years ago?" Nate said.

"The stroke was just a little over seven," Desirae corrected him. "More precisely, two months before Jennifer was killed in Osaka."

Tessa's mother, Desirae told them, had been Rostov's mistress. When she became pregnant with Tessa, he had sent her away to appease his wife, promising his mistress he'd take care of her and Tessa, and acknowledge the child as his own at some point in the future. The money had come, but the public acknowledgment had yet to materialize when the stroke cut him down. In his diminished capacity, Rostov was no longer able to run the company, so his wife, Jacqueline Rostov, took on the role of CEO. She had been the one who had used the company's defense connections at the CIA to find someone who could handle a delicate matter for her. This turned out to be 525, Gavin Carter's group, and the job was to terminate Tessa and Jennifer.

"But why?" Nate asked.

"I couldn't figure it out at first, either," Desirae said. "His wife had inherited the company. What did she care anymore? At the suggestion of my hacker friend, we infiltrated the system belonging to the law firm that represented the Rostovs. It turns out that while Frank Rostov hadn't publicly acknowledged Tessa, he had added her to his will a few weeks before he became incapacitated. If Tessa showed up, half the estate would be hers. Mrs. Rostov is clearly not interested in sharing. She made a bad choice, though, by hiring Carter. He might have been greedy for the money the project would bring in, but he wasn't able to stomach the idea of killing a little girl and had come up with an alternate plan.

"What he didn't realize was that apparently Mrs. Rostov had a separate plan to eliminate anyone associated with the deaths so they wouldn't be able to talk about them later. There's no doubt in my mind that's where McCrillis first came in. In the process, either McCrillis or Mrs. Rostov herself must have realized something odd was going on. Otherwise, why continue looking for Tessa?"

They all fell quiet as they digested this last bit.

"They may never find out about this place," Orlando said.

"I can't take that chance."

"Do you have somewhere else to go?" Quinn asked.

"I have backups."

"Is there anything we can do to help?"

"The best thing you can do is leave us alone." There was no malice in her words. She was only stating a fact.

Abraham rose from his chair. "Can I at least tell Tessa good-bye?"

"Of course," Desirae said. "Her room's last one on the left."

He had barely disappeared into the hallway when somewhere toward the front of the house a buzzer sounded.

CHAPTER
THIRTY THREE

DESIRAE TURNED TOWARD the noise, startled.

"What is that?" Quinn asked.

"Driveway intercom," she said, and then headed across the room.

The buzzer went off again as she reached a panel by the door. On it was a speaker, a few buttons, and a small video screen. Though Desirae blocked most of the screen from view, Quinn could see it flicker to life when she pushed one of the buttons.

"Yes?" she said.

"Detective Baker with the county crime investigation unit," a woman's voice said. "Wondering if I could have a moment of your time?"

Quinn moved quickly across the room so he could see the monitor.

"About what?" Desirae asked.

"It would be much easier to do this face to face. Could we come in?"

Though the camera appeared to be mounted several feet above the gate, it was angled enough that Quinn could see most of the driver's face. He grabbed Desirae's hand as she was about to push the button again.

"It's them," he said. "McCrillis."

She looked at the monitor. "Are you sure?"

"That's the woman responsible for Eli's death."

Desirae thought for a second before pushing the button

again. "Now is not really a good time for us. Would it be possible for you to come back in the morning?"

On the monitor, the woman hesitated before she touched the talk button again. "Of course. Would eight a.m. be all right?"

"That would be fine," Desirae told her.

"We'll see you then," the woman said. She pulled back inside her vehicle and backed out of camera range.

"They're not leaving," Quinn said.

"I know," Desirae said, turning. "Follow me."

"NOW IS NOT a good time for us," the woman inside house number six said. "Would it be possible for you to come back in the morning?"

Alarm bells clanged in Gloria's head. The woman was hiding something. But did it have to do with the phone call or was she worried because Gloria had said she was the police?

"Of course. Would eight a.m. be all right?" Gloria asked.

"That would be fine."

Gloria pushed the button again. "We'll see you then." As soon as her window was up and the Suburban was rolling backward, she said, "Everybody ready. We're going to check this one out."

DESIRAE GRABBED HER Tavor assault rifle and quickly led Quinn, Orlando, and Nate into the hallway.

"Please tell us you have more of those," Quinn said, motioning to her weapon.

Instead of answering him, she yelled, "Terri, code red."

Before they reached the end of the hall, Tessa, pulling Abraham by the hand, came rushing out of her room, looking scared but in control.

"Is this practice?" she asked.

"No, honey. You know what to do. Take Abraham with you."

Tessa nodded and led him down the hallway and into the guest bathroom, while Quinn and the others followed Desirae into the master bedroom.

"Where's Tessa taking Abraham?" Orlando asked.

Desirae flung open the door to a walk-in closet and hurried inside.

"Tunnel under the house," she said, pulling an old trunk away from the wall. She yanked back the carpet, revealing a trapdoor. "Comes out in the jungle behind my neighbor's place." Using a key on a chain around her neck, she unlocked the door and pulled it open. "There's a path that goes to the next valley. We stashed a motorcycle there."

"Tessa knows how to drive one?" Nate asked.

Desirae leaned into the opening. "She can drive pretty much anything in a pinch. Here." She handed out three more Tavors and then pulled out four GLOCK 9mm pistols, suppressors, and extra magazines. When she was through, she jumped back up and shut the door.

As she connected the suppressor to her GLOCK, she said, "I'd rather not freak out my neighbors too much if we can help it. So rifles only if you have no choice, okay?"

Once they were all ready, they moved back into the hallway. Quinn was expecting them to go into the guest bathroom and join Tessa and Abraham in the tunnel, but Desirae kept going toward the living room.

"We need to get out of here," he said.

"In a second," she said. "I just gotta grab something."

Quinn motioned for Nate and Orlando to wait by the bathroom, and then headed after Desirae.

GLORIA PULLED TO the side of the road a hundred feet down from house six's driveway.

"King, you and Andres go to the other side and work your way in. Nolan and I will take this end."

They jumped out of the car and rushed around to the back, where they equipped themselves with pistols and ear-mounted radios.

"Backpack?" Andres asked.

Gloria nodded. "Bring it."

The pack contained several specialized items such as

flash bangs, tear gas, disposable gas masks, lock picks, and knives. Since they didn't know what they were getting into, it was best to be prepared.

As King and Andres hustled off to their assigned entry point, Gloria and Nolan moved into the jungle near the back of the car. Since they were far enough away from the house, Gloria decided to sacrifice stealth for speed, not slowing until she estimated they were level with the house.

While she expected to find a fence, it was telling that the one surrounding house number six's property was topped by two strands of razor wire. Since the wire cutters were in the pack with Andres, she looked around for an alternate way over and spotted a tree that would do the trick. It didn't have any branches that went over the fence, but its trunk was solid enough for her to push off from as she leaped over the fence. After Nolan joined her, they continued toward the house.

From the driveway gate she'd been able to see one car parked in the driveway, but her new vantage point revealed there were two. She crept between the vehicles to the lanai that surrounded the house. Lights were on in the room at this end, but the windows were covered by a sheer fabric that made it hard for her to see anything distinct inside. She moved to the back of the house to check for a better way of getting a glimpse of the interior. Before she got there, she noted a structure near the back corner of the lot, half hidden among the trees. A shed maybe, or a guesthouse.

She sent Nolan to check it out and returned her attention to the main house.

The back had large windows but they were all covered by opaque curtains. Quietly, she climbed up on the lanai and moved back around to one of the windows covered only by sheers. As she neared, she heard a man's voice in the house, which meant at least two people were home.

She moved directly under the window and slowly rose enough to look inside.

ABRAHAM WATCHED TESSA open the bathroom cabinet and press something inside. She then grabbed the top and pulled.

The whole cabinet swung out as if it weighed nothing at all, revealing a three-by-three-foot hole in the wall.

"This way," she said as she slipped through the opening.

Abraham had to crouch way down to follow her, something his body wasn't exactly happy about, but he made it through with only a small scrape of his shoulder. On the other side was a set of narrow wooden stairs leading down into darkness.

"Tessa?" he asked.

"Down here," she said.

A flashlight winked on a dozen feet below him, lighting up the girl's face and part of a passageway leading to the left.

"Where does this go?" he asked when he reached the bottom.

"Shh. We're not supposed to talk," she whispered.

As she started to move off, he said, "What about the way we came in? Do we need to close it?"

"Mom will get it. Now come on, and stay quiet."

He followed her down the tunnel.

"Careful," she whispered about a minute later. "Slopes down here."

She shone the light above her and he saw what she meant. Not only did the floor angle downward, but the ceiling did, too.

"How far does this go?" he asked once they were level again.

"Shh. I told you—no talking."

After another dip, the tunnel went on for an additional fifty feet or so before ending at a second set of stairs. Like the others, these had been cut right into the dirt and covered by boards. At the top was a trapdoor.

As Tessa started up, Abraham said, "Let me go first."

She considered it for a second before nodding and moving out of the way.

"There's a lock," she whispered into his ear. "Twist to the right and pull down."

"Got it."

As soon as he had a hand on the lock, Tessa doused her flashlight. Following her instructions, he twisted and pulled, then ever so slowly pushed up the door.

Small clumps of dirt and dried leaves rained down on him as the opening widened. The door, though, was remarkably quiet. When it was high enough for him to stick his head above ground level, he took a look around. The dark jungle was everywhere, not only to the sides but above, too, blotting out most of the sky. As for noise, the only thing he could hear was the gentle wind whooshing through the trees.

With a wave for Tessa to follow, he climbed out.

"Where are we?" he whispered, after she shut the door.

She pointed to the right. "My house is over there, but we go this way."

She turned in the opposite direction and flicked her flashlight back on, keeping the beam pointed at the ground right in front of her.

"Stay close," she whispered as she started walking.

THOUGH THE OUTBUILDING was only a garden shed, Nolan knew better than to return to his boss without giving it a full inspection.

As he turned along the back side, he heard voices, too low to understand. They had come from beyond the back fence. He cocked his head.

There it was again. A quick little spurt.

Then quiet.

What he heard next was not talking but the movement of bushes, like someone passing through.

He moved back around the building, putting it between him and the noise, before activating his mic.

"There's someone in the jungle beyond the fence," he reported.

"A neighbor?" his boss asked.

"Not sure," he told her. "You want me to come back or check?"

"Check."

DESIRAE RACED INTO the kitchen with Quinn only a few feet behind her. She opened a drawer, cursed, and started opening others.

"What are you looking for?" he asked.

She angrily pushed another drawer closed. "My tablet computer. It should be right..." She froze, her gaze on the ceiling. After a second, she groaned and said, "Right."

Reversing course into the living room, she ran over to a cabinet next to the back wall. There were several books on it, mostly textbooks by the looks of them, along with spiral binders and a thin stack of loose pages. Desirae began rifling through everything, finally finding the computer under a white three-ring binder.

"I hope to hell that's important," he said.

"All my pictures of Terri are on here. I'm not leaving it for them to find."

She grabbed the empty book bag that was lying on the floor, stuffed the tablet in it, and slung it over her shoulder.

"That it?" he asked.

She nodded, and together they raced back to the hallway.

GLORIA LOOKED THROUGH the window just in time to see a man run into a room on the left. She could hear muffled voices and the slamming of a drawer, and knew the woman must be with him.

The receiver in her ear emitted a soft beat, and then Nolan reported hearing someone in the wild area beyond the property.

"You want me to come back or check?" he asked.

"Check," she said.

A few seconds later, as she continued observing through the window, a woman ran into the main room, carrying a Tavor assault rifle. High end. Not easy to obtain. When the man followed her out, Gloria saw that he was similarly equipped, but that was not the most interesting thing about him.

He was none other than Jonathan Quinn, the same son of

a bitch who had disabled her team and almost killed her.

She sank below the window ledge and turned on her mic. "You're going to like this, boys. One of our friends from the other day, the main guy—he's inside. The other two may be here, too, but I haven't seen them yet. Nolan, after you check out that noise, get back here as soon as you can. Unit two, meet me on the east side of the house."

NOLAN USED AN empty barrel near the shed to get over the fence, and was well into the forest when Gloria made her announcement.

Despite her orders, he almost turned back. He didn't want to miss any of the action, especially if it meant getting some licks in at the men who'd surprised them in Virginia. But orders were orders.

He found a trail about thirty yards back. It went down a gentle slope for a hundred feet or so before going over a ridge to the right. The valley on the other side was dark, no signs of habitation. Once more, he almost turned back, but a brief but very real flash of light on some bushes farther down the slope stopped him. He increased his pace as much as he could without drawing attention.

About a minute later, he saw the light again, but not only the beam this time. The person holding the light source walked through a gap in the brush.

The halo was wide enough that he could see a second person, too. Judging by their shapes, the one following was a man, maybe six feet tall, while the one holding the flashlight was considerably smaller. His first thought was a petite woman, but she seemed small even for that.

Then it hit him.

A girl.

No, he thought. *It couldn't be.*

But back at the house was a man who was tangentially connected to the girl they were hunting. Nolan kept watching, hoping to get another look at the two people, but they had been swallowed up by the jungle.

She *had* been about the right size.

He let the thought stew for another moment before clicking on his mic. "This is Nolan. I may have found something you'll be very interested in."

CHAPTER
THIRTY FOUR

"THE BOTTOM STEP lifts up," Desirae said. "You'll find some flashlights underneath."

They were in the guest bathroom, standing near the entrance to the escape tunnel.

"Nate, take point," Quinn said.

Nate ducked through the hole and vanished down the steps.

"You next," Quinn told Orlando.

GLORIA RENDEZVOUSED WITH King and Andres less than a minute after she'd called for them.

"Consider all targets hostile," she said. "All I need is one of them alive enough to talk. Understood?"

Both men nodded.

"They're somewhere in the back of the house," she said. "We locate first and then neutralize the problem. You two go back around the front, I'll take the rear, and we'll meet on the west side."

Staying on the lanai, Gloria hurried past the living room to the only window between it and the far corner, and peeked in. No lights on, but enough illumination leaking in from the hallway to discern the shape of a twin bed and a dresser. This room was too small to be the main bedroom. Turning down the west side, she found another window looking into the same bedroom, but it provided no more help.

A moment later, King and Andres appeared at the other

end.

When they met in the middle, she whispered, "I take it they're hiding in the master bedroom."

"You didn't find them?" King asked, surprised. "They weren't in the rooms we checked."

"You're sure?"

"Yes, ma'am."

"Dammit."

She motioned for Andres to turn around, then pulled out the lock-pick set, three disposable masks, a couple of flash-bang grenades, and a tear gas canister. The last she kept for herself, while handing a flash bang each to the two men.

They hurried around to the door into the living room. Gloria picked the lock and they all pulled on their masks.

Just loud enough for her men to hear, she said, "One, two, three."

She shoved the door open and rushed across the living room to the hallway entrance. Immediately, Andres and King tossed their grenades toward the bedrooms.

Bang! Bang!

The double explosion filled the house with sound and light.

Gloria pulled the pin on the tear gas canister and lobbed the can to the back of the hallway. With a hiss, smoky gas began to fill the rooms.

She waited for the first cough, knowing it would come in a matter of seconds, but all remained quiet. She gave it another few moments, and then raised her gun and led her men to the back of the house. When they reached the end of the hall, they each took one of the rooms.

"Clear!" King called from the hallway bathroom.

"Clear!" Andres called from the smaller bedroom.

"Shit," Gloria said as she stood in the deserted master bedroom, then added, "Clear." She reentered the hallway. "Where the hell did they go?"

Before anyone could venture a guess, her earpiece beeped.

"This is Nolan. I may have found something you'll be very interested in."

"I sure as hell hope so. We haven't found crap here."

He told her about the man and the girl, and then floated the possibility of who she might be.

Andres's eyes widened. "In here," he said, then disappeared inside the second bedroom.

"Did you hear me?" Nolan asked.

"Just a second," she told him as she followed Andres.

Lights were now on in the room, so there was no mistaking it for anything but what it was: a preteen girl's bedroom.

Not proof. Not even close. But in her bones, Gloria could feel everything aligning.

I'm so close.

"Nolan, stay on her," she ordered.

"Yes, ma'am."

"We're on our way."

Gloria and Andres returned to the hallway and found King waiting for them. As they started toward the living room, she noticed something odd.

The haze in the bedrooms had hung in the air, hardly drifting at all, but in the hall, it was being drawn into the bathroom.

She looked inside, thinking the window must be open, but it wasn't, nor was the gas moving in its direction. It was drifting toward the sink. More accurately, it appeared as if it was being sucked in *around* the cabinet the sink was in.

"Hold this." She shoved her rifle at King and then pulled the cabinet doors open. She was fully expecting to see no back panel, but it was there like it should be. Odder still, there was no smoke in the cabinet.

She ran a finger along the seam where the counter met the wall and felt a slight separation that continued all the way around the side. She gripped the countertop and gave the cabinet a yank but it didn't move.

"Give me a hand," she said.

King and Andres set down their weapons and grabbed

on. The cabinet creaked when they pulled, and the gap between it and the wall increased to nearly a quarter inch, but that was all they got.

"There has to be a release," she said, checking under the lip of the countertop.

Nothing there, so she felt along the sides of the box, and then opened the doors again and searched the inner frame.

"Ha!" she yelled as her finger touched a button.

She pushed it and felt the vibration of something releasing.

When she yanked the cabinet again, it moved effortlessly away from the wall, revealing a hole and the top few steps of a staircase.

"Grab your guns. Time to go hunting."

THE MUFFLED BOOM of the grenades echoed down the tunnel, but they were all too well trained to stop and look back.

"How much farther?" Quinn asked Desirae.

"Not too much."

Another minute on, they heard a noise in the distance, a kind of groan.

Quinn looked back at Desirae, an eyebrow raised.

"Keep going," she said.

Several moments later, they heard footsteps on the planks covering the stairs behind them. Without saying anything, they picked up their speed. As soon as they reached the end, Nate raced up the stairs and, following Desirae's directions, shoved the door open.

"Nate and I can pin them down here while you two catch up to Tessa and Abraham," Quinn said to Orlando and Desirae as soon as they were out and the door was closed. "Let me know as soon as you've gotten them out of here and we'll join you." He looked at Nate. "Pistols only, and spread out so if they throw a grenade it doesn't get both—"

A faint but unmistakable scream cut him off.

Desirae twisted toward the sound. "That's Tessa," she said as she ran into the jungle.

Orlando took off after her.

Quinn and Nate hesitated. The trapdoor provided the perfect chokehold to tie down their pursuers, but the others must have split their forces and sent some into the jungle. How many? No way to know, but the most pressing danger was clearly to Tessa.

Quinn looked at his partner and saw Nate was thinking the same thing.

Without a word, they headed into the jungle.

AS ABRAHAM REACHED out to push a branch to the side, his foot slipped on a loose bit of ground. He staggered forward, the branch he'd been trying to avoid slapping him in the face, and was just barely able to keep himself from falling.

"Are you okay?" Tessa asked, looking back.

"I'm fine. Don't worry about me," he said. "Let's keep going."

She eyed him, as if unsure whether or not to believe him, before turning back to the path and moving on.

It was surreal, him being here with her on the run again. Hell, him finding her, seeing her once more when he thought he never would—that was the most surreal part. In those times when he felt sure she was still alive, that he couldn't have transported her thousands of miles only for her to be killed later, his mind would still not give him a happy ending. An endless string of horrible alternate possibilities intruded— neglect, violent and mental abuse, forced servitude, prostitution.

Thank God none had been true. It was obvious Desirae loved the girl and had given Tessa as close to a normal life as she could, while preparing the girl to deal with the very real possibility that the danger that had taken her birth mother would return.

"Careful here," Tessa said, pointing at some roots that had grown across the path.

Abraham watched his step, not wanting a repeat of the near disaster from a few minutes ago. A moment after he cleared the root, he heard the rustle of brush from somewhere along the path behind them.

He rushed forward. "Kill the light," he whispered.

As the beam flickered out, he heard the sound of a step. He put a hand on Tessa's back and ushered her off the path into the wild. He wanted to keep going but knew they were making too much noise, so they crouched as low as they could about a dozen feet off the path.

"Maybe it's Mom," Tessa whispered.

"I hope so. She'd want us to play it safe, though."

She nodded, her brow creased in worry. He put an arm around her. After a slight hesitation, she leaned against him, shaking. For a moment he was taken back to Japan, when, though scared, she had put all her trust in him.

A crunch.

Abraham peered through the foliage back toward the path, but saw only indistinct shapes of plants and trees. Several quiet seconds passed before he heard steps again. They were light, almost imperceptible, the movements of someone trying very hard to not be heard.

Quiet again, three seconds, and then the crunch of dirt and a man passing through Abraham's field of vision. He was mostly a shadow, but Abraham could see the man well enough to know he was neither Quinn nor Nate.

Abraham could feel Tessa's shuttering breath as she, too, saw the man. Abraham squeezed her shoulder and moved his mouth to her ear. "I need you to stay here."

She jerked her head back and looked at him in horror. "No," she mouthed.

"I'm going to see where he's going, that's all," he whispered. "I'll be right back."

She shook her head. "Don't leave me."

The words drove a knife into his heart.

"Okay," he whispered. "Don't worry. I'm not going anywhere."

She leaned into him hard and he put his other arm around her.

"I'm not going anywhere."

NOLAN'S CONCERN GREW with every passing second.

Tracking the girl and the man had been relatively easy. They were surprisingly quiet but not completely so, and he was able to follow them without keeping them in sight.

About two minutes earlier, there had been an increase in noise for a few seconds, and then nothing. He figured they'd passed through a section that was more overgrown than others, but as he continued down the path himself, he found no such area, nor could he hear them ahead of him anymore.

He stopped, realizing they must have turned off the path somewhere behind him. Either there was another path he'd missed or they were hiding. Using the illumination of his cell phone, he studied the ground. The only prints were his.

With extreme care, he retraced his route, stopping every few seconds until he finally spotted the others' footprints. After he determined the exact spot where they disappeared, he pulled out his gun and turned toward the jungle.

SOMETHING DIDN'T FEEL right.

Abraham looked toward the path but it was empty. He listened but could hear nothing unusual. Still, that old sense of impending danger that had kept him alive for so many years was on alert.

He whispered in Tessa's ear, "I want you to quietly crawl back until you find a good hiding place."

She looked at him, silently asking, why?

"Please," he said.

Lip trembling, she nodded.

As she backed away, Abraham concentrated on the path again. Still nothing there. So why had his sense—

A sound about halfway between the path and where he was. Without another thought, he moved to his left, slipping between two bushes. It wasn't quite as easy as it should have been. His right leg was stiffening from all the walking and crouching, but it was by far not the only ache and pain he felt.

Suddenly, a shadow of a man slipped out from the brush, low to the ground, and in his hand was a gun. When he reached the area where Abraham and Tessa had been, he paused. In his other hand was a glow, shining on the ground.

Our tracks, Abraham realized.

The man moved the light in an arc before looking in the direction Tessa had gone. He started creeping forward.

Letting his old instincts take over, Abraham launched himself forward with as much speed as his sore legs could generate, slamming into the man's back as the guy was twisting around. They rolled through the brush, Abraham ending up on the bottom with the man's back in his face.

An elbow whacked into Abraham's side. He tried to throw an arm around the guy's chest, but the man easily batted him away.

Abraham pushed and rolled just enough to get the guy off him.

The gun.

He reached for the man's hands, knowing he had to keep the guy from pulling the trigger. But both the man's hands were empty.

Abraham spotted the weapon lying on the ground a few feet away and lunged for it, but the man had seen it, too, and got there the same time Abraham did. They struggled, each getting a temporary grip on the handle, but in the end it was the man who slipped his finger over the trigger.

Abraham latched on to the suppressor, pushing it as hard as he could so the barrel couldn't be turned on him.

The man pulled the trigger.

A *thup* echoed softly through the jungle as the bullet drove harmlessly into the ground several yards away. Abraham yanked his hands away from the now white hot suppressor.

As the man started to aim the gun at him, Tessa screamed from somewhere in the jungle behind them. The shooter turned his head toward the sound, giving Abraham the opening he needed.

He rammed his knee hard into the man's groin. As the guy cringed, Abraham hit him with an uppercut under his jaw, rattling his teeth and dazing him. Abraham then wrenched the gun away and put it against the man's chest. The double *thup* as Abraham pulled the trigger twice were nearly silent this time, the body absorbing most of the sound.

He straightened up. "Tessa?" he said in a loud whisper. "Tessa? Are you all right?"

He ran back in the direction she'd gone.

"Tessa?"

"Here," she said, her voice small and shaky.

He turned around and spotted her curled against the back of a rock, trying to look as small as possible.

"I thought he was going to shoot you," she said.

"I'm okay. Everything's fine. Just like I told you."

"Is he…"

"He's not going to bother us," Abraham said, and held out his hand. "Come on. We need to keep going."

CHAPTER
THIRTY FIVE

GLORIA LOOKED UP the earthen stairs at the trapdoor and grimaced.

If the others were smart, and she knew they were, they'd be waiting above for her and her men to stick their heads out.

"Back the other way?" King asked.

That solution sucked, too. By the time they worked their way out of the tunnel and then all the way back here at ground level, the others could be long gone. Sure, Nolan was out there somewhere, but she put his odds alone against Quinn and his friends at zero.

She grabbed King's shoulder, turned him around, and dug out the last two canisters of tear gas from the backpack.

Once they had their masks on, she said, "Now."

With a shove from King, the door flew open. Gloria sent the first canister flying out to the left and the second to the right. They waited until the gas drifted across the opening.

"Go," she said.

King went first, Andres second, both swinging their guns left and right as they raced out of the tunnel.

Gloria hung back until she was sure there was no gunfire, and then joined them.

"No one here," King said, after finishing a sweep.

Apparently Quinn wasn't so smart after all. Too bad she had to waste the last of the gas to find out.

"There's a path on this side," Andres said. "Lots of footprints."

THE TRAIL WAS not without its obstacles, especially when running flat out like Quinn was. Fronds and leaves and branches swiped at him from the top, while roots and rocks and mud attacked from the bottom. So far he had been able to keep from falling, but there'd been a few close calls.

Ahead, Desirae had come to a stop and was scanning the jungle to either side of the path.

"It was around here somewhere, wasn't it?" she asked when he reached her.

"About right, I think." He looked behind him to see what Orlando and Nate thought, but neither of them was there.

The last time he'd seen Orlando was when he'd passed her on the uphill slope. She'd waved him ahead, saying she'd be right behind him. He took four quick paces back down the trail, and she and Nate suddenly appeared around a bend. They were jogging at best, Orlando first, looking winded, with Nate right behind her.

He ran over to them. "What happened? Are you all right?" he asked, putting an arm around her waist and taking some of her weight.

She seemed glad for his help. "Not quite up to sprinting condition at the moment," she said.

He hadn't been thinking. He should have found her someplace safe to wait it out. He gave Nate a nod of thanks for hanging back with her and then guided them over to Desirae.

"We should fan out," Desirae said. "She had to have been around here somewhere when she screamed."

They didn't find Tessa or Abraham, but Quinn did find the body of one of the men he and Nate had dealt with in Virginia. Two shots to the chest had done the job.

In a hushed voice, he called to the others.

"Jesus," Desirae whispered, then quickly looked around. "Any signs someone else was hurt?"

"A definite struggle," Quinn said. "But the only blood is here."

"They must have kept going," Orlando said.

310

"Let's go, let's go," Desirae said and took off back to the path.

"Slow down," Quinn called to her. "We need to be smart. This guy might not have been alone."

Desirae made no attempt to slow.

"Dammit," Quinn said. "Nate?"

"On it," Nate said and took off after her.

Quinn turned to Orlando. "Do you need more rest?"

"No, I'm okay," she said. "Just go. You don't have to babysit me."

"Yeah, well, tough. You first."

GLORIA HEARD NOISE about two hundred yards up ahead. Running, more than one person, the sound fading fast.

"Double time," she said. "King, you're in front. Andres, you're rear guard."

"I NEED A second," Abraham said as they neared a rock he could lean on. The fight had once more reminded him he wasn't a young man anymore.

"You're not having a heart attack, are you?" Tessa asked.

"No," he said, trying to smile. "Just...need to catch my breath."

"How old *are* you?"

"Old enough." He huffed, rapidly at first, drawing in as much air as he could. When his breathing was closer to normal, he said, "All right. I'm ready."

They moved farther into the valley, their pace about half as fast as it was before. As the path began to level off, Tessa whipped around and looked back beyond Abraham.

"What is it?" he asked.

"You didn't hear that?" she asked, fear returning to her eyes. "Someone's back there."

He followed her gaze. While they were walking, he hadn't been able to hear anything above the sound of his own labored breathing, but now he could pick it out—someone coming fast down the trail.

"Quick," he said. "Into the brush."

As he followed Tessa off the trail, his toe caught on a thick root. One second he was up, and the next he was sprawled on the jungle floor, his knee throbbing in pain and the gun he was carrying gone.

Tessa skidded to a stop a few feet in front of him and looked back.

"Run!" he said. "Go!"

From down the path he heard bushes part. He tried to see who was coming but there were too many bushes in his way. He twisted his head back to make sure Tessa was gone. But she was still there, aiming the gun he'd dropped toward the path.

"Whoa!" a male voice said. "Tessa, it's okay. It's Nate. I'm a friend, remember?"

"Terri, put it down."

Tessa lowered the gun a few inches. "Mom?"

"Sweetie, put the gun down."

Tessa let the gun drop to the ground and ran to her mother. As they threw their arms around each other, Nate knelt down next to Abraham.

"What happened?" he asked.

"When we heard you coming we tried to hide, but I tripped," Abraham said. "Stupid."

"Are you hurt?"

"Tweaked my knee, I think."

"Roll on your back."

Abraham did so, but not without pain. As Nate gently probed his knee, Quinn and Orlando showed up.

"What happened?" Orlando asked.

Nate repeated what Abraham had told him.

"Let's see if you can walk," Quinn said.

He and Nate helped Abraham to his feet. As Abraham applied pressure to his injured knee, a jolt of pain rushed up his leg. He staggered, wincing, and would have fallen if the other two hadn't been holding on to him.

"I think that's a no," Nate said.

Abraham sighed. "Not my best day, I guess."

"We've got to keep moving," Quinn said. "Nate and I can help you."

Abraham shook his head. "Path's too narrow and I'd slow you down. You go. I'll hide out here. You can come and get me later."

Quinn looked at Orlando.

"Not a choice," Abraham said. He used Nate to lower himself to the ground. "Get Tessa out of here. I'll be fine."

Orlando did not look happy, but she held out her pistol to him. "At least take this."

"Don't need it. Got my own," he said, nodding back to the gun Tessa had dropped. "Now get the hell out of here.

He turned before anyone else could say anything and crawled toward the gun and the safety of the deeper jungle. It was a moment before he finally heard the others returning to the path.

They had barely reached it, though, when a female voice called out, "That's far enough."

GLORIA HEARD THEIR voices a moment before she spotted Quinn and his people standing about a dozen feet off the path. She made a quick count. Four adults.

And one blessed child.

Could this really be it? Could she really be the one to close the books on the Rostov assignment? If so, she could write her own ticket at McCrillis from now on.

She clicked on her comm to get King's attention. When he looked back, she pointed to a spot on the other side of the group."

With a nod, he was off.

She activated her mic again and whispered, "Andres, need you up here with me."

"On my way," he replied.

She edged down the path as far as she could without exposing her presence, and watched as one of the women held out her gun. Why wasn't clear. A moment or two later, the woman pulled it back and the group headed back toward the path.

"King?" she asked.

"I'm about fifty feet beyond them."

"All right," she said. "Here we go." She cupped a hand over her mouth and yelled, "That's far enough."

The group immediately collapsed into a circle around the girl, their rifles up and ready. Gloria let off a well-aimed shot that cut through the jungle to their left.

"Guns down," she yelled. When they didn't comply, she keyed her mic. "King, warning shot."

King sent his bullet sailing a few feet over their heads.

"Put your weapons down," she said. "Or we won't miss next time."

GLORIA CLARK.

Quinn had recognized her voice immediately. And though he couldn't see her, the flash of her gun had given away her position.

"Anyone have the second shooter?" he asked, not moving his lips.

"My right, seventy-five feet ahead," Nate said from the other side of the protective ring they'd formed around Tessa.

"Do we see any others?" Quinn asked.

"No movement here," Orlando said.

"Same with me," Desirae said.

The car Clark had driven up to the gate was a sedan and could hold up to five passengers. One man down thanks to Abraham, and the two shooters meant one or two more were still out there somewhere.

"Very well, then," the woman said. "Mr. Quinn, we'll start with you."

The use of his name was clearly meant to show that by knowing who he was, Clark was in a superior position. It wasn't the first time someone had tried that trick with him, and it was something he could use to his advantage.

"All right," he said, sounding as if he were admitting defeat. "I'm putting it down, okay?"

As he dropped his rifle to the ground, he slipped his

other hand behind his back, retrieved the pistol, and tucked it against his leg. Around him, he heard his friends drop their rifles, too.

"No need for anyone to get shot," he said.

A tense few seconds passed before Clark said, "Send the girl down the path toward my voice."

Quinn heard Tessa take in a jittery breath.

"She's just a kid. A nobody," Quinn said.

"You're lying, Mr. Quinn. If I'm not mistaken, the girl is Tessa Kagawa. Or does she go by Rostov?"

"You've got the wrong girl," Desirae said. "Her name's Terri Drake."

"Terri. Cute. Personally I would have tried a little harder to get something a little less Tessa-like. Now send her over, or we'll kill you all *then* walk over there to get her ourselves."

Quinn noticed a bush move in his peripheral vision, about twenty feet from Clark.

"Get ready," he whispered. In a louder voice, he said, "Isn't that your plan anyway?"

"Excuse me?" Clark replied.

"If this girl is who you think she is, you'll have to kill all of us because we know too much."

Another tremble of a branch, a few feet closer to the woman.

"The things I heard about you weren't wrong after all. You *are* a smart man. Have it—"

"Now!" Quinn shouted.

JUST A LITTLE closer, Abraham thought.

He had crawled as quietly as he could toward the woman's voice. Though at some level he knew his injured knee was hollering in pain, he felt nothing, his fear for Tessa's life and his anger at all this woman represented masking anything that would hinder his movements.

There. He could discern the outline of shoulders and head on the other side of the bushes in front of him, less than ten feet away. As he repositioned to bring his gun up, his arm bumped against a plant. He froze.

"...*are* a smart man. Have it—"

"Now!" Quinn yelled.

As if the cleaner were speaking to him, Abraham pushed to his feet and pulled his trigger.

He saw the woman's shadow twist as she screamed in pain and fury. As he was about to pull his trigger again, he lost her for a moment in the vegetation.

Then, two bright flashes and the double *thup* of the woman's gun betrayed her position. He fired two shots before finding himself on the ground again.

At first he thought he must have tripped as he fired, but that wouldn't explain why he was suddenly cold and his shirt wet.

And then the barriers in his mind began to break, allowing the pain to rush in.

QUINN RACED TOWARD Clark, his gun whipping up in front of him. Behind him he could hear Desirae rolling into the brush with Tessa, while Nate and Orlando opened fire on the second shooter. As Quinn was about to pull his own trigger, Abraham rose out of the brush and fired almost point blank at the woman.

The woman yelled and returned fire.

Abraham's body twisted from the impact, but he remained on his feet long enough to send off two shots before collapsing into the jungle. Quinn kept going, knowing he had to get to the woman before he could do anything for Abraham.

There was a dark splatter on the bushes in the area Clark had been, but the woman was gone. Quinn lowered to a crouch and eased forward, following a trail of wet spots on the ground. Twenty feet farther on, the path bent around a half buried boulder.

He heard her ragged breaths coming from the other side of the rock. He inched forward, his weapon at the ready, and found her sitting on the ground, her back against the rock. In her hand was her pistol, but she didn't even try to lift it. As he drew closer, he saw why. One of Abraham's shots had torn through her upper arm, and she was lucky to have held on to the gun at all. Her real problem, though, was the gut shot that had turned her shirt into a glistening mess.

She eyed Quinn. "You're a real asshole…you know that? I was…"—she coughed—"just doing my job."

He crouched in front of her and looked at her for a second before saying, "If your job is to kill a child, which one of us is really the asshole?"

"People like us…it's not our…place to question an assignment."

Quinn heard a noise, close, but he kept his gaze on the woman. "Who taught you that?"

She tried to scoff but ended up coughing again. "They'll come for you….They won't stop until…you *and* the…girl are dead."

A shifting of dirt.

"Who? Your friends at McCrillis?" he asked.

"You…don't have…a chance. They're too…big."

"I've dealt with bigger."

Before she could reply, he twisted to the side and fired into the jungle.

A gurgle and a thud.

He relieved the woman of her gun, and then cautiously moved into the brush where the noise had come from. Parting a few branches with his leg, he found the man he'd shot lying on the ground. The bullet had caught him square in the throat, and while he still had a bit of life in his eyes, it was quickly draining away as blood pooled around his shoulders.

Quinn took the man's weapon and returned to the woman. She was looking at him again, but whatever strength she'd had was gone. He knew it would be only minutes before she took her last breath.

He found Abraham on the ground, wincing in pain.

"Where were you hit?" he asked as he knelt down.

"Nowhere good, Johnny," Abraham said.

After a quick examination, Quinn knew he was right.

One bullet had entered just below his rib cage and the other in his chest. From the wheeze of the older man's breaths, Quinn was sure one had punctured a lung. He was equally sure there was little he could do for his friend.

Raising his voice, he said, "Clear on this end."

"Clear here, too," Nate said.

"I need Orlando."

A moment later, he heard her cutting through the brush.

When she saw Abraham, she said, "Shit," and dropped down on the other side of him. "Dammit, Abraham. What the hell did you do?"

"I thought…that was pretty obvious." He winced again. "Did we get them?"

"We did," Quinn said, "but it would have been a lot harder if you hadn't taken out the woman."

As the others approached, Quinn caught Desirae's gaze and shook his head. She got the message and tried to stop Tessa from approaching, but the girl kept coming.

"Abe?" Tessa said, her eyes wide. "Oh, no. Are you…"

Despite the pain Quinn knew Abraham was feeling, the old op smiled and said, "Are you…okay?"

She knelt beside him. "Yeah. But you—"

"I need you…to promise me…something."

With effort, he lifted his hand toward her and she grabbed it.

"I need…you to just have fun…be a girl…enjoy every…"—he coughed—"moment. Can you…promise me that?"

Her lower lip trembling, she said, "I promise."

As he coughed again, Desirae put her hands on Tessa's shoulders. "Why don't we give Abe a little room?"

Abraham moved his gaze to the woman, the look on his face asking if Tessa was indeed okay.

"She's fine," Desirae said. "Thanks to you, she's just fine."

"I brought the others to you.…You would have been…safe if I left…it alone."

"They would have come for us whether you were

looking or not. You helped us stop them. Thank you." She smiled. "Come on, Tessa." She led her daughter away.

Abraham seemed to drift off for a moment.

Orlando squeezed his hand, tears running down her face. "Hey, stay with me." When his eyes opened again, she tried to smile as she said, "You know, you were wrong earlier."

He looked confused. "Wrong?"

"Yeah, what you said about it not being your best day," she said. "You saved Tessa. Seems to me this *is* the best."

A twinkle flitted through his eyes as a smile touched the corner of his mouth. "Orlando," he said, his voice no more than a whisper now, "my best day…was the day I found you."

As far as last words went, Quinn thought Abraham's were pretty damn good.

CHAPTER
THIRTY SIX

WHEN THE SUN came up, Quinn and Nate got down to the business they were best at, and before long the bodies of the McCrillis crew were buried deep in the jungle where they would never be found.

Abraham was another story. A call to Helen Cho—the first of what would be several—resulted in a no-questions-asked death certificate and a sealed coffin ride back to California.

But Abraham and the bodies of the others were not the biggest issue. Despite what Desirae had said to Orlando's mentor, Clark and her men had been a symptom of Tessa and Desirae's problem, not the cause, so the danger still existed.

After Quinn and Orlando promised they would continue their working relationship with Helen's organization, she was more than willing to provide them with the assistance they required to finish things. It would, after all, clean up a mess the CIA—one of her internal clients—would be very happy to be rid of.

"Big house," Orlando noted.

"You expected something smaller?" Quinn asked.

The house was in an exclusive neighborhood of San Mateo, California, the heart of Silicon Valley. Surrounding it was an eight-foot-high stone wall with a solid wooden gate across the driveway entrance.

They had no problem getting someone inside to open this gate for them. As a respected reporter for a leading lifestyle website and her freelance photographer, Orlando and Quinn were ostensibly there to interview Jacqueline Rostov, CEO of Rostov Dynamics.

The house was a three-story French chateau, which, according to the information they'd been given, was a brick-by-brick copy of a home in the Loire Valley of France. As they neared the front, a suited man standing in the driveway directed them to a parking spot before leading them up to the front door.

Inside, an older gentleman took them to a lavishly decorated office on the second floor.

"Mrs. Rostov will be with you soon," he said. "She's finishing up other business. After you finish the interview, I've been instructed to give you a tour of the grounds."

"That'll be great," Orlando replied. "Thanks."

"Would you like something to drink while you wait?"

"We're fine."

To ensure they would have a little extra time before the "interview" started, they had arrived fifteen minutes early. As soon as their guide left and closed the door, Quinn opened his camera bag and he and Orlando set to work.

Thirty-two minutes passed by the time Mrs. Rostov finally walked in and found Quinn and Orlando seated in the guest chairs in front of her desk. While her bio listed her as fifty-nine, the head of Rostov Dynamics had clearly spent a sizable chunk of cash on doctors and clothes to look younger.

Businesslike smiles and quick, firm handshakes were shared, and then the woman settled into her chair behind the desk.

"I'm having some tea brought in," she said. "If there's something else you'd rather have…?"

"Tea is fine," Orlando said.

"Works for me, too," Quinn said.

They had prepared for the contingency of someone bringing refreshments, so Orlando started in on her list of questions, while Quinn walked around the room under the pretext of checking the lighting and looking for good angles to take some pictures.

He was still walking around when the tea arrived. A young woman in a dark suit brought the tray in, set it on the desk, and left. Quinn arrived at the double doors just as she closed it. With his back to the desk, he slipped the double-looped lock over the two handles and pushed the button that silently tightened the carbon-fiber straps. He then walked toward the window at the other end of the room, pulled out his phone, and sent the pre-typed text.

Commence transfer

Casually, he returned to his chair. Orlando was in the middle of asking the woman about her favorite vacation spots but stopped as soon as he sat down.

Rostov looked at her for a moment, waiting, then said, "Was there a question?"

Orlando smiled, but said nothing as Quinn removed a laptop from his bag and set it on the desk.

Rostov looked confused. "What's going on?"

Quinn held up a finger. "Just a second."

"I'm sorry?" she said, clearly unaccustomed to being told what to do.

A video chat window opened on the screen. In it was Desirae Rosette.

"Who is that?" Rostov asked.

"We'll get to her in a moment," Orlando said.

"I'm not sure what this is all about," the woman said, "but if this is some kind of—"

"This is not some kind of anything," Quinn cut her off. "It *is* a discussion about your future."

"My future?" She stared at him for a tense second before her face relaxed and she said in a calm voice, "Murphy, get in here." She donned a smug smile and leaned back in her chair. After several seconds, puzzlement crept into her eyes. "Murphy? Now."

"I'm afraid no one's coming, Mrs. Rostov," Orlando said as she picked up the small device she'd put on the desk when the interview started. "I'm not actually using this to record you. We know you have this room bugged." She glanced at Quinn. "How many?"

"Seven, not including the one in the private bathroom," he said.

"This thing is a signal jammer," Orlando went on, "but not just any old signal jammer. In addition to keeping your people from hearing what we say, it's playing back to them an interview you gave to a reporter two days ago in New York. I should probably tell you she wasn't a reporter, either, so don't expect to see that article anytime soon."

Rostov picked up her phone.

"Sorry, that doesn't work, either," Quinn said.

Not believing him, she put the receiver to her ear before slamming it back into its cradle and rising to her feet. "I am not a fan of pranks or whatever this is you're doing. You can explain yourself to the police."

As she rounded the desk, Quinn said, "Sure, and you can explain to them why you put a hit on a four-year-old girl and her mother."

Rostov stopped. "I don't know what the hell you're talking about."

"Jennifer Kagawa and her daughter, Tessa? You remember who Tessa is, don't you? Your husband's daughter?"

A crack in her control. Not much, but enough.

"I believe you were going to get the police," Orlando said. "We're happy to wait. They'll love the information we have."

Rostov narrowed her eyes. "What information?"

"Sworn affidavits, video testimony, bank records."

"What records? What testimony?"

"That would be the testimony of Don McCrillis, CEO of McCrillis International. I'm sure you've heard of him."

Rostov placed a hand on the desk as if she needed help maintaining her balance. "I don't believe you."

"Of course you don't," Quinn said.

He moved Desirae's video window to one side and clicked open another file. Up popped an image of McCrillis International's president. Quinn hit PLAY.

"State your name," an unseen man said.

"Donald Wayne McCrillis."

"And the date?"

McCrillis stated a date from three days earlier, the interview having taken place immediately following the completion of negotiations between McCrillis and the US government under the direction of Helen Cho. The negotiations really only came down to whether McCrillis wanted to keep his company, albeit in a considerably less powerful form, or spend the rest of his life in jail. An easy decision, to say the least.

"We are here to discuss the Rostov-Kagawa matter, is that correct?"

"Yes," McCrillis said.

"I believe you have a prepared statement?"

"I do."

"Proceed."

McCrillis picked up some papers off the table in front of him and began to read. "Earlier this month, I became aware of a rogue operation run by Ethan Boyer, our recently deceased vice president of special operations. The operation was contracted by Jacqueline Rostov, head of Rostov Dy—"

"That son of a bitch," the woman said. "Turn it off!"

Quinn clicked the PAUSE button. "No sense in going over details you're already familiar with, right?"

Rostov slumped back into her chair, her right hand trembling.

"I believe it's introduction time," Orlando said. "Mrs. Rostov, this is Desirae Rosette. Desirae is the woman who raised your husband's daughter. Someone had to since you killed the girl's mother."

Rostov drew back against her chair as if Desirae was going to leap through the screen and strangle her.

"You'll excuse me if I don't say it's a pleasure to meet you," Desirae said.

"What is it you want?" the woman whispered.

"First, you or anyone acting on your behalf will never attempt to harm Tessa again," Desirae said.

"Let me interject something here," Quinn said. "If anything does happen to Tessa, anything that can't easily be explained to all of our satisfaction, then that same something will happen to you, Mrs. Rostov. Am I clear?"

The woman's hand continued to shake, but otherwise she didn't move.

"Am I clear?"

Finally, a nod.

"Please continue, Desirae," he said as his phone vibrated with an incoming text.

"Second, since you have no children of your own, eighty percent of the Rostov estate will be kept in a trust for Tessa, while the other twenty percent will go to the Abraham Delger Memorial Education Fund."

Rostov nearly flew out of her chair as she said, "If you think I would *ever* let you take my money away, you all are beyond delusional."

Quinn gestured to the frozen image of Don McCrillis. "You've lost it one way or the other. Or would you prefer the government takes it away when you're given the death penalty?"

"You'll have to do what the rest of us do," Orlando said. "Get a job and live off of that."

Rostov gritted her teeth. "I have a job."

"That brings us to the third point," Quinn said. "The board of directors has decided it would be best if the company were not associated with someone who hires hit squads to kill children."

"The board can think whatever they want, but *I'm* the majority stock holder! My vote is the only one that counts."

"I believe you misunderstood point number two. Your assets aren't waiting to be transferred out of your name. The transaction completed..." He checked the new message on his phone. "Thirty seconds ago."

Rostov stared at them, dumbfounded. "Bullshit."

"Go ahead," Quinn said, motioning to Rostov's own computer. "Check one of your accounts. It doesn't matter which one."

She pulled her keyboard toward her and did what Quinn suggested. The account in question had a current balance of $43.71.

"There's a little bit left in each," he said, "to give you a fresh start."

"You can't do this," she whispered.

"*We* can't, no," Orlando said. "But friends of ours can, and did."

Quinn asked Desirae, "Anything else to add?"

"One more thing," she said, then looked offscreen and raised her voice. "Terri!"

A few seconds later, Tessa squeezed into the shot with her.

"There was something you wanted to say, wasn't there?" Desirae said to her daughter.

Tessa looked into the camera. "You're Mrs. Rostov?"

The woman's mouth hung open.

"Answer her," Quinn said.

"Yes," Rostov replied.

"I know what you did to my first mom, I know what you did to my friend Abe, and I know what you wanted to do to me. You're not a good person. My mom…"—she glanced at Desirae—"says I should forgive you so I can move on. I'll try, but I don't know if I can." She paused and looked at her mother again. "That's it."

"Okay, sweetie." Desirae kissed Tessa's cheek and then said into the camera, "We're done here."

"Thanks," Quinn said. "We'll talk later."

He closed the computer. After he and Orlando gathered their things, they stood up.

When they reached the door, he stopped and looked back. "An accounting team arrived while we were chatting and started inventorying everything. My understanding is that they're beginning on the ground floor, so if you want any clothes, you should probably grab them now. Nothing valued over a hundred dollars, though. Believe me, they'll check."

As he and Orlando drove away a few minutes later, his phone rang.

"So how did it go?" Helen Cho asked.

"Exactly as planned."

"So the matter's finished?"

"One more thing."

"How much longer?"

"Give us three days."

"Call me when you're ready. I have a job you'll be perfect for."

CHAPTER
THIRTY SEVEN

FROM ABRAHAM'S GRAVESITE they could hear the waves crashing on the beach, a gentle metronome marking time for those to whom time didn't matter anymore.

Quinn had thought only he and Orlando and Nate and Daeng would be at the service, but a surprising amount of others had shown up—including about a dozen old colleagues from the business and Quinn's sister, Liz. She had never met Abraham but knew he'd been important to Orlando and that was enough for her. Perhaps most surprising were the kids, nearly thirty of them, all from the afterschool tutoring center where Abraham had volunteered.

"Did he realize how many lives he touched?" Quinn asked Orlando after the crowd had drifted off, leaving them alone with her mentor.

"I doubt it. He never thought of things that way. He just did what he did."

When he put an arm around her waist, she laid her head against his shoulder and they looked past the grave, out at the sea.

"It's beautiful here. He'll be happy."

She nodded and they fell silent again. The ordeal and the loss had exhausted her. He made a vow to himself that until Orlando was fully recovered, he would do whatever it took to convince her not to go into the field.

He pulled her into his arms and held her tight. After a few minutes, he said, "Ready?"

"Just a second."

She knelt beside the open grave.

"I've never been keen on Abraham as a first name," she said, "but I've been thinking it would work well as a middle. I mean, if it's a boy."

"Wait, what?"